MAXINE'S
STORY

MAXINE'S
STORY
PETER RITCHIE

First published in the UK in 2015
By PR Publishing

This revised edition first published in 2019

ISBN 978 1 91622 912 9

Typesetting and cover design by Laura Kincaid,
tenthousand publishing services
www.tenthousand.co.uk

Printed and bound by Amazon

For the women who have no voice

'Anger is a killing thing: it kills the man who angers, for each rage leaves him less than he had been before – it takes something from him.'

— Louis L' Amour

PART 1

1

'Christ,' she hissed in a cloud of iced breath. Only one punter all night and she was freezing her arse off dressed in a short leather skirt that was never designed for mid-December in Scotland. Stamping her feet like a tap dancer who'd forgotten their next move, the cold had drip-fed into her bloodstream and there was nowhere in her body that felt like it had retained any heat. One of the other girls walked past, coughing smoke in all directions as if her lungs were coming up, and staggering along the pavement on stiletto heels she obviously wasn't used to wearing.

'Fuck this, Maxie; I'm dyin' in this cold. Headin' for the boozer. You comin'?'

Maxine Sarah Welsh did her best to smile, but her lips felt numb. The thought of a nice warm bar with a double vodka and blackcurrant in her hand felt like her idea of heaven at that particular moment, but she'd been ripped off by her last punter and was up to her arse in debt to every bad bastard on the street. There were no plan Bs left – someone was going to cut her up and leave her for the medics if she didn't produce some serious wonga.

'I'm broke, Connie. Bad times, honey, but have a double for me and if I can get a punter I'll see you there.'

Everyone knew Maxine Welsh was a gem, but the girl never caught a break and the whole world just seemed to take from her – except the other poor cows that were in much the same place half the time.

'Leave it, Maxie. They're sittin' wi' the central heatin' turned up an' lookin' at next year's trip to the Med wi' their wives.'

Maxine grunted and tried again to refuse the offer, but Connie McGinn had pulled three regulars and a drunk tourist who hadn't twigged that she'd dipped his wallet.

'Come on, Maxie – drinks on me.'

'Could you throw in a meal?' Maxine smiled at Connie, who barely touched five foot when she stretched.

'Cheese an' onion or salt and vinegar, honey?'

Connie was full of it; she had more cash in her bag than she'd taken in weeks thanks to the mug tourist. As far as both girls were concerned, if the punters were daft enough to pick up business off the street then hell mend them if the contents of their wallets were chored. They could afford it anyway – it was just some payback and no worse than avoiding income tax.

They both snorted a laugh, thrilled they'd be off the street for a while and could forget that their lives were shite. The girls shivered in sync, and for them there was only that moment when their spirits began to lift at the thought of getting off the freezing Leith streets. There was nothing to look back on like the 'nice time' they promised the paying customers – there was fuck all nice about what they wanted from the working girls. Even the most recent punters barely formed a shape in their memories. They were wired to forget so they could go on living. The future? Well, that was just something that other people had, people who didn't have to wait around damp cold streets to pretend to some guy that he was special. Do it and forget, do it and forget, over and over again – that was their life.

Maxine looked at her cheap wristwatch, which was all she could afford and not worth pawning. It was nine o'clock and normally that would have been early doors on the game, but it was Christmas and the punters were all up to their hypocritical arses in domestic bliss or pissed at their office parties like the rest of the city.

Connie was right up for a laugh, which was normally the case anyway, and although there were no festive treats in their world, just for that one night she wanted to catch something of the mood and excesses going on in the rest of the city. She pulled Maxine into a nearby convenience store and asked for two of everything. Two packets of smokes, two bars of milk chocolate, two packets of chewing gum and two Lotto tickets. She always picked the same numbers and was convinced that one day it would happen for her. She bought Maxine a ticket with exactly the same numbers as hers and, as a bonus, stuck a twenty-pound note in her friend's pocket.

'Happy Christmas, darlin'. This is about as good as we'll get it.' She grinned and squeezed Maxine's hand. Maxine returned the gesture and choked back the tear that was trying to acknowledge her friend's generosity, but that was just how Connie was – live for the moment and the future will definitely be brighter. 'Fuck knows when,' she would say with a shake of the head, 'but eventually, Maxie – trust me.'

'Jesus, Connie, have you ripped off Santa Claus tonight?' Maxine rarely saw kindness dispensed in her life and what her friend had done was more than she could have imagined – the girl had so little in her own existence that was worth celebrating. Her man was Banjo Rodgers, who'd never risen above small-time dealing and lacked the bottle or street cred to move further up the division. In fact, Banjo was quite a gentle guy with women, but his head had been fucked up by Billy Nelson, a Belfast loyalist who'd created havoc in the city for a while and driven Banjo's woman at the time to OD in a Leith back street. Connie knew she should have shown him the door months earlier, but he was the closest thing she could get to someone who cared. Banjo looked after the flat, watched TV, smoked some grass and swallowed beer till she came in at night. She lived with the forlorn hope that he might just get a grip, because she was convinced there was a decent-enough guy underneath the self-pity and occasionally heavy drug use.

Connie grinned and said, 'Let's get to the boozer before my nipples fall off.' It was her favourite line and Maxine nodded – the trip to the pub was an offer she wasn't going to refuse. The future was a big empty hole, so she might as well make the most of the chance to forget who she was for a few hours.

They took each other's arms and steered for the pub, heads down against the freezing wind and driving sleet. They didn't hear the patrol car coming up slowly behind them then pulling in just ahead. They tensed and slowed a pace, heads up till the driver's window slid down and they saw who it was.

Charlie Brockie had served in the Leith division his entire career and was just part of the furniture. Most people would have been shifted to other stations or divisions at some time during their service, but the bosses just turned their heads from the page anytime they were doing a review and saw his name. Leith needed Brockie and he needed Leith. When he was nightshift, he always made a point of making sure the working girls were as safe as they could be when he was about. He never judged them, but he did judge the men who knocked them about.

Over the years there had been a few unexplained incidents where punters were found with painful injuries that they refused to explain. The street legend was that they'd all hurt girls when Brockie had been on nightshift and he'd dispensed some rough justice in return. No one was sure if it was true, and although there was strong circumstantial evidence, the CID investigators never put too much effort into finding an answer. No one wanted to make an official complaint anyway and have to explain to their good ladies what had happened. It was much easier to make up a story about an accident and avoid a messy and expensive divorce.

'Hi, girls. Want a lift? You'll freeze to death there.' Brockie squinted into the cold wet air and tried his best to grin.

'We're fine, Charlie.' Connie pointed towards the boozer that was in sight now and glowing its welcome into the December night. 'You comin' to buy us a Christmas drink?'

'We'll see, hen. Finish a couple more shifts then that's me day off. Watch yourselves.' Brockie closed the window of the patrol car then moved off into the night, spinning the blue light a couple of times like a goodbye wave to the girls.

'He just needs to ask me for anythin' an' the answer would be yes… anythin' and I wouldn't even charge. Love that man.' Connie dug Maxine in the ribs and sniggered like a schoolgirl.

A few minutes later Brockie locked up the patrol car and cursed the weather, shuddering as a heavy gust of sleet-filled wind lashed him from head to toe and drew the remaining heat from his bones. Two young probationers left the station and shouted a greeting to the ageing PC, a man they both admired and at the same time regarded as a relic of a bygone age.

'Hope you've got the long johns on, Charlie. Don't want to take chances at your age.' It was just police piss-taking, part of the job, and Brockie had done enough of it in his time when he'd started his own probation, always delighting in winding up the old legends. It showed you'd grown balls, had gone past basking in the former glories of the old men who sat and told endless war stories.

'Just make sure the neds don't mistake you for a couple o' lassies. Now piss off, children.'

Brockie grinned at the two young men. He liked them both. They were mustard on the street and just loved getting into the action. Unlike him, they were destined for bigger things eventually, and it was enough for him to know he'd helped smooth off some of the rough edges and shown them how to work the street. It made him feel old though, and his stretched bladder confirmed that to him. He headed straight for the bog and wished he could go more than a couple of hours without needing a Jimmy.

When he got into the toilets, he caught his reflection above the washbasin and wondered who the fuck was staring back at him. In his head he was still in his thirties, but the guy in the mirror was a couple of decades older.

Brockie washed his hands slowly, wondering where it had all gone and wished he was starting over – wished he gave shit again.

'Fuck.'

He splashed some warm water onto his face and at least it brought a bit of colour back into his cheeks. The two girls came back into his mind and it was as if his subconscious had just warned him to lighten up. He nodded a couple of times, remembering what life was like for some people – and it didn't get much worse than what those girls had to do to survive. He shuddered and thought about his own daughter, a law graduate married to a guy who cared, with a couple of grandchildren who just asked to be loved.

'Get a grip, Charlie boy,' he said before leaving the bathroom and heading to the kitchen, where a couple of the team were chewing on sandwiches and catching up on paperwork.

'And a very fuckin' Merry Christmas to one and all,' he said to them.

Brockie was together again – there was no other way but to just get on with it.

2

When they pushed the boozer doors open, a tsunami of warm beery air wafted towards them. It was all mixed in with arguments about Saturday's result and 'What the fuck are the Hibees playin' at?' Or alternatively 'They were fuck-in' magic, man!'

The atmosphere was thick with every expletive the locals had sown into their vocabulary as the two girls grinned and felt the heat wrap itself around them like blankets warmed at an open fireside. The barman and licensee was Big Tam Logan, a tolerant guy brought up in Leith who knew the score from a lot of personal experience. Some of the upmarket bars wouldn't let the girls in the door now, but he was old school and one of his own cousins had fallen off her perch years before, working the streets before she'd ended up beaten into disability by the serial killer Thomas Barclay.

Logan was one of those quiet legends who'd earned respect even among the detectives who'd once wanted to see him inside the guest rooms in HMP Saughton. He'd been blessed with a good physique since he was a kid and learned how to fight as a Hibs casual in the Granton mob.

He just loved to get it going, and what made him stand out was his quiet nature, even when everyone was wound up tight before a battle. He looked absolutely at peace with himself before weighing into the opposition like a raging animal – it was just his life and had seemed normal at the time. He had size, speed and lifting weights in the gym most days made him stand out even among the casuals.

The Flemings – the local gangsters who had mattered at the time – knew talent when they saw it and had signed him on as muscle. He graduated to the big league ahead of schedule, but although he kept his mouth shut, he never really liked the life of a professional villain. There were far too many arseholes who thought they were the lead man in a gangster movie.

Minding was fine, but hurting ordinary citizens or some poor bastard who couldn't pay their loans back was another thing. Fighting as a casual had seemed fair enough – the enemy turned up for a square go because they wanted to and took their chances just like him.

He hadn't known it at the time but Lady Luck had intervened on his behalf when, years later, he'd done a bit of time after a couple of rival villains had tried to take him on for no reason that made sense. They'd ended up in plaster while he'd been lifted and given an unpaid holiday in the big hoose. He'd been released just weeks after Billy Nelson's Belfast psychos had put the Flemings out of business and three feet underground.

He often thought about that – that he could have ended up lying in the same dirt with old man Fleming and his firstborn. They were a couple of heartless bastards, but in those days Logan had been the kind of mug who would have gone to war for them when the rest of the Flemings' gang couldn't be arsed to take on the Shankill men. Logan shook his head when he thought about what might have happened. The Flemings would have been poor company for eternity.

Although the police had him on their radar in those days, he never did time for anything after that, and retiring into civilian life hadn't been too hard because a woman had stepped into the picture. Old man Fleming didn't like anyone leaving unless he retired them himself, but when he'd disappeared from the picture there was no one to complain – though if there had been, they would have realised Logan was a bit special and would have created a lot of casualties – so he passed into civilian life without a ripple.

3

The two girls who came into the bar never caused him a problem and he liked them more than most of the loud-mouths and sad fuckers who frequented his place. They just hadn't caught the breaks, and he was the last person on God's earth to judge them for what they did. Men were the problem on this earth, not these girls. He knew what they had to endure each and every day and wondered what the tabloid readers would think if they really understood the deal they'd been cut in life. He was no fool though and knew there was always the potential for trouble around them, so the non-negotiable house rule was that the welcome mat was removed the first hint of bother.

'Two vodis, Tam, with the usual mixers.'

Connie picked up a flyer for a local Chinese takeaway and studied it as if she was in a Michelin-star restaurant. Running her finger up and down the stained page, she went into her little routine. 'Then I think we'll just have a main course and that'll be one cheese an' onion for *moi* and…' She looked at Maxine and raised her eyebrows. Her friend giggled like a schoolgirl and told her she was a mad cow. Connie was in the zone though – she loved this kind of play-acting.

'Yes, barman, I think my friend here will go for the salt and vinegar straight from the bag.'

Logan played along as he always did. 'Will madam be requiring any side orders?'

'No, I think the crisps will be lovely on their own.' Connie nudged her friend and winked at the barman, who shook his head; for such a serious man, he enjoyed his small exchanges with Connie.

'Coming right up, madam.'

Although he'd heard the same patter a hundred times, Logan smiled, which was a rare thing for a man who was tired of his line of work. Actually, it was people who tired him, and he ached for the old world of Leith to come back, but he knew that was no more than an ageing native's dream now. He shoved the drinks and crisps over the bar and pushed Connie's money back towards her.

'On me, girl – it's nearly Christmas and I always give the regulars one on the house. That's one though, Connie, and there's no free bar, so keep the money warm for the next round.'

'You're a good man, Big Tam. Doesn't matter what folk say.'

She turned then did an exaggerated wiggle to a couple of seats at the back of the bar that faced the door. The two girls knew through hard training that they needed to keep an eye on the door in case one of the bastards who inhabited their lives came in with some reason to piss over them – as if they needed any more misery.

They sat down then Maxine leaned her head back after the first mouthful and let the heat of the spirit wash through her. With the sensation coming back into her bones, it felt almost like a dope hit. The heat made her realise how tired she was and her eyes suddenly felt heavy with exhaustion. She slugged back the rest of the drink and her friend watched some colour flush her cheeks.

Connie's life was bad by normal standards but not the worst compared to most of the working girls. As for money, it was just whatever she scraped off the street each day, though Banjo did his bit of dealing to his regular customers, so they survived. There was a saving grace in her case because she was almost unique among the girls on the street in that she didn't use drugs. She could never explain why, but it was probably from watching her baby brother become a dedicated junkie then shrink into his skeleton before expiring to hypothermia. They'd found him in a condemned flat surrounded by so much filth the cops who discovered his body had both thrown up when they found what the rats had left. She clung on to the belief that she could make it off the street one day and was convinced that she just needed the spotlight to fall on her once. When it did, she'd walk away and never look back. Why wouldn't she? She asked her friends that question over and over again but none of them believed it – there was too much evidence to the contrary.

Maxine didn't have that luxury. She'd gone through a patch where she'd used whatever dope she could get her hands on and had run up debts all over the city. She didn't kid herself; she knew she was probably beyond rescue and Connie was one of the only people who would risk being seen with her. In their game, she could get the same message as Maxine if she was in the wrong place at the wrong time when the collectors came for their pound of flesh.

'Enjoy that, honey?' Connie gulped her drink then signalled to Logan for a refill and blew him a kiss at the same time.

'God, Connie, I just want to stay here for the rest of my life. Is that so much to ask?'

She tried to open the crisp packet but her hands were still shaking. She needed to overdose on sugar, but the drink would do the job. The shakes were so bad at times that she couldn't pick things up, although she was trying hard to cut down the dope and was down to the occasional bit of weed. If anyone did notice, she just made light of it.

'Jesus Christ, I'm a fucking' junkie. Comes with the territory.'

4

Maxine Sarah Welsh was a bit different from most of the girls who sold it on the streets. Anyone sitting near her in the pub might have noticed that she didn't drop her *g*s or picked up on the other little clues in her vocabulary that showed she'd had a different upbringing from nearly all of the other women reduced to hawking themselves just to survive.

Maxie was what she called herself now. She didn't actually like the name, but it made her feel more like her street friends and hid a past that embarrassed her, because unlike them she'd been born with opportunities and thrown it all away. Women like Connie had come to the streets with a story that mirrored the girl working on the next street corner, and so it went on. They were nearly all born into shit lives and brought up to expect nothing as a future – they were like the condemned who hadn't actually been sentenced in court. It was their birthright, although no one ever explained that to them.

Maxine, on the other hand, had been born into a lower-middle-class family who'd hauled themselves away from their own working-class backgrounds and worked to give their offspring a decent break. They'd offered their kids an education if they wanted it and all the love in the world. Her two brothers had grabbed it with both hands and Maxine had gone for nursing, which her parents thought was a natural course for their wee girl. She seemed to be a born carer from the time she was old enough to dress up in her favourite nurse's uniform, and her father had loved telling his friends how, when he'd been recovering from an accident, his girl would appear every day after primary school dressed in her Nurse Nancy uniform, ready to treat him as a special patient.

Everything had gone according to plan and her early years of nursing were all she could have asked for – she was seen as a talent and 'one for the future'. That was it; life seemed to have been marked out and, on top of all that, she was attractive, with copper-coloured hair that was so thick and full of life that it drew envious looks from most every woman she met. Her eyes were chocolate brown and she was one of those rare creatures whose face broke into a smile almost anytime she met another human being. Sometimes she tried but struggled to understand how she'd got into drugs though, looking back, it was about the same time she'd realised that whenever there was a man in her life, something went wrong.

The one who'd done the damage though was off the Richter Scale, and although it had just seemed like a game at the time, it wasn't till she ended up on the street that she realised how naive she'd been – she'd thought being a nurse meant she was already wise and ready to take on all of life's challenges.

He was a nurse on the same ward. No Brad Pitt, but he was ten years older and had honed his patter over the years on his native Glasgow's streets. If he saw vulnerability combined with youth, he was like a rat up a drain.

Maxine never understood how she could have been taken in by his lines – which would have been laughable now – but somehow or other they'd worked at the time. Now half her punters were just like him; they talked a good game, but it was all piss in the wind.

When she'd found out he liked to do a bit of dope, it had seemed like a taste of something exotic, and of course she'd felt her life had been a bit dull, so where was the harm? She hadn't been able to think of a single thing in her past that was close to risky, and even her first sexual experience had still been her first till she'd met him.

It was the old story – a bit of weed then a dabble with smack. She remembered the first hit whacking her like a warm cloud of pleasure that almost made her pass out from the rush. It was like everything she'd missed all wrapped up in a ten-pound bag of brown powder. It was just that easy.

When Maxine injected for the third time, her story became much like those of the other girls, all now part of the same class as they headed downwards into the gutter. There was panic when she realised that she had an addiction, trying everything to get money to feed the beast and then stealing.

When they caught her in the hospital, the shame almost drove her to suicide. It was remarkable how quickly her life completely disintegrated. She lost it all – family, work, self-esteem and the tosser who'd introduced her to the beast.

By the time she was gagging into the gutter after being with her first punter, the male nurse had already hooked up with another woman who believed his every word. Maxine had even protected the bastard who'd introduced her to dope right up to the point where she'd walked out of prison and worked out that he'd never been in touch. He was a predator, pure and simple, and she'd never believed to that point that a predator could wear a nurse's uniform and care for sick people. That was about the time it had finally dawned on her that most men's words tended to mean little or nothing.

By the time Connie had ordered their fourth drink, they'd both stopped worrying for the time being. The next morning would bring fresh pain, but they enjoyed each other's company, and Connie could always get a laugh out of Maxine, which wasn't easy these days.

Nothing lasted though in their world, and as Big Tam laid the drinks in front of them, the door opened, the rush of freezing air momentarily grabbing everyone's attention. Fat lumps of sleet blew in with Andy Dillon – a man Maxine needed to see like she needed a dose of the crabs.

5

Dillon was an arsehole and never came near this boozer normally, but tonight he had business. He was strictly a small-time dealer from the little county town of Dalkeith, although he liked to pretend he was a real gangster to the halfwits who bought gear from him. The fact was he couldn't punch his way out of a nursery, but he was careful to sell to people who were so fucked up they were a walk-over, and he especially liked selling to women who were in the shit. That way, he could get what he wanted, when he wanted it. The real bonus was that he could paste the odd female; that really got his juices going – slapping someone about who couldn't fight back was playtime for him.

There were a few villains current and retired in the bar already and a retired detective called Mick Harkins who was as wide as they came. If they'd taken a straw pole to describe first impressions of Andy Dillon in one word, 'wanker' would probably have come top or close to top of the list.

He'd come from quality criminal stock on his father's side, but his mother was a waster who ran out on his old man after six months of Friday-night beatings. Dillon had tried everything to build up his frame, but he was a lazy bastard by nature and just couldn't be arsed to lift enough iron, so he took what he thought was the easy option and swallowed steroids, forgetting that you still needed to lift the iron. All it did was make him aggressive when he didn't have the kit to take on all comers, and he took a few kickings before it dawned on him that he was no heavy-weight boxer.

He still had the family brand name though and decided he would stick to dealing with losers who he could control. He was just under six foot, painfully thin and shaved his thinning red hair, which, together with his almost-haunted eyes that were placed too close together, gave him an almost Dickensian look. His dress sense and hygiene didn't help the picture, but apart from his endless desire for porn and violent video games, he didn't really care. The women and junkies he preyed on couldn't complain without con-sequences that would hurt, so he could spend most of his waking hours in a state of semi-delusion that he was a name, a player on the big park. That's what made him such a dangerous bastard to the souls who owed him, because he could pay mad bastards to hand out the violence if he wasn't handy enough to do it himself.

A long time before Maxine met Andy Dillon, she'd run out of dealers in the city who'd sell to her on the strength of goodwill – then she'd heard about the Dalkeith source who always had gear available. It was like the poor bastards on the street who thought loan companies or the shark version were the answer to their debt problems. The delusion that a handful of cash would make all those problems go away just before reality kicked in and some bad fucker with a shaved head and too many tattoos arrived at your door with a negative attitude and a mandate to cause physical harm.

At the time, she'd thought it was worth a bus ride out to the country, and Dillon had been all half-toothless smiles when he'd handed over the gear. She was still attractive, obviously broke and if she'd headed out to the sticks to buy gear, it meant he could own her from the very first deal. He didn't need a degree in business management to work out that she'd run out of credit in the city.

She managed to pay Dillon the first couple of times, then the third time, when she was potless, he'd pushed her into the back of his van and grunted on top of her for about a minute and a half. She'd stared upwards and forced herself to think of her first and only foreign holiday. That had been one of the happiest times of her life, and she used that memory like a sedative when she couldn't face reality. All she could remember was that he'd wheezed his way to the big moment and it had sounded like he had some kind of chest complaint.

Dillon was never going to be the man of her dreams, but she needed him and his supply of happy bags up to the time she started to seriously come off the gear. She could almost cope with his performance, which was feeble, but the first time he couldn't make it to the top, he'd sat back on his knees, rapped her with two hard shots to the face and told her it was her fault. Assaulting Maxine had seemed to get him going again and he'd almost fallen on top of her before getting his moment. That's when she'd worked out he needed violence to get the sex bit completed.

Maxine was beating the dope, but she owed Dillon more than she could pay back, even on her good weeks on the street, and now she had debt all over the city plus this creep on her case. In a way, he seemed the least of all the evils; the city boys were proper gangsters and would simply beat her unconscious – extras from her wouldn't have made any difference to them.

Dillon was different. He was as much an addict as most of his clients; he just hadn't worked that out yet. His drug was power over people who wouldn't see him in their road in another life, where he could play out his fantasies of being someone who mattered. Maxine had almost learned to switch off whenever he was on top of her, but in the moments when reality whacked her round the head, she was repulsed by what she'd become. She wanted to do a runner, but the question she had to ask herself on a regular basis was where do you run to when you don't have a light? The answer was obvious, and it was that she'd run straight into the same problem in some other city full of exactly the same kind of sick predators.

6

Dillon sucked in the atmosphere and slowly scanned the bar left and right in the way he imagined a real gangster would. Despite his own self-delusion, he actually looked like what he was – a small-time dealer with no real cred among the professional villains. The only thing that kept him in one piece was that his old man 'Bear' Dillon was a name, respected and – more importantly – feared in the past as a hard man, robber and talented thief. He dealt gear now in a modest way on his own, and even though he would have agreed that his only son was a wanker, he wouldn't let anyone fuck him over. That was family so a red line. Other than that, he told his son to get on with his own life and, as far as possible, 'Do your business but keep the fuck away from my mine!'

Young Andy Dillon made a decent profit selling gear because of his father's name, and to prove he was a total wanker he'd bought and customised a red Beamer, souped up with a ridiculous spoiler. He loved to roar along the streets of the county town imagining he was in L.A. and part of a real crew.

He spotted Maxine and grinned, showing what was left of his rotting teeth. He had a pathological fear of dentists and preferred pain to the chair. He started towards the two women and Connie saw the smile disappear from her friend's face. She had a rough idea what it meant. Dillon looked like the kind of twat they all had to deal with at one time or another, but she knew straight away he was a pretend hard man, so she was ready to jump in for Maxine.

Big Tam Logan worked Dillon out about five seconds after he came into the bar. The Big Man, as he was known locally, had been quality in his time, knew all the strokes required to survive in the game and clicked straight away that the boy was nothing for him to worry about. He guessed correctly that he was probably more than a problem for one or both of the girls though. His radar was switched on and, as he did so often, he cursed the men who preyed on these girls. Logan never looked for trouble, but if it came, he dealt with it quickly because that's how you did it on the street.

'What you buyin', sunshine? Hope you're not just in here for an orange sash?'

Logan said it loud enough to stop Dillon in his tracks and most of the punters were already tuned into the vibes. The only one who didn't get it was the fuckwit who'd walked into the Leith boozer thinking he'd make an impression.

Dillon had done a couple of lines of his own coke before he'd cut it to fuck so he could sell it on. His brain was lit up like a Christmas tree, so he had all the confidence he needed and wasn't about to take pish from some antique beer dispenser. He looked at Logan and took in his size but thought the guy was ancient – there wasn't a hair left on his napper.

'Take it easy, auld yin. Just here to see ma wee pals in the corner there.'

In his coked-up brain, Andy Dillon believed that the words he'd just uttered carried weight – that the man behind the bar had to be impressed and maybe just a bit spooked.

If he'd really studied the bar and the man behind it though, he would have spotted that Logan was actually shaved as bald as a nun's arse – a choice, not a consequence of age. Another thing that should have rung a bell was that he had forearms like Popeye and they were covered with tattoos – one of which declared 'Hibee till I die' – but the final clue was that he had 'the look', that confidence that came from years staying alive when you ran with the hard men.

Logan just gave away a hint of a grin, like a predator who sees a small furry animal that has absolutely no fucking chance in a skirmish.

'That's fine, son.'

Logan wiped the bar, which was as clean as a whistle.

'Still need to buy a drink though – them's the rules. Everybody knows the rules. That right, Mick?'

He directed the comment to Mick Harkins, the retired detective at the end of the bar who was pretending to mind his own business and reading the sports section of the *Herald*.

Harkins looked up from the paper as if he'd just heard his name being called, but that was just part of the act. Harkins was ex Crime Squad, knew these games back to front and how to join in the fun. Retired after nearly being killed in the job, this was his favourite boozer because everyone talked football and the local gangsters used it. Mick liked a bit of banter with the opposition. He was a rare breed in that the local villains respected him because he knew every stroke in the book and then some. He was one of the few detectives who could do that and avoid aggravation. They saw something of themselves in him, and *he* was wise enough to know that the line between him and the men he used to lock up was a thin one.

'The rules is the rules, Tam. No exception – even for people wi' learnin' difficulties,' Harkins said straight-faced as he stared up at the TV screen and sipped some foam off a fresh pint.

There were a few barely suppressed laughs round the bar, and although Dillon didn't quite get the message, it started to dawn on him that maybe he hadn't impressed the barman or the old fuck with the smart mouth. He tried a kind of a laugh, as if he was part of the joke, but suddenly felt lonely and took the sensible course of action.

'Pint o' lager then, chief.'

Dillon felt like he was suddenly caught in a spotlight, naked, and that the customers were examining him as if he was something unpleasant that had just blown in off the street.

Logan poured the beer slowly and kept steady eye contact with Dillon, who started to twitch uncomfortably because he didn't like close examination. When the beer was poured, he told Dillon how much and then leaned on the bar. That was the moment Dillon noticed just how much meat was on the barman's forearms.

He gulped a couple of times because those forearms were impressive and wished he could stop walking into these problems so often. He felt like a small child in a room full of adults, but another problem for Dillon was that reality only lasted as long as the chemicals in his blood would allow.

'Listen, son.' Logan lowered his voice to a whisper, but the pub had gone quiet because they all liked this kind of thing and wanted to tune in.

'You drink your beer like a good wee boy, but see they lassies? They're regulars an' I like them, so when they're in ma boozer they get peace 'cause life's hard for them. So, you drink your drink but no bother. You hear me, son?'

'Sure thing, chief. Just a kinda social call, if you know what I mean?' Dillon gulped some beer because he realised he needed it.

'That's fine, son – an' happy Christmas when it comes.'

Logan went back to wiping the bar and ignored Dillon, who was pissed off – as he was so often when he got things wrong. He looked round at Maxine and Connie, saw them grinning, then vowed he'd wipe the smile off Maxine's coupon the first chance he got her on her own.

Dillon shuffled towards the girls' table and watched their eyes lock on to him all the way across, but if they were pleased to see him then they had a strange way of showing it. He was a lightweight in every sense of the word, because a real player would have realised that there were a number of men in the bar who were all equipped to hurt him, and they were watching his every move – just wanting him to provide an excuse. The bar had a reputation to keep and letting arseholes in lowered the tone of the place.

'How's it hangin', Maxie? Miss me?'

Dillon grinned, showing off what was left of his teeth to full effect and sat down opposite Maxine without being invited. In his mind, he didn't need an invite from a hooker he owned from the feet up.

'Same old, same old, Andy. Take it this is more than a social visit and if it's money you want, then sorry but my friend's buying. I don't have a light.'

She said sorry again to finish off but knew that saying it twice would make no difference to the slug who'd decided to join their table. Her voice was strong for about half the sentence then the nerves clicked in and a tremor took hold.

Dillon heard it and grinned; he loved it when people who were poorly equipped to defend themselves showed fear. It was the substitute he used in place of respect from A-list criminals. He could only dream about those boys giving him the look that meant he was a man with balls instead of a bawbag, which was the consensus of opinion.

He'd heard himself described that way one day in the boozer when he'd passed a couple of retired gangsters who'd nudged each other then made the comment – just loud enough for Dillon to receive the message. They were in their late sixties, but Dillon could do fuck all about it because they would still cover the walls with his blood if he made a move. It hurt and just made him angrier, and his only release was with people like the two street girls watching him now, like some bug that had just crawled into the light. The disgust in their eyes was barely concealed because even Connie knew exactly what he was, despite the fact she'd never met him before.

'You don't mind if I sit, girls?' he said, though he was already resting his arse on the seat. Connie was to his left and she moved her seat a foot further away from him.

'Would it make any fuckin' difference if we objected, like?'

Connie gave him the wee hard girl look before she weighed in again.

'Maxie told you the truth – she's got fuck all apart from what I gave her. OK?'

Connie had enough vodka in her to stifle any fear of what Dillon might try. If anything kicked off, there was enough support in the bar to make sure the bastard would end up in the gutter pissing blood from his ruptured kidneys.

The rest of the customers were in listening mode and at DEFCON 1, although Dillon still thought they were in their own little bubble at the table. He gulped too much beer all at once and the alcohol hit his system hard; it was already overheating with the high-quality cocaine. He leered at the sight of Maxine's face, which always got him going. In any other life, a woman as attractive as she was would have crossed the road to avoid him. That gave him a big buzz as well as making him angry, so punishing her for all his own inadequacies was always the default position of his deluded mind.

'It's OK, Connie. My problem.'

Maxine put her hand on her friend's forearm; she didn't want to be the cause of one more problem in Connie's life. The girl just didn't need that.

'You go to the bar, chat up the Big Man and I'll talk business here. Please, Connie – it's no problem.'

Connie saw the look in her eye, knew that she meant every word and that sticking a glass into the guy's face wasn't an option Maxine was considering at that time. For all the problems in her friend's life, she knew how to talk so maybe she could convince the arsehole who'd just dampened a good night to fuck off back to whatever rathole he called home.

Connie lifted her glass and stood up. 'I'll be right there at the bar, darlin' – just shout if you need me.' She gave Dillon a look that was the equivalent of a mouthful of gob in his eye. His leer widened. He liked that – hookers giving him the evil eye was like a compliment because for all his own problems, he was above them on the food chain.

'Nice meetin' you, hen?' Dillon winked at Connie, who ignored him and wobbled to the bar on those heels.

'Nice girl, Maxie. Where'd you find her? In a fuckin' skip.' Dillon pissed himself and it made no difference that Maxine didn't join in. That was the whole point.

Logan heard it too. It was unusual for him to bother himself with what came out of the cakehole of dross like Andy Dillon, but he'd watched the girls come in and grab an hour where they'd enjoyed themselves, and now this bastard had walked in and robbed them of a bit of peace and quiet.

'How did you know I was here, Andy?'

Maxine swigged back what was left of her drink and resisted the temptation to stick the empty glass in his face.

Even though he hadn't laid a hand on her, she felt as if he was assaulting her – he'd broken into their peace, their brief time forgetting, and it was all reality again.

'A hoor workin' along the road gave me directions for a bag – no honour among slags, eh, hen?' He was feeling good again and self-delusion had reinstalled in his fevered brain.

'What do you want, Andy? I told you I'm broke. Simple as.'

Maxine turned her palms up to confirm the statement, but she knew there was more to his visit than collection.

'Got a nice plan where you can cancel the debt, hen. Need you for a wee job in the mornin' – well actually the afternoon. Keep forgettin' slags like you don't get up till it's dark'

He sat back and waited.

'And if I can't be arsed?' She knew the options would be all bad.

'Thing is, Maxie, you do this or it's time to collect, and I've already paid a guy to slit your nose up the middle.'

He took a long slug of his beer and winked over the top of the glass as if he'd just delivered good news. Despite the bit of courage delivered to her system by Mr Smirnoff, Maxine felt her gut squirm as she pictured the outcome of the threat the bastard had just delivered. Even with her chaotic lifestyle, she still had her looks, although her complexion was suffering and premature ageing was no doubt on its way. She could still look in the mirror and see that young woman who only the year before could have taken her pick, and the image of one side of her nose slashed up the side made her wince. Dillon saw it and lapped it up.

'Wi' a puss like Frankenstein, the punters'll drive right past you, hen, and then where the fuck are you?'

He was grinning from ear to ear. She stared at his decaying teeth and felt revolted that the creep had crawled all over her whenever he felt like it.

Suddenly her eyes flicked upwards – she hadn't seen the Big Man arriving and Dillon had definitely missed it because he was just so pleased with himself. Logan appeared behind Dillon, laying a paw like a bear's on his shoulder and squeezing – hard. It was remarkable the way Dillon almost crumpled in on himself, and Maxine realised just how strong the Big Man was as he lowered his head down to the side of Dillon's and talked slowly into the boy's ear.

'Seein' as I'm the gaffer here, son, I can refuse to have or serve anyone I don't like. Understand? That right, Mick?' He looked again towards Harkins, who was still staring at the telly. Harkins looked round and nodded seriously.

'Absolutely right, Tam, an' there'd be chaos without law an' order. The man's right, son.' He locked eyes with Dillon, who wished he'd just stayed in Dalkeith that night.

Dillon looked sideways – he could hardly speak with the pain shooting from the nerves, muscle and bone that seemed about to collapse under the Big Man's grip. His eyes were wide with fear, but he managed to nod because Logan obviously wanted some acknowledgement that he was being understood.

'Thing is, son, you're upsettin' the customers, so you're barred, and I'm about to throw you on the pavement because I think you're a menace. Understand?'

Dillon knew it was better to agree and as he nodded again, some dribble spilled from the side of his gob.

Logan was as good as his word – never releasing his grip, he guided Dillon to the door as the two girls stared open-mouthed. Maxine knew that Logan was trying to be noble, but the rat bastard he was ejecting from the premises would blame her, and on top of every other problem, she didn't need another. But she wouldn't say anything to Logan because he was one of the few people who seemed to care that she was alive.

'Say goodbye to the big people, son.'

Logan paused at the door he was holding open with his free hand. Harkins tore his gaze away from the TV screen and waved as if it was one of his best mates leaving the premises.

Dillon hit the pavement and landed on his skinny arse, which sent pain coursing through his body. It hurt like fuck and he screwed up his face, waiting for it to subside.

It just wasn't Dillon's night though because a couple of unfriendly jakies wandered past at exactly that moment. They'd survived by taking every opportunity that came their way to get the next day's supply and some eejit lying injured outside Logan's boozer was too good a chance to miss. They were all over Dillon like a rash and by the time they were finished his wallet, iPhone and loose change were chored. At least they'd left his car keys, wise enough to know that if they tried to drive, they would probably be killed.

If there was a positive, it was that the jakies were so pissed that the taller one's rallying cry of, 'Let's batter the bastard, Sandy,' didn't really come to anything and there was no real power in the swings and badly aimed kicks that quickly exhausted the two robbers. The tall one eventually called his mate off before they died of exhaustion.

'That'll do, Sandy – he's had enough.'

They disappeared into the shadows and Dillon lay prostrate, coughing his guts up with the additional pain in his ribs, neck and hips. His bottom lip was split vertically and dead centre. He rolled over onto his side and spat some blood onto the wet pavement as he heard the pub door open behind him. The light from the warm interior reflected on the soaking ground, which sucked the heat from Dillon's aching body.

Mick Harkins stood in the doorway and squinted into the night as he lit up a smoke. He pulled up the collar on his overcoat and rubbed his hands as he glanced down at Dillon, who turned his head to look up at Harkins.

'You want to get somethin' on the lip, son – looks painful.'

He stepped round Dillon and walked a few steps before stopping and turning around. 'Sorry, son, I forgot to say have a lovely time an' I hope Santa's good to you.'

He turned again and walked in the same general direction as the jakies with the smoke from his cigarette billowing in the freezing air.

Dillon said 'fuck' several times and pulled himself onto his hands and knees. He was hurt, angry and pictured his revenge, which if it had been real or an option included the big barman, the jakies and the smart arse at the bar who'd walked past him as he lay on the pavement.

The problem was that they were all in the 'too difficult' box, so instead he fixed on Maxine as an achievable target – she'd get it for all he'd taken that night.

'Fuckin' bitch.'

He pushed himself up onto his feet and headed for his car, his mind raging with the humiliation. He said 'bitch' a few more times before he pulled the car door open, spat some blood onto the pavement then sank into the driver's seat and tried to calm the shakes that had gripped him.

7

In the pub, Logan had almost forgotten Dillon, and when he looked at the clock he felt another one of those moments of panic that hit him every night since the death of his wife the previous year. He was fine when he was working at the bar, but the attractive stone-built house he lived in seemed frightening and dead. It was almost as if their home had died at the same time she'd passed away quietly in the hospice. He tried, but life just wasn't working anymore. His dreams were all of those days that just wouldn't come back.

When Logan had been in HMP Saughton as a young man and his employers – the Flemings – were wiped from the criminal map, she'd given him the choice of going straight or never seeing her again, so he'd walked away from the only life he'd ever known. It had never occurred to him that she might go before him and now he was lost with only the pub to keep him from walking into the sea.

'Fancy comin' back to the flat for a Christmas drink, ladies?'

Connie and Maxine hadn't noticed him coming to the table. They looked up, surprised because no one invited working girls for Christmas drinks unless they were looking for services. Both girls felt a moment of disappointment because they wondered for a moment if he was just like everyone else. He saw the look, felt almost embarrassed and the girls watched his face redden, which for a man who always seemed in control surprised them.

'No strings, girls. I'm askin' some o' the boys and their girlfriends over there as well. Honestly. Just a few bevvies.'

There was enough in his expression and colour for them to know he was straight up. They looked at each other for a second before Connie tilted her head up, grinned and seized the moment.

'Free drink, Tam? You know how to charm a girl, so you do.' She nodded to Maxine who shrugged, but an invite to somewhere warm and friendly was a positive bonus.

'What're the options, Connie?'

For Maxine there were none available apart from worrying who might call in a debt. She was never more exposed than when she was working on the street and spent her nights wondering whether each punter was there for business or to settle matters for someone else. They told Logan just to give them the nod when he was ready. He looked pleased and the red flush calmed.

'Never thought I'd see the Big Man embarrassed, Maxie. There's a good man there.'

Connie needed a smoke and walked to the door as Maxine stared at Logan's back. He walked over to the few regular drinkers left, including the Campbell brothers, who were up and coming gangsters in the city. Young, good-looking and smart, they had a certain charm few in their profession possessed. They liked the Big Man, but most importantly they respected him, and his pub had become their part-time office. They never caused a moment's bother, spent well, dressed like celebrities and attracted some nice female company. Logan accepted them and they brought in trade because their mates started to use the place, with the added bonus that it kept the bampots away. If there was any smell of bother then the offender was taking on the Campbells as well as Logan, and that was never a contest.

'Nice one, Tam. We'll come for a drink.'

Rab Campbell was the oldest of the brothers and tended to do the talking. He was occasionally guilty of saying the wrong thing and had a habit of shooting from the mouth. His sibling Colin, or 'CC' as he was known, had a quieter nature and was the business brain.

Logan felt a moment of relief that at least for one night he would have company and not spend the dark hours running the same memories on a loop in his mind. He almost felt embarrassed – a strange emotion for a man who rarely felt pressure from another human being. His home had been silent, almost still, like an empty church since his wife had died. Now he'd invited a bunch of people he knew more or less through the bar – hardly bosom buddies but he'd almost blurted out the invites and it was too late now to rein back.

Logan finally admitted to himself that he was lonely. In the old life he wouldn't have known what that meant, and there were times he almost felt angry that she'd died before him – he would sit at the side of her bed and beg her to live. She just used to smile, wondering if any of the hard men he knew had ever seen this side of Big Tam Logan.

8

Logan was nervous because there hadn't been another person in the house since his wife had died. He wondered if it was wrong to bring this bunch of flash gangsters and working girls into the home that had meant so much to her, that was almost sacred to them – the place they had always dreamed of. But the long nights alone were killing him slowly, and he needed this, regardless of the ghost that tugged at his feelings. He wondered if she would be angry but knew that just wasn't the way she was – she'd hate to see how he was now, all that suffering inside one man who had to pretend he was different, harder than the rest.

Connie and Maxine walked beside the Big Man while the Campbells, a few of the other boys and a couple of girl-friends tagged a few yards behind. They were all slightly under the influence, bordering on half pissed, but they babbled like teenagers and there was a good mood among them. Maxine thought it almost felt the way Christmas used to be for her and she pushed her own problems away. *Live for the moment, girl – there's nothing else*, she thought and would keep telling herself until those old dreams came true.

Logan opened the door to the home that looked onto the ancient ground of Leith Links and switched on the light in the hall. Maxine was behind him, followed by Connie, who dug her friend in the ribs and raised her eyebrows in surprise.

Even in the hall, the place took them by surprise. Maxine expected a 'man alone' tip with the usual array of debris scattered around by someone living without the balance of another human being. Not Logan's place. The smell of polish hit their nostrils with a kick because that level of housework was something from a previous life, though in Connie's world, the chance of Banjo rubbing polish into the furniture was about the same as him joining the Hare Krishna movement.

Logan shoved open a beautifully varnished door and steered them all into the lounge, which was illuminated only by the street lights. He started to flick on the switches of the various lamps in the room. It was pleasantly warm, the timer having switched on the central heating half an hour before the door opened.

For the next few seconds, the crowd that had been on the edge of a party mood fell quiet, looking at a room that was full of the touches of someone who wasn't there and never would be again. It wasn't just the furniture, old-fashioned but made for the place; it was the pictures. Logan, the one-time hard case, tamed by the serious-looking, diminutive woman in the photos who seemed dwarfed by his size. The ornaments were almost themed and the paintings – though not expensive, not works of art – were good pieces bought on their travels. She loved to travel and he loved to take her to all those places that had never interested him before they met.

Perhaps the biggest surprise was the old upright piano. It wouldn't have occurred to the visitors that it had never been played since her death; in fact it probably wouldn't have occurred to them that it had been played before her death. Pianos didn't really figure in their family homes.

'Jesus, Tam. We in the right place?' Rab Campbell said just to make some noise. They all knew that Big Tam had never recovered from his wife's death and what Rab had said was thoughtless, but at least it broke that brief moment when they were dealing with their surprise. Maxine was struck more than anyone because she recognised a home that reflected much of the one she once belonged to. She put her hand to her mouth for no more than a second and felt her throat tighten with emotion. Whoever had inhabited this place, the Big Man had loved her and what came with her.

'Do you play?' Maxine said without thinking. It seemed almost a daft question to the rest of them, but Logan just saw it as reasonable. He remembered the nights his wife had tried to teach him a few notes as he struggled to get those beef fingers to flick across the keys. He would have loved to have played and had managed to string some notes together, which had made him proud in a way he'd never experienced before. It was an achievement that didn't include criminal activity, and he'd been almost shocked by the experience. That was when he'd realised how much he'd missed and that she was showing him the way to a different, better kind of life.

'Tried, Maxie, but wrong kinda fingers. That's my excuse.' He smiled and she saw the vulnerable boy in the man's body again.

'Do you mind?'

It was Maxine's turn to pull the surprise. She walked almost gingerly towards the piano, lifted the lid slowly and then tapped out a few simple notes with one hand, but enough for everyone in the room to know she could actually

41

play. She put the lid down quickly as if she was guilty of something and turned back to face the rest of them.

'Right, boys and girls, what'll you have?'

Logan knew something had touched Maxine and that it was time to resume normal services, at least for the moment.

The moment was gone and the noise level rose as everyone got in their orders and Rab Campbell kicked things off with a joke about homosexual jihadists. Appropriate was a word he'd only heard on the telly and definitely didn't understand.

Logan came through with treble vodis for Connie and Maxine and it was a typical atmosphere of post-pub partying where time left the room. The noise, music and laughter seemed to merge into a swirling mixture of enjoyment and overindulgence. Even Logan got stuck in for the first time in months, and for a couple of hours, he felt young again.

Rab Campbell more or less stole the girlfriend of one of the pub regulars. There wasn't much the poor guy could do but grin and bear it. He would treat her like a lady for a couple of days. She'd believe every word the lying bastard told her then that would be the end of that and the guy could have her back, if he wanted. It was one of the fringe benefits of being a gangster that you could more or less rob who you liked, when you liked.

9

It was strange because Maxine and Logan couldn't remember the party winding down and the last of the guest leaving the house. He'd put the fire on earlier and the flames from the burning coal danced for them. Maxine kept closing her eyes so she could just feel the heat on her skin and nothing else. She'd sunk more booze than usual, but it'd had little effect and she was OK. Better than OK – sitting cross-legged in front of the fire was a special moment among endless days where morning till night all she felt was misery.

They'd both drunk a lot, but they'd hardly spoken and didn't need to for the moment. Logan was just enjoying the warmth of female company while Maxine could pretend this was a normal night – the she was just a normal girl spending time with an old friend.

Maxine had always interested Logan, while others ignored her, as if working the street erased personal history and meant the women were all exactly the same once they'd sold themselves for the first time. They were the untouchables – at least that's what people pretended, especially the punters who led normal lives, whatever the fuck that was. But Logan had always seen her as different, though he had never asked about her past. Unless someone offered up those details, he'd found it was best to avoid the subject. He suspected that in her case, it had to hurt.

'Play something, Maxie. Anything.' His words broke the long, comfortable silence. She looked round at him and, despite her instinct to say no, she nodded. Logan had been kind and she'd heard the stories from Connie that he was wounded, so she decided that he deserved something for what he'd done for her and her friend that night.

She grinned. 'I'll play, but can I ask a favour?'

He nodded and hoped she wouldn't spoil it all by asking for money. He'd give her it if that's what she wanted, but he hoped it wasn't.

'Can I have a hot bath? Don't know when I had one last. I'll go after that – promise.' She felt her cheeks flush, although he wouldn't notice in the half light and shadows thrown around the room by the fire.

'Last thing I expected, Maxine, but you go ahead, girl. Tell you what, it's the middle o' the night. There's two spare rooms to pick from an' I'll no' come near you, so you might as well bed down here. No worries if it's a problem.'

Maxine had no intention of arguing. A hot bath and a clean bed had a stronger pull than dope, the way she was feeling.'

'You sure?' She hoped he was.

'Go on, girl. I'll show you where everything is. A wee tune first though, Maxine – that'll do for me.'

'Do me a favour, Tom.' He looked straight into her eyes because no one had called him Tom since his wife had died. She'd always refused to call him Tam.

'What is it?'

'Can you always call me Maxine? I used to have another life.' She paused and seemed to be somewhere else for a moment before she spoke again. 'I was Maxine back then.'

Logan smiled. He wanted to know more but her request held an intimacy that pleased and surprised him at the same time. 'Of course, that's easy enough... Maxine.' His smile widened. 'Still want that tune though – price for the B&B.'

She pushed herself up onto her feet, the same tremors in her stomach she'd felt every time she'd gone for music exams all those years ago.

Her parents had been so proud when she'd passed. She'd only ever seen her father cry once – when she'd played 'Ae Fond Kiss'. He was a Burns man and watching his only daughter play a song that had touched so many hearts had been too much for him. She remembered that moment as one of the most precious in her life.

'There's only a few I can tap out from memory, Tom.'

She looked over her shoulder as she spoke and he watched the shadows and light flicker across her skin, thinking it was hard to believe this was a young woman who sold herself on the street. He knew she was up to her armpits in trouble, but all he could see was the girl behind the mask. It was only her clothes that gave her away. All wrong for her, but the girls used what they wore like an advertising board saying 'cheap and cheerful, come on in!'

'You know any Beatles songs, Maxine? Still a fan after all these years.' He sat down and waited, hoping the moment wouldn't disappoint. So many of these girls became preda-tors and grabbed what they could, when they could, just to survive – a warm smile appearing at exactly the same time they were dipping your wallet.

'A couple – my dad loved them as well.'

She sat down at the piano, lifted the lid again and stared at the keyboard. For a moment she panicked and it was as if she was dreaming, staring at something that was only a memory. Could she still do it or had the dope ripped up too many circuits in her brain?

She took a couple of breaths and pretended it was just another one of those exams that used to give her sleepless nights. She had passed them all so why not?

Her mind drifted off as her subconscious took over and her hands did the rest. She played the old McCartney classic 'Here, There and Everywhere'.

Logan closed his eyes and let the notes drift around him in the lights that moved around the room conducted by the dying flames. He imagined his wife was back, that it was her playing again, and even if it was just for a moment, it was what he'd asked for.

When Maxine played the last notes, she smiled, pleased that she'd managed it with barely a mistake and turned to see him with his face in his hands, sobbing quietly as if he was ashamed of the raw emotion. She knew he had a past but there was so much good in him. What he was doing needed privacy so she closed the door quietly behind her and left him to his grief.

An hour later, her skin still glowing from the hot water, she almost nervously opened the door into the lounge to find the flames low and Logan standing with his back to the fire.

'Thanks, Maxine – and sorry you saw that.'

'Don't be, Tom.' She meant it.

'Right, I'll show you where the room is and see you in the mornin'. I like a good breakfast so hope you've an appetite.'

He smiled, his grief once again buried away in the compartment he'd kept sealed till that night.

Minutes later, Maxine sank into a bed that was clean and a warm piece of heaven. It was like falling off a cliff into a deep safe place. She was asleep in a moment and didn't dream.

10

Maxine's phone was running low on charge but there was still enough life in it to spring to action and lift her out of a kind of sleep heaven. She woke struggling to lift her eyelids and the reason was obvious. Her body and mind were exhausted. The full six hours of repair had been a wonderful break from her cares, but she needed much more of the same. The text alert purred for the second time, and she rolled over wishing she could keep turning the clock back to the minute she'd fallen asleep. It took only a few seconds to read the message from Andy Dillon and re-enter the cold world of reality.

'Shit, shit, shit.'

She squeezed a handful of bedcover and felt her stomach knot up. He wanted her to do a job in the afternoon. There were no details but he was heading into town in a couple of hours to pick her up and, if she wasn't there, 'to order a plastic surgeon'. *He does love his little jokes*, she thought.

Logan was moving about downstairs as she let the shower turn her skin pink again, and she realised how much she'd missed these luxuries most people treated as nothing more than a normal part of life. There should have been a hangover from the booze, but she was alert and didn't feel like she needed any chemical assistance to get her day going. She had no idea what Dillon wanted her to do, but it wouldn't be Christmas charity work. Maxine hated him, no question, and it was a feeling that was new to her. It wasn't in her nature to hate, and the people she owed money to would come to hurt her eventually, but that was all her fault. There was something else about Dillon that turned her stomach. He was a weakling feeding on the weak. A rat.

She padded into the kitchen wrapped in one of Big Tam's old dressing gowns, which looked like it was designed for two people. The smell of bacon unlocked her saliva glands and she found she was hungry, which seemed strange because the desire to eat had been suppressed for someone who never had anything left after buying smokes and dope. Logan looked slightly embarrassed, as if she'd take the piss after what she'd seen in the early hours, but she did her best to smile and move any conversation away from his grief.

'Did you sleep, hen?'

He cracked a couple of eggs; he obviously knew how to cook. In truth, he hadn't made breakfast for months, but like Maxine he had an appetite for a change and had headed out to the local market long before she woke up. The papers were on the kitchen table, and it was a picture of normality that was far from the truth, though they both ached for that version of life.

'Slept like a log, Tom.'

He looked up from the spitting rashers and watched her glance down at the paper. He liked it; he liked the fact that she thought about him in her own way and not just as Logan the barman. Sitting with his oversized dressing gown on, she looked almost comical but completely at home. It wasn't some older guy trying to recapture his youth with a younger woman. Just the pleasure of having the cold empty space in his life inhabited by someone who made sense to him. Logan had never been that interested in chasing women. The Hibees and a bit of criminal activity had been all he'd ever wanted or thought about till he met the woman who'd changed all that.

He dished up the breakfast without asking what she actually wanted – he could see that she was as hungry as he was. She tried hard not to rush the food, but it was difficult, and he wondered when she'd last eaten a square meal. He loved to see a good appetite, and he went for his own plate in much the same manner. They hardly spoke as the full-fat breakfast disappeared.

When she was done, Maxine sat back, gulped down some black tea and sighed.

'Honestly, that was as good as it gets.'

She knew that there was an awkward moment coming about what happened next. There was no vibe that Logan expected her to pay back, and she felt absolutely comfortable with him. A lot of the girls would have offered him a turn and tried to get what they could, but that wasn't an option. She wouldn't ask and definitely wouldn't take from him. He felt the same and decided to get to the point.

'What you up to the rest of the day, Maxine?' He paused then said what he really meant.

'Look, I know you've got problems, so if I can help, just say the word.' He waited and wasn't even sure what he wanted her to do or say.

'You've done enough for me, Tom – best night I've had in a long time. I'll go in a bit.'

'Do you need some money?'

'No. I'm in enough trouble with money.'

'That wee shite in the pub last night, Maxine… I know the kind. That type feeds on lassies like you. You want me to speak to him?'

Maxine knew he meant every word. But Dillon had an old man who'd go to war over the boy if someone like Logan intervened, and then there'd be a line of stretchers rolling up at the A&E just because she couldn't pay her debts. One of those stretchers would be carrying the big man opposite, and he'd done nothing to deserve being dragged into her mess.

She put her hand over the table and clasped his huge wrist.

'You don't need to do any more, Tom. I need to get myself sorted out. No idea how, but coming here last night reminded me what I've lost. God knows how, but I have to find a way back. There's stuff I need to do and maybe try my parents. They gave up on me but it's worth a try. Even if they'd just talk to me again, it would be a start.'

She took a deep breath and knew it was probably all talk. Dillon wanted her for something she'd hate, it might all go so wrong and she'd be flogging herself back on the street before the day was done.

'Tell you what, Maxine – the room's here if you want it and still no strings attached. Anyway, I'm way past my best and you're safe enough.'

They both grinned almost politely and wondered at the same time.

'You do a bit of work here and that'll do me fine till you get on your feet. One condition. You come off the street.'

'Let me think, Tom. That bastard Dillon wants me to do some job to pay off the debts an' then I'm clear at least where's he's concerned. Not much choice really.'

She frowned and felt trapped by what she had to do. The offer to live in Logan's house was something she couldn't have imagined only a day ago, but she didn't know what the outcome of Dillon's plan would be.

'He'll no' let you go, hen. His type can't afford that. You change your mind an' I'll give him a house call. The Campbells will weigh in. They owe me.'

'I'll get dressed, Tom.' She stood up and turned to head for the bedroom, then stopped.

'Tell you what – if I can get through this day then we'll talk again. Truth is, I'd love to stay here.'

Logan watched her disappear and felt the danger in his gut. He knew how the game worked, had seen all the casualties, the ones who didn't have the extra sense for scanning the environment they lived in. The red light was flashing for Maxine, but she couldn't see it – or maybe she could but she was determined to move into the danger zone regardless. He shook his head and hoped she'd take the offer he'd given. He thought maybe they could help save each other.

Dressing in her old clothes almost repelled her. They weren't clean, but her skin was, and it felt wrong pulling on what was just about all she owned. It was as if she was pulling the street onto her back once again. Those clothes had been touched and in the company of the punters who used her every night, and it felt wrong in this house.

'Christ.' She struggled to finish dressing, and when she went back to the kitchen she was almost ashamed that Logan would see her back in working gear. She had her head down when she joined him as he cleaned up and finishing another coffee.

'I'm off, Tom.'

He knew exactly what was bothering her, stood up, wrapped his arms round her and told her to come back when she was ready. It felt wondrous, a good man holding her because she needed it. He let her go and sat down again.

'I'll be in the pub if you need anythin', hen.'

11

Maxine walked out onto the street to find a winter sun doing its best in a clear sky. Some kids were knocking a ball about as a couple manoeuvred a pram past her and the baby exercised its lungs at full volume. She smiled at them and they smiled back, and the world looked fairly normal. She'd sent a text to Andy Dillon and had a spare half hour before he was going to pick her up.

What she didn't know was that, hurt as he'd been the previous night, Dillon had decided to wait and had followed the group back to Logan's house, counting them in and out – apart from her. He would have killed her if he could have wrapped his bony hands round her throat for what he saw as an insult after his treatment in the pub at the hands of the Logan, but there was a job to be done that was potentially a real earner. Once that was finished, he was going to make her beg to stop the pain.

What he'd imagined had excited him – even with all the aching muscles he'd been turned on to full volume and couldn't control himself, so he'd leaned back, closed his eyes and tried to let his imagination get to work on his fantasy.

He'd said 'bitch' over and over again, and hadn't noticed a local wide boy walk past with his new lemon. The young lady had cackled at what she'd seen him doing, while the wide boy had assessed the build of the tosser in the car, realised he could take him with his eyes closed and decided it was a real chance to impress his new squeeze.

'Ya durty bastard.'

He'd jogged round to the driver's side, yanked open the driver's door and pulled Dillon out of the car – forcing him from the edge of ecstasy to cold reality in a moment. The wide boy had then forced him back over the bonnet, where he'd enjoyed watching the panic on Dillon's face as his chinos had descended in a pile round his ankles. The wide boy hadn't been able to work out why the perv already looked like he'd had a beating, but his new girlfriend had given him the green light.

'Stick the fuckin' heid on him, Stevie.'

Her young man hadn't needed any further encouragement, drawing back his head to give it the full welly and cracking Dillon right in the middle of his nut, splitting the skin and knocking the cement out of his legs. He'd slumped to the ground, only just aware of the young woman whooping in delight at her boyfriend's martial skills.

'Kick his heid in, Stevie!

She'd wanted more – and her hero had been only too happy to oblige, rattling his feet into various parts of Dillon's torso and head till honour was satisfied and the happy couple had headed off to a Christmas party, arm in arm. If Stevie hadn't been sure the lemon would do a turn before he'd battered Dillon, he'd definitely been on course after it, the way she'd held him close. Christmas had come early for him at least.

Dillon had lain still for a couple of minutes, groaning at the nausea wracking his body. He'd thrown up then struggled onto his knees for the second time and felt an anger that had almost overwhelmed him and needed release.

'Fuck!'

He'd wanted to go home and get cleaned up, so he'd buckled his trousers and, once his brain had stopped spinning, got back in the car and sat with his head on the wheel till he'd felt able to drive. He'd had more than enough for one night, but at least he knew where Maxine was resting her head. Tomorrow, she would pay for everything that had happened to him in Leith.

12

Dillon was already in position about three hundred yards from Logan's place when Maxine stepped onto the street. He leaned forward and winced at the pain shooting through his ribcage. Dillon glanced up at the mirror and saw his face again. It looked like a Rottweiler had been chewing his puss, and he'd lost another one of his few remaining teeth. He snarled. As far as he was concerned, Maxine had more than her debt to pay back. He just wished it was time to show her what he was capable of.

She walked slowly across Leith Links, glancing at her phone then tapping in her parents' number before deciding against it. She knew that if there was a chance to live again, she had to try with them. Convince them that all she wanted was to speak, even if they could never forgive her. She tried again to give herself the courage and pushed the 'call' button, then panicked and felt like throwing the phone away and running.

'Hello.'

Her mother's voice was from another world – the one she sensed in Logan's home. A safe place where good things happened.

'Mum.' That was all she managed before she broke down. Her mother didn't hang up, gripping the phone till her fingers turned white, listening to her only girl break her heart. She waited because she'd wanted the call – every day since she'd told her only daughter she never wanted to see her again. Her husband would never come to terms with what Maxine had done, but she couldn't live without knowing where her girl was and what she was doing. Every time she read or listened to a report about a drugs death she almost choked expecting the worst.

What she couldn't know or even understand was that Maxine hadn't touched H for weeks. She was still spending money she didn't have on weed and tabs to take the edge off, but she was staying a few steps away from the dragon's grasp. It was impossible for Maxine to explain everything that had happened and she wouldn't want to. Her mother inhabited another world and it was better to leave her there. She couldn't control the release of emotion though, and it all came out standing on the wet hoary grass in the middle of Leith Links.

'Maxine.'

Her mother only ever used her full name and she said it again, feeling helpless, but her anger was long gone. She'd tried Maxine's old number a few times, but it had been ditched not long after she'd run from the family home. Her mother was convinced that she couldn't be in Edinburgh. It wasn't a big city, and eventually you had to bump into even those people you wanted to avoid. It was that kind of place.

A couple of times she'd walked the streets till she was exhausted, hoping for the chance meet so she could pretend it was accidental. But in a way she was right and her daughter was in different city. Her mother lived in the day while Maxine inhabited the night. They were different places.

When Maxine recovered enough to speak, the emotions washing through her overwhelmed her ability to string a coherent sentence together. She just kept saying she was sorry and it was all that would come.

'Maxine, listen to me.' Her mother found some strength. 'Let's meet and talk. I want to see how you are, alright?' She put the palm of her free hand flat against her breastbone as tension squeezed her heart.

'I'm glad you called; I worry every day.' She couldn't wash away the words that she'd hurled at her daughter that last day, watching the girl crumble under a verbal assault that she'd regretted every day since, but she could let her know how much she regretted them.

Maxine heard the words 'I'm glad you called' and felt like getting down on her knees and thanking the God who'd deserted her a long time ago.

She controlled her sobbing, but those few words of comfort were almost too much to handle. She needed to speak to her mother again once she'd survived the day and she was calm.

'I promise to call back, Mum… Tomorrow… we'll meet… I miss you and Dad.'

She put the phone down, grateful the battery had held out, and fumbled with the packet of cigarettes that refused to open. Her hands were shaking, and she tried to work out all that was happening around her. Logan, Andy Dillon and the chance to repair some of the damage she'd inflicted on her family. Nothing could stay the way it was; she knew that, but her life could be better than it had been on the street.

She managed to get the cigarette into her mouth and burning. She pulled two longs draws, but it tasted foul for some reason, and she flicked it into the gutter as she made her way to meet Dillon at the foot of Leith Walk.

Dillon had watched her from a distance, lightly tracing his forefinger over the swellings and cuts he'd picked up in the night hours.

'What the fuck is she on?' He gripped the wheel and felt all of his suppressed anger almost close his throat.

He drove the long way round to the pick-up point and felt that stirring again when he thought about what he was going to do to her later. *After all*, he thought, *who the fuck's going to worry about a street hooker?*

13

She hissed through clenched teeth when she saw the van approaching, any hope that he just wouldn't turn up in the gutter with the cigarette she'd tossed away in frustration. She was shivering with cold but felt a glimmer of hope after what had happened with Logan and the conversation with her mother.

Maxine had one foot on the sill and was about to pull herself into the van when she clocked Dillon's coupon.

'Jesus, what happened to you?' It was only said through surprise – it wasn't like she gave a shit about his state of health.

'Get the fuck in and keep it shut,' Dillon snarled. His face was a mess and he didn't need the cow to remind him what he could see in the mirror.

Maxine did as she was told but would like to have thanked the guy who'd rearranged his face. Her trailing foot hadn't even left the deck when he gunned the engine, pulling away from the kerb, and the manoeuvre almost threw her back on the road.

'Move your arse.' Dillon was right in his comfort zone, throwing his insignificant weight around with a woman who couldn't fight back, much as she wanted to. And she wanted to – there was no doubt about that where he was concerned.

'What's the deal, Andy?'

They were moving slowly past the Festival Theatre on the south side of the city and he still hadn't spoken. He was angry; it was all over his mangled face. He had to speak, but he was struggling to control the rage that hadn't subsided since he'd received that double tanking in Leith. He needed a release, but it wasn't time yet.

'There's an auld fucker lives on his own in the sticks. On a wee farm. He's a fuckin' perv,' Dillon said without a trace of irony. 'Thing is, I picked up a story from some wee junkie burd. I sell her gear so she talks, know what I mean?'

Maxine could see he was excited – it was that look she despised and had seen too often.

'She's stampin' his card on a regular basis an' the boy can't get enough.'

He looked at Maxine and grinned as if she'd enjoy him sharing the story. Her blank expression barely registered with him as he told her the rest.

'Turns up this guy is an elder o' the fuckin' church, Round Table an' a' that shite. Fuckin' pillar o' the community. Thing is, he's loaded, lives on his Jack an' can't get enough o' the wee junkie. So, he just asks the wee burd if there's any chance she can fix up a threesome an' as soon as I hear that then it's Bob's your fuckin' Auntie!'

Again, he looked round at Maxine, who stared straight ahead because she already knew part of what was coming next.

'Well, I thought, Andy boy, if I need a cheap ride, I know the very fuckin' slapper.'

'Is that it?' Maxine said, and although it turned her stomach, she thought it might not be the worst thing she'd had to do in her time on the street.

Dillon could see that she still didn't get how sharp an operator he was. 'See.' He tapped the side of his head. 'You just don't get the big picture, hen – the plan. That's why you hawk the mutton in Leith an' I drive a nice set o' wheels.'

He was enjoying himself and honestly believed he was some kind of criminal mastermind.

'It's blackmail, Maxie. We bleed the boy till he's dry. Get it?'

'Blackmail?' She knew then that the situation was a shit storm waiting to happen. They would be facing serious time if the bizzies got involved.

'What the fuck, Andy? You're having a laugh.'

Maxine knew as soon as she'd opened her mouth that the words were all wrong to a man who believed that he had a gift. His anger simmered barely under control, and he needed no encouragement to show what he could do.

They were on the long Dalkeith Road, one of the arteries leading out of the old city to the newer estates on the southern edge of town. Dillon pulled the wheel to the left and squeezed down hard on the brakes, burning a lot of rubber before stopping with the nearside front wheel on the pavement. He gripped a handful of Maxine's hair and pulled her head down and over towards his lap. He lowered his face close to her ear and dripped saliva from his swollen lips.

'You do what I tell you, do you hear me?'

He waited and heard her groan the words, 'OK, Andy.' Her breathing was rapid, and he felt the heaving movement of her breasts and pictured again what would come later, once he was finished with her. She felt him stir and gagged at the smell of his unwashed clothes.

'Now here's what'll happen. You'll meet up wi' the other slag, go see the boy an' do exactly what he wants. Wee burd says he never closes the front door. When the two o' you are

61

near the happy endin', I come in wi' the camera and that's fuckin' that.'

He pulled harder and watched Maxine wince, trying her best not to cry out.

'She's only fifteen, so when she's doin' the business, I want you to take some pictures as well, an' of course there'll be DNA on the wee hairy.'

He let her go.

'Now, you fuck this up, darlin', and the junkie I've hired to cut you up for a few free deals gets the nod. I'll be alibied up to ma tits when he's openin' the old nasal cavities. We clear?'

Maxine pulled herself up and wiped a couple of stray tears forced out through pain as much as emotion. Her face was tight and her own anger had taken hold. Dillon was out of control and going to get them all locked up if he went ahead.

It was worse than that though, and she realised in those few minutes that at some point, he was intent on hurting her himself. Logan had been right, streetwise – he knew what Dillon was and that in one way or another, the bastard would never leave her alone. Even if this job came off, he'd keep his claws buried deep inside her. She should have listened to the Big Man and taken up his offer. Dillon was barely able to contain what was inside and she was his release, the one who couldn't fight back. It might have been selfish, but the realisation that she might be disfigured or worse hit home, and she felt frightened and helpless.

As he started the van, she decided she had very little time to think and needed to use every second to make the right decision.

They headed out of the city as Maxine's mind circled the options and found there wasn't a good one among them. Her heart fluttered rather than beat, and she felt she was going to pass out with what was close to an anxiety attack.

Every couple of minutes Dillon would mutter a few obscenities, and it was as if he was talking to someone else. She wondered if the beating he'd taken had dislodged a few of his remaining brain cells, because he looked close to a meltdown, and she didn't want to be there when it happened. The bastard seemed completely unfazed that the other girl was only fifteen. He was happy to get a kid in on the act and worse – a kid with a habit.

She ground her teeth and her own anger started to bubble near the surface. Whatever happened, she wasn't playing this game – not with a kid involved. She glanced over at Dillon, who seemed to be leaning too far forward as he drove and staring, almost as if he wasn't registering what was actually in front of him. Twice he drifted into the other lane and she said his name – he didn't look at her but her voice registered and he pulled back to his side.

As they passed the outskirts of Dalkeith and onto the old A68 route to the Borders, Dillon seemed to focus again, scanning the road ahead for something. Dillon's phone rang. He stopped and answered it, said OK twice, then moved off again, before turning onto a side road and pulling into a layby.

He said nothing as they waited – just lit a cigarette hanging from his cracked and bloodied lips. Lowering the driver's window, he stared across the fields, constantly running his fingers over the damage to his head and face. He was still muttering under his breath, and Maxine was tempted to bolt, but he would have her before she got twenty meters.

She froze when her door was pulled open, then registered what was happening when she saw who was standing outside the van.

'You awright?' It had to be the accomplice. Fifteen going on thirty and probably a lifetime of experience in all the wrong things.

She ticked all the boxes – she chewed gum like her life depended on it, had an attitude that almost radiated heat and dressed like a stand-in for Vicky Pollard. The girl's complexion was somewhere on the grey spectrum – a diet of crap and cigarettes had clearly taken its toll.

Maxine knew the type, neglected since birth with nowhere to go but the streets. She almost winced at her own thoughts. *'The type' – Christ, what does that make me?* she thought. A cheap hooker who owed more than she could earn working twenty-four-seven down Leith. At least she'd seen another life and thrown it away – this girl had never had the chance.

'Hi, Kylie.' Dillon seemed to have cheered up at the sight of the kid and couldn't quite hide his leer. Maxine knew exactly what the sick bastard had been up to with the girl.

'Hi, Andy.' She looked sideways at Maxine; she seemed like she was ready to go to war with her at a moment's notice.

'Jump in the back, hen.' He stepped out onto the grass verge, pulled down the driver's seat and grinned. 'Ye ken where that is, eh? Been in there a few times wi' Andy boy. Eh?'

He did a kind of wheezy laugh that didn't seem to faze young Kylie but nearly made Maxine throw up. She walked round the front of the van, still giving Maxine the evil eye, even though they'd never met. It was just the way these kids thought they were supposed to act. She wished she could talk to the girl alone and tell her exactly where she was headed in a few short years. It wouldn't be that day though; Dillon had other plans.

'Okay?' Maxine tried an opener when Kylie clambered into the back.

The first thing that was obvious was that the young girl wasn't into daily showering, and the smell of the unwashed wafted round the van. Was this how this old punter liked them?

Maxine tried to put the thought out of her head and concentrate on getting out of this Mickey Mouse plot without being arrested, cut up by Dillon or whichever junkie was waiting for the nod.

Kylie continued to look coldly at Maxine and grunted something that might have been 'awright'. She snorted up what looked like the ends of a number eleven trying to escape from her nostrils then lit a cigarette, before leaning over the driver's seat and nibbling Dillon's ear, though he was definitely no great shakes in the hygiene department either. Maxine did her best to ignore it, fixing her eyes on the road ahead as Dillon moved off slowly.

After about half a mile, he turned left onto a single-track road, pulled into the edge and switched off the engine. Kylie had moved to sit on the floor after her work on his ear and was now smoking a roll-up. He turned halfway round, took the cigarette from her hand and dragged deeply.

'Right, here's the plan. The place at the end of the road is the auld perv's. Nice wee spot an' he owns all the land here. His missus died a couple o' years ago and he's on his own there. It's a dead end, so if anybody comes in, we should get warnin' an' I'll be ready for that. He's a fuckin' loner anyway.'

Kylie snorted at the end of his sentence to recapture the number eleven, which was trying to escape again.

'Right.' Dillon looked slightly agitated at the interruption and carried on. 'According to wee Kylie here, he's fuckin' minted and must be to own that place.' He grinned, which did nothing to alter the mess his face was in. 'He's a big cheese in the church an' charities an' a' that shite. Tell Maxie how he met ye, hen.'

Kylie had mastered the art of chewing a mouthful of gum and talking at the same time.

'Ma fuckin' mother's right intae the church, right? So, the auld boy used tae come roond the hoose now an' again when they were daein' charity stuff, right?'

Kylie stopped. She'd had enough of the number elevens and drew her nose along her sleeve as Maxine struggled to remain expressionless.

'Well, the auld shite cannae keep his eyes off ma erse. So, I gies the boy a wee flash up the mini an' he's gaggin'. Course, Ma thinks he's the dugs baws an' disnae see a thing. So, she keeps tellin' me aboot a' this dosh he's sittin' on, so Ah'm interested right? So I starts tae visit the place, an' well guess what come next? Durty auld bastard starts feelin' me up then slippin' me a length. Minger, but he keeps slippin' me a nice wee earner so I'm fuckin' happy, right?'

Dillon nodded, staring at the girl as if he was proud of an outstanding student. Maxine thought the risk of doing whatever the plan was held far more danger than not doing it. The question was how to get out of it?

She noticed her hands shaking again. The shakes had never worried her before, and there had been a time in the depths of her drug problems that she'd lain on the kitchen floor and shook as if an electric current was being forced through her body. She gripped her hands as if they were guilty of some offence and squeezed them, trying to force out the demon that had taken possession of them.

'Are you fuckin' payin' attention, Maxie?' Dillon snarled and she realised she'd drifted off from Kylie's lurid story about the pillar of society they were about to turn over.

'I'm fine, Andy, just seems risky, that's all.' Maxine chewed her lip, trying not to think where this might end up.

She was staring straight ahead at the distant rooftop of the old farmhouse where this man she'd never met was waiting for her and an underage girl who seemed older in mind than she was.

Dillon punched the soft top of her arm, one knuckle protruding in a wedge, and she wheezed with the pain that ripped through her nervous system. Bent over, her arm hanging straight and deadened with the force of the blow, she gripped her shoulder and dipped her head a few times in an unconscious reaction to the pain. She forced open her eyes, which were trying to squeeze out the light and the reality of her situation.

'You fuckin' keep the ears an' eyes open – no fuck-ups allowed on this one. This is a big score, an' any problems an' I'll tell the junkie just to start cuttin'. Hear me?'

She nodded, then opened her eyes and glared at Dillon. Her fear was gone; his cruelty had seen to that. She was in pain but decided that she either fought back now or she was dead already. There was no plan; she just acted.

The van was a tip, rubbish covering the floor, and earlier she'd noticed an old spanner and screwdriver lying at her feet among the empty crisp packets. Maxine had never wanted to hurt someone in her life, and up to that moment that included Dillon. But if there was a chance of getting her life back, she had to act decisively.

She knew enough about anatomy and pain to pick her target. She gripped the spanner with her free hand, and although the space was too restricted for a full swing, she managed to whack Dillon's left elbow with enough force to give him a dose of what he'd just given her. He snarled the word 'bitch' but was in enough pain to give her at least a few moments to make her next move. She was acting on the instant messaging from her subconscious and there was no time for considering options. It was a case of act and hope to fuck she could find a way to put some space between her and the two basket cases in the van.

As she fumbled with and released the door lock, Kylie acted on her own instincts. For reasons that defied logic, she felt loyal towards Dillon simply because he'd given her something almost alien to her in the whole of her existence. He pretended he cared, although she couldn't see that his only interest in her was confined to selling her dope and using her body, nothing more. That made no difference to Kylie though, because she lived without affection, so just showing interest bought her temporary loyalty.

In the instant after the spanner connected with Dillon's bony elbow, Kylie was drawing the Stanley knife she kept close for the protection she thought she required on the street. She knew nothing about Maxine, which meant she was just like everyone else and thus a potential enemy – someone who was likely to do her harm. People had been doing her harm all her life, and this logic was no more than a safety mechanism. The people she'd trusted as a child had abused her, and her mother had always managed to look the other way or pretend that bad things couldn't happen because God wouldn't allow it.

'Fuckin' cow!'

Kylie lifted the Stanley knife, but she was the wrong side of the seats and trying to get across was a minor problem that at least gave Maxine enough time to get out of the van and put a few yards between her and the clear threat that Kylie presented.

Maxine lifted her phone and called the police with no idea what she was going to say, but she needed to save herself first then worry about the consequences. Millions of tiny circuits fired in her brain, stimulated by the threat to her life. Stories of Police Scotland's problem of failing to answer calls from distressed victims set off alarm bells, and she realised that if the phone just rang endlessly while some stressed-out operator dealt with a backlog then it was all over.

Panic flooded through her as she remembered how low on battery her phone was, and she prayed it would hold out long enough for the call to go through. She couldn't run any distance, and it wouldn't take Dillon long to recover enough to get the van going then do God knows what, never mind Kylie and her Stanley knife.

'Police Scotland.'

It felt like a minor miracle. She looked up to her left and the next small miracle appeared, because she had no fucking idea how to describe where she was. It stood on top of a ten-foot post like a biblical vision – a sign saying 'Deep Glen Farm'. She knew they'd travelled through Dalkeith and turned off somewhere on the road to the Borders, where she had cousins her family had rarely visited, but beyond that, all she could be certain of was the farm name, and she threw that information at the operator in rapid-fire bursts.

The operator, who was pissed off at someone not talking in the same bored monotone as herself, tried to clarify, but Maxine couldn't do clarification. She could see Dillon recovering before her eyes and Kylie was in the passenger seat now. They exchanged a few words before he pushed open the driver's door, and what she saw in his face told her all she needed to know about his intentions.

Maxine kept backing away as she watched Dillon close the door, exposing the claw hammer in his hand. Kylie managed something like a grin and Maxine realised just how dangerous the girl was. She screamed the next line of information down the phone and actually managed to make the operator interested.

'A man called Andy Dillon is going to kill me! Please send someone. It's Deep Glen Farm – please hurry.'

She pushed the loudspeaker button and held the face of the phone up towards Dillon and Kylie. The girl looked like she didn't give a fuck, but he hesitated and had only taken a couple of steps when he heard the tinny but discernible sound of the operator's voice.

'There are two cars on their way. Please stay on the phone if you can and talk to me.'

Maxine grinned, but it was overwhelming stress that caused the reaction rather than any sense that they were involved in a comical bit of theatre. She put the phone to her mouth once more, shouting, 'Please hurry,' before thrusting it out in front of her again like a Hammer Film actor keeping a vampire at bay.

'They're only a couple of minutes away. Stay calm.'

The operator's voice was the guardian angel Maxine needed and Dillon was frightened to move.

'Wait, Kylie, for fuck's sake!' He was unsure, seething with rage, but enough of a coward to know that this could all end badly. The bizzies might take long enough to get to them, and they probably had more than enough time to do Maxine, but the bitch had given them his name. It was all a gamble. He could survive and just wait, but as far as he was concerned, he was fucked if he was paying the junkie to cut her. He was doing her himself. There had been so many affronts to his reputation, and clearly Kylie wasn't impressed.

'Are we gonnae dae this or no', Andy?' She looked like a dog on the way to its bone then told no.

'Get in the fuckin' van. I'll deal wi' the cow later. The fuckin' bizzies are on the road. You stupid or somethin'?'

In that moment, Andy Dillon lost his one and only fan in Kylie. She looked disgusted; clearly the thought of being arrested for doing Maxine was fine with her.

The three players all looked up at the same time at the distant sound of the two tones. Kylie looked Maxine straight in the eye and spat on the road before turning and jumping back into the van. Dillon drew his finger across his throat and followed Kylie into the van. He gunned the engine, spun round on the narrow road then burnt rubber in the opposite direction to the sound of the police blues and twos.

Maxine was almost hyperventilating, but she was alive and that had been the first priority. She didn't want the police anywhere near her now she had some space and headed into a thin line of woods on the other side of a drystone wall. She was about eighty yards into the wood when she heard the cars pass and the driver's windows must have been open because she could hear the radio traffic with the control room.

She sank down onto a mound of soft grass in the middle of a small clump of bushes that looked like they were in the wrong place. It was cold but dry, and she heard the cars make several passes in the area, and she was sure it sounded like one had headed along the gravel path to the farm where Dillon's master plan was to have taken place.

14

She woke gasping for air and frightened by the strange surroundings. Despite the cold, she'd fallen asleep but was shivering now in the half light as the winter darkness turned the wood into a million skeletons surrounded by deepening shadows and the small indistinct sounds created by the wind dancing around the trees. She heard something scuttle in a pile of drying leaves, decomposing for the new life to come in the canopies above them.

Maxine climbed unsteadily to her feet and walked back to the road. It was quiet, and she knew she must have slept for hours, but how could that be? It was December, but a winter sun had been shining earlier in the day, and the fact shocked her. She must have been exhausted, but she could have died lying there in the chilled air.

Her muscles ached and she groaned with the effort of climbing back over the wall. The light had gone and she headed back the way the van had travelled into the road. One thing was certain – this wasn't on any bus route, so she had a long walk in front of her. That wasn't a problem; she was alive, and at least for the time being, Andy Dillon was off her back.

It didn't matter in the long run though, because as sure as God made little green apples, the bastard would come back for her, and the few options open to her were disappearing by the hour.

She could leave Edinburgh, but that would be without a bean to her name and she would no doubt end up back on the game in some shitty inner city south of the border. If she took that route, it was more than likely she'd be trapped by one of the widespread parasites who fed off the working girls in so many of these ratholes. So that wasn't really an option.

Going back to try to patch it up with her parents would take time, diplomacy and a great deal of compromise, but then the risk of bringing Andy Dillon to her parents' door was out of the question. Men like Dillon would wreck her parents' lives and see it as a bonus.

She shook her head, wondering if the only real option was to walk up to Andy Dillon and invite him to do his worst, or just kill herself, but she wasn't ready for that. Suicide had crossed her mind often enough in the previous months, but for all that was happening to her, there was still a spark inside her that craved a way out of the life she was living.

One thing that played on a loop in the back of her mind was Tom Logan. She was confused about him because she trusted him, and that was something she wouldn't have believed could happen again. No matter what, she would talk to him. He seemed to want something from her, but she wasn't sure what it would involve. It was clear that there was a void in the man's life, and seeing his home had confirmed what that was – or rather who that was.

She saw it sometimes in the punters who were OK and nothing more than lonely, through divorce, death or the common complaint that they lived with someone who didn't care anymore. There were men who paid her to sit and talk, and she saw the tragedy in those situations where the loneliest place on earth could be in the company of another person who'd been loved at some time in the past.

She was floundering in a storm that threatened to drown her, and the Big Man was the distant haven just on the crest of the dark horizon. If she could just make it to his door, she would be safe as long as he was there. All she had to do was find him and she could at least rest till the night had passed.

15

The problem for Maxine was that Andy Dillon was closer to the rat family than the human race, and all he wanted to do was find her and hurt her. Not just hurt her; it was more than that now – a primeval drive that ignored all the consequences that would come from the act he kept running through his raging imagination.

Like a man intent on suicide, all his old terrors had passed and his greatest fear of all had appeared to him in sharp relief. In those few hours since his humiliation in Leith, his delusion had cleared as if a heavy mist had lifted from his mind. He saw what he was and it terrified him – more than that, given there was no way for him to change. The hard men he so admired who took the piss were on the money. He was a wanker and always would be.

But that truth lifted his fears, and he accepted that some things were much worse than death. What became of him after he was finished with her didn't matter anymore. Everything that had happened to him had forced him to look into the mirror of his soul and see that weakness and a sense of injustice was all he could give to the world. He would be forgotten as soon as his miserable life was over.

Dillon had decided that one glorious act would at least get the criminal community he so admired to say his name, and his rat instincts told him there were only two places Maxine could go unless she slept in the gutter – Connie's place or the big bastard from the boozer where she'd spent the previous night.

As Maxine shivered her way towards a bus route, Dillon had already found out where Connie lived. It wasn't a problem – dealers were always on the phone doing business, exchanging favours or chewing the fat.

He waited, chain-smoking and twitching with the flood of nicotine, adrenalin and speed polluting his system. The palms of his hands were soaked with the results of the nervous tension that made his heart thump and rattle to dangerous levels.

About the same time as Maxine stepped into the warmth of a city-bound bus, Dillon was watching Connie and a short-arse who matched the description of the twat she was supposed to be living with. Dillon recognised him as Banjo Rodgers and had run into him a couple of times to do a bit of business. They left their front door together. The light had gone off in their flat about one minute earlier.

He followed them to Leith, but it was clear she was just going to work the street. He waited for a while, but there was no sign of Maxine, so he started up the engine and headed for Logan's place.

16

Dillon pulled the collar of his jacket up as if it would make any difference to the temperature in the van. The heating system had been fucked for weeks, but he could never be arsed to fix the thing or pay the money needed to sort the problem. He'd picked up the old van so he didn't spook Maxine when he found her. She knew the new van too well now, having been in it earlier in the day.

If things went the way he wanted, he'd probably need to torch these wheels – and what was inside – when he was done anyway. He just hadn't factored in freezing his balls off while he waited for her – if she even turned up, which he was beginning to doubt.

He kept muttering quietly, the increasing cold making him unsure how to carry on. He couldn't keep running the engine every five minutes or some concerned citizen or a passing patrol car would stick their neb in and ruin what he'd planned. His thin jacket was no protection against the night frost, which seemed to creep into the van through every little space, and each time he exhaled it was as if what strength he had left was vaporising in front of him.

He felt ill, sick in the stomach, but didn't want to throw up. It was like the worst of hangovers, and he wasn't sure how much longer he could last in this weakened state. Dillon hadn't eaten for a full day, and the self-administered poisons swirling in his bloodstream were taking him to the edge of collapse as he clenched then unclenched his hands, trying to keep them from stiffening up.

His control broke like a dam, and he screamed into the walls of the van. There were no words, no blasphemies, just a guttural roar and a torrent of suppressed anger that poured out then tapered into a long wail of despair. He leaned forward and thumped his forehead on the dashboard, opening up a couple of the small cuts that were there already. He leaned his head back, tears streaming down his cheeks and spit trailing from both corners of his mouth.

'What the fuck? What the fuck?'

He was asking himself a question he'd already answered.

He looked across to the line of smart stone-built homes along the edge of the Links. Hundreds of Christmas lights sparkled different colours through the windows where families did normal things, shielded from the terrors that followed unfortunate souls like Andy Dillon and Maxine Sarah Welsh.

He looked in the rear-view mirror and saw a woman's dark shape form and grow in the glass. It was her walk, her posture, that gave her away, and he sat bolt upright and snorted the last bit of powder he'd been saving for the occasion. Suddenly everything had changed and he felt the immediate kick from the good-quality gear he'd kept just for his get-together with her.

She was tired; she'd walked for three miles before she'd managed to find a bus stop. It was a limited service at that time of night, and she'd shivered till she was nearly blue before the lights of the bus had appeared in the distance.

When she'd dropped into the seat, the heat had almost overwhelmed her, and she'd hardly been able to control the urge to let the lights go out in her head. But through half-closed eyes, she'd looked at her hands and found they were steady, and she'd decided then and there that if she survived whatever Dillon had planned for her, she was going to clean herself up and start living again.

Now, her breath billowed smoke clouds in front of her and she was shivering again. Like the man who was waiting for her in the shadows, the cheap thin clothes she wore were no match for the bitter cold.

Five more minutes – that's all it would take to get to Tom's door. She prayed that he was at home and not still in the pub. It wouldn't take her long to get there, and her feet tapped out a rhythmic beat on the glistening pavements. There was hardly a soul around as the Christmas crowds tended to congregate in the centre of the city, although the party season was almost over and people were settling down for the rundown to the twenty-fifth.

Maxine looked at the line of Christmas trees illuminating the windows and remembered how excited she used to get at this time of the year. As a child, she had never been able to sleep, and maybe Christmas was all an illusion for some people, but it was one of those memories that made her want to live. She felt ashamed when she spoke to women like Connie and saw that their lives were built on struggle and desperate attempts just to survive in a world that sneered at them for working the streets for a living. Life had given her so much compared to her friend, yet that girl still believed that life held possibilities. Connie was the one who made her think, proved every time the human spirit could battle on and hope, and if Connie could hope, then so could she.

She walked along the tree-lined border of the Links as the moonlight glowed across the frosted grass on the open parkland. It was so quiet – no people and hardly any traffic, the world clearly settling down for the holidays.

There was nothing unusual about parked cars there, and she'd picked up a few punters in the same area herself who would give up circling the streets, park up there and avoid the risk of attracting the attention of the bizzies. They knew that if they waited, there was a chance that one of the girls would pass by, and the old police station at Leith was only a minute's drive away.

That hadn't stopped some horrific attacks and murders over the years, and Maxine knew that anytime a girl was out working, there was the potential for something to go badly wrong. Unfortunately, Maxine's antennae were dulled by exhaustion, and her thoughts overwhelmed her as she tried to analyse and come up with a rational answer to all the problems she faced.

Dillon's timing was perfect – when she was about six feet from the rear nearside corner of the van, he pushed the driver's door open quietly. He'd released it a few inches as soon as he'd spotted her in the mirror.

Maxine was deep in her own thoughts and almost excited by the idea of seeing Tom Logan, imagining the bear-like warmth he generated. She was parallel with the passenger door of the van and glanced up as the faint hit of tobacco smoke hit the back of her nose. That made no sense – the night air was freezing, and you would have to be close to a smoker to register what was hitting her olfactory organs. It set off alarms, but it was already too late. Dillon was right behind her and he'd already decided that there wouldn't be any mistakes this time. His life was one big fuck-up after another, but this time he'd leave nothing to chance because he was going all the way.

Killing someone was a fantasy he'd dreamed about often enough. Night after night, behind the curtains of his bedroom, he'd lived through endless computer-generated battles and survived unscathed. His favourite video games always involved the heroic slaughter of cyber enemies or game victims who fell in waves from the barrel of his pretend guns.

Dillon was broken; he'd moved from being a sad wanker who dreamt of being a contender to accepting the awful truth that he just didn't count. But for his old man's name, he would have been ripped apart by just about anyone who wanted to take him on. That revelation that he'd finally accepted and the beatings had torn up his mind till all that was left was a wounded predator intent on a final kill.

Dillon grabbed the collar of her jacket and put his Rambo knife against her throat. He had control and it felt good.

'No fuckin' around this time, Maxie. Think I was finished wi' you, hen? Eh?'

He pushed the knife against her neck and even a fractional increase in pressure meant cutting. She stopped moving and froze, her eyes popping with fear.

He turned her round slowly, holding the blade steady across the front of throat, and seemed to be studying her eyes. He brought his face close to hers, and the rank smell of tobacco and decay made her want to gag.

When he was satisfied, he punched her low in the gut. The blow connected right on target and with enough force to almost take her legs away, completely disorientating her long enough for Dillon to push her into the passenger seat and slam the door shut. The child lock was on and the rear doors were locked. He'd left the driver's door wide open, but there was no chance of her reaching over and closing it on him before he was round there himself. Especially when she was doubled up with the force of his blow.

He closed the door, lit up a cigarette and felt like a million dollars. He had the back of the van prepared and had put an old mattress in earlier so they could be comfortable for a little while. He was heading somewhere quiet so he could have peace to kill her then dispose of the evidence. In other words, a nicely planned Christmas murder, but this was different. He grinned as she moaned and tried to focus her eyes.

'That's it, darlin'. I love it when they moan.' He blew a cloud of smoke towards her. He didn't feel cold anymore, the sickness had passed and he was all good to go. He felt wonderful, the way he had years before he'd started feeding various forms of recreational dope into his system. It was the ultra-high that he got at the thought of extreme violence. It happened to a degree with video games or when he slapped the junkies about, particularly the females, but this moment was pure high-octane-level exhilaration. He drew his head back, snarled like a beast then pulled out the syringe he'd made up with a whack load of H.

'This'll do the trick, Maxie. High-quality shit. The fuckin' best.'

One minute later she felt the warm tide sweep through her and she shuddered with the electric thrill of the gear sending her all the way up. Her eyes flickered and all she wanted was to lean back, feel the pain in her gut drift away and let it all just happen…

17

Logan had finished early because he couldn't get Maxine out of his head. He'd made the offer and felt foolish, but she hadn't sneered at him; in fact, her reaction had been warm. He was confused by his thoughts, wondering again why he'd become so interested in a working girl who might bring nothing but problems into his life – as if he didn't have enough to deal with already. The same thought looped again and again in his head. Would she come and see the sense in what he'd told her?

He paced again and stood at the bay window looking out over the Links. The world outside looked picture postcard with the almost ghostly lunar shine illuminating the broad grounds of the ancient park. He scanned both ways, hoping Maxine's figure would come into sight – then he could take her in and protect her.

Dillon's van was on the edge of his vision but would mean nothing to him. As far as Logan was concerned, the world outside seemed to be at peace. He lit another cigarette and headed to the kitchen to brew up some coffee at the same time Dillon was wallowing in the high that had engulfed him.

Watching Maxine struggle to breathe and feeling in complete control for a change was like being God. The van engine rattled like an old tractor, but he wasn't concerned that some taxpayer might pass by and alert the local cavalry that a woman appeared to be in distress beside him. What he had in mind wouldn't take too long. Then he made his first mistake – he was so high he decided to call Kylie rather than getting on with the job, even though she was pissed off that he hadn't followed through in doing Maxine.

'What the fuck, Andy? I'm wi' ma pals.'

Kylie didn't seem overjoyed at the sound of Dillon's voice. It wasn't the response he'd expected, and his extreme high dropped a couple of levels at her talking to him as if he was some kind of fuckwit. But, of course, he knew he was, and his brief high started to crash in flames again, his mood swinging like a hanged man. All the time he was giving Maxine seconds to absorb the initial hit from the H.

It hadn't occurred to him that Kylie had seen him for what he was when Maxine had legged it from the van earlier. Kylie's ability to care about people was a fragile emotion at best. She could love and hate someone several times all in the space of a day. What she admired was whoever was the strong man on the street or who could give her stuff she couldn't afford herself. Dillon had turned out to be a tosser, so emotionally she'd dumped him already and was taking the call from the bed of the old man they'd planned to turn over earlier on.

Dillon would have cracked up if he'd realised that she was in bed with the guy and had just been about to bring matters to a close when the phone had killed their moment of passion. She'd decided that if they weren't going to black-mail the bastard then she certainly wasn't going to throw away the fringe benefits of stamping his card when the mood took him. She'd given him a story that the threesome had to be cancelled because the other girl was in hospital. It wasn't true, but Kylie reckoned that with the way Dillon was acting, it wouldn't be long before it actually happened – if Maxine was really lucky and survived.

She pressed the end call button on the phone and chewed furiously on her ever-present wad of gum as she tried to get the old guy back on course for a happy ending.

'Who was that, honey?' The old man didn't like the way she spoke sometimes.

'Lie back and shut the fuck up.' Kylie didn't do romance.

For a moment, Maxine thought she was just coming out of a deep sleep, then she realised she must have lost consciousness for a moment, though it couldn't have been for long. She was slumped over in the passenger seat, and as her vision cleared she looked up and saw Dillon cursing and pushing his phone back into his jacket pocket.

She wanted to say, 'Andy, don't do this please,' but her mouth was taped. Her lower abdomen ached and pounded where he'd delivered the blow.

Dillon sniggered and tapped the ash from his cigarette onto her hair.

'Relax, Maxie – you'll love what's comin'.'

His original plan had been to take her somewhere quiet, but he felt brave, something new for him, and he kept muttering, 'What the fuck,' under his breath. He smoked the cigarette all the way down till it burned his fingers, feeling almost nothing, and giving her more previous seconds.

He tossed the fag end onto the road and decided it was time for the big show. He gripped her hair and yanked her head up with one hand, forcing her head round towards the rear, where an old sheet had been taped from the roof and hung loosely to the floor. He pulled the sheet back so she could see the filthy mattress, but it was what was underneath it that made her suck in air as if she was in danger of drowning. Plastic sheeting had been taped across the floor under the mattress and on the walls and roof of the van. Four lengths of rope had also been tied to the sides of the van, two a side, and there was no doubt what they were for.

He kept a grip of her hair with one hand and scrambled to the back of the seats, then pulled her over and forced her down onto the floor, straddling her. He grinned – it was all going to plan.

She tried to say the word 'no' but there was nothing more than a moan deep in her throat as her brain struggled to cope with the attack.

He held her hands down and stared at her, savouring the moment.

It seemed as if there was nothing but full-volume radio static in the van, and only Dillon's laboured breathing made its way through the scrambled noise generated in her brain. Her will to live was strong though, and giving up her life without a struggle couldn't happen. The H had been a big hit, but the first rush was passing now. Her revulsion and that ancient instinct to fight rather than die poured enough strength back into her body for this final struggle to survive.

He leaned down towards her shoulder and started to bite like a rabid dog at her neck and shoulders. The pain was excruciating and made her grit her teeth as she tried to push him with her free hand, but it made no difference. Dillon was physically weak, but he was enraged and was finding energy and the strength that came from the madness that had gripped his mind. He'd thought that he had it all covered for the final act, but he'd left a gap, and now she was fighting for her life. His vanity and remaining self-delusion made him believe that his earlier blows would leave her far too weak to resist. It was why Dillon would always be a failure in life and even in the way he would die.

He leaned back and let her hands go while he fumbled with the zip on his jeans, instead of using the rope ties he'd taken so much time to prepare. Maxine's fingers stopped trying to push him and skittered along the edges of the van floor like a demented spider looking for something, anything.

Of course, Dillon had made many mistakes in life, and one of them was that he lived like a pig. He was a serial offender when it came to fucking things up but could never have guessed that when he dropped a cheap biro in the back of the van six months earlier, it would come back and kill him.

Maxine's fingers felt something long, hard and thin, then almost without thinking she gripped it and drove it up towards his head. The small metal point was sharp enough with the force behind it to push deep into his flesh, and although Maxine only drove towards the neck, her luck was in as much as Dillon's was out. The pen managed to tear into his carotid artery and he began the process of dying.

She pulled it out and plunged it in again. He could have survived the second blow with treatment but no fucking danger with the first.

She left it in after the second strike, watching his back arch, and his body seemed to snap rigid for a few seconds as blood geysered into the semi-darkness of the van. When Dillon had actually used the pen months before, he'd had a habit of chewing the end through his constant battle with stress. The boy just collected bad luck.

Maxine drew her hand away as if it had been scorched, tore the tape from her mouth, pulled her lips back and started to scream.

Dillon clutched at the exposed end of the pen but only succeeded in the badly fractured end breaking into pieces. Maxine could see his eyes glaze as he started to twitch, spasm then fall to the side, cracking his head on the side wall of the van. Somewhere far away he could just make out the sound of her screaming and the door pushing open.

The evening light made a grotesque display of the scene inside the van as Maxine started to run towards the centre of the Links. She could see Dillon was down and out, but she was crazed through fear and dope and wanted to be in the middle of the park, where at least she could see anything approaching that might hurt her.

That definitely wasn't going to be Dillon though. His heartbeat was now no more than an odd flutter and no medic was going to save him.

18

Logan was staring at the kettle as it came through the boil again – then his head snapped up at the distant sound of a woman screaming. He paced quickly back to the front window and tried to see where it was coming from. Deep inside, he knew who it was. It was one of those things – it had to be Maxine; it was almost written before it happened. He knew when she left that all the omens were bad, but he'd hoped that this would be one of those occasions where his feelings for her were clouding his judgement and street instincts.

He slipped on his shoes, pulled on a hooded jacket and headed out into the bitter night air, towards the sounds of distress. They had reduced to a low moaning, but it carried across the still, open parkland.

Logan was a bull, physically strong, and he'd proved a hundred times he was a match for anyone in a one to one. When he closed in on the figure he knew had to be Maxine, he watched her drop to her knees as he approached. He stopped a few feet from her and tried to understand what he was seeing, puzzling at the black patches and streaks covering her hands, clothes and face. It came to him quickly because he'd seen blood in moonlight before.

'Jesus girl what…?' He didn't know how to finish the sentence. He pulled off his jacket and stepped carefully towards her. She was terrified, and he wasn't even sure she recognised him.

Maxine stared somewhere into the distance and seemed to go limp as he kneeled down on the grass, ignoring the freezing damp that sucked in through the knees of his trousers. She whimpered like a child and let him pull the jacket over her shoulders. He put his arms round her, talked quietly, and told her she was safe.

Looking up, he watched the blue lights start to converge and saw them pull up at the van sitting with its doors wide open. Voices carried over the Links, and the crackled messages on police radios started to attract the attention of the locals. Dog walkers seemed to appear from all directions.

Logan managed to get Maxine to her feet, though she was shivering uncontrollably. He felt sick and knew whatever was attracting all the attention in the van was about to change her life forever. They walked slowly till they reached the pavement, and he wanted to take her across the road to his house when a uniform appeared at his side.

'Tam. You alright there?'

The uniform walked in front of Logan, who recognised him straight away. Charlie Brockie and Logan had had their run-ins over the years, and he'd gone nose to nose with the Big Man on a couple of occasions in his younger days for battling in the street. Well, for leaving some challenger unconscious on the street. But they respected each other, and Logan knew when Brockie did the business it was always fair and square.

'Don't know, Charlie. You tell me.'

He knew how it must look. He was smeared in a lot of Andy Dillon's blood, which had transferred from Maxine onto his hands and the sweatshirt he'd worn under the jacket.

'Need to get this lassie warm. Know what I mean?'

Brockie hated what he had to do at times, and wherever he could, he used common sense rather than the laws passed by men who rarely understood the world of people like Logan or Maxine. All he knew was that there was a body almost drained of blood in the back of a shitty old van and he was speaking to a man and a woman covered in what looked like good evidence. He wished he was off for the holiday.

'You know the score, Tam. The suits are on their way, and at the moment, you and Maxine are making it look like it's an open-and-shut case.'

He struggled to look Logan in the eye because he wanted to help Maxine, who had to be a hospital case. He pulled out his radio and called for medical assistance.

'It's nothing to do with him, Charlie. He just came over the Links and put his coat on me. I was in that van.'

Her voice was level, calm and it surprised the two men. She straightened her back and asked Logan for a cigarette. He lit it in his own lips because her hands were shaking.

'I killed him, Charlie. I'm glad. He deserved it.'

'Don't say another thing, Maxine.' Logan knew his law, and Brockie nodded in agreement.

'He's right, Maxie. Save it till you see your lawyer,' Brockie said, without recording what should have been good evidence.

Two cars arrived, one a marked patrol car and the other with a couple of suits. An ambulance arrived at almost the same time. For a moment, Logan thought about kicking off; he wanted to take out some of his frustration and disappointment on the plain-clothes bizzies. But Maxine saw what was in his eyes and put her hand on his arm. She didn't need to say anything and he calmed down.

'I'll take care of it, Tom. I'll be fine.'

'Right, split these two characters up and cuff them.'

The taller of the two suits was an arrogant bastard Brockie had disliked since the day he'd met him. He pulled him to the other side of the road and spoke quietly to him. Maxine watched Brockie stab his finger towards the detective a few times before they walked back over the road.

'Look this lassie over first,' Brockie barked at the ambulance crew, who helped her into the back of the vehicle.

'Tam, you need to go to the station with these guys. No need for a battle here. Doesn't help this lassie. You hear me?'

Logan stared at Brockie then took a long look at the detectives, and much as he wanted to nut the suit with the attitude, he put it away and nodded.

'Let's go, Charlie, but make sure she's alright. She's had enough.'

'I'll make sure, Tam,' Brockie said and turned to the detectives, shooting them a look that told them exactly what he expected. It was enough.

19

Maxine was in a detention room with a female uniform who was a member of Charlie Brockie's fan club. She was young, and like a few of her contemporaries, she wanted to be just like Brockie, who seemed to have all the street knowledge in the world.

Maxine's clothes had been taken, and the blood staining on her hands and face had been photographed and swabbed. She was deathly pale, but she'd stopped shivering, and although she was wearing a sterile suit, she'd been given a blanket to put round her shoulders. The uniform had also sorted her with a brew, and the hot liquid seemed to have calmed her down. She was exhausted, but her terror had at least passed for the time being. The effects of the smack were also fading, and she'd already accepted that her life was changing again – maybe not the way she'd hoped for hours before, but she wasn't going to fall over and die or tie a rope round her neck. Whatever was coming, she'd take it on because she wanted to live so much.

Brockie came into the room and nodded to the young officer to take a break.

'How's it goin', Maxie?' He sat opposite and wondered, as he'd done all his service, at how easily good people could end up at the bottom of the cesspit.

'I'm OK, Charlie. Tea's the best ever.' She managed a smile and he nodded.

'I'm off after the next shift, love. That's me till the New Year.' He looked at the floor and struggled to find words that meant anything and wondered why he was mentioning holidays to someone locked up for murder.

'What do you think, Charlie? What'll happen to me?'

He should have said that he couldn't comment, not for him and all that officious shite. But Brockie was always a human being first and a street cop second. It had done hee-haw for his promotion chances, but it helped him sleep at night. Not every night but most nights.

'Well, Maxie…' He paused and waited for the next words to form. He didn't want to lie, but he'd give her the truth with something to hang on to.

'The suits'll charge you with murder – they always do. Then it's up to the court. Truth is, I've never had a clue what goes through jury's minds, and they can do daft things.'

'But what do you think? I need an idea. I'm not scared anymore. I'll take whatever it is.'

He looked at her and believed what she said.

'I'm not involved in the case, Maxie. Suits do this one. Apparently, the boy in the van's all bad news but suppose you know that. My guess is you'll walk from a murder conviction, but he's still potted so there's no knowing how it'll turn out. Possible you'll do a bit of time on a reduced charge once they hear your side of the story. Christ, the back of Dillon's van was done up for a killing or rape with the mattress and ropes.'

Maxie realised then that if Dillon had taken his time and tied her up, she would be dead now.

'You can take whatever they throw at you,' Brockie said wearily 'Christ, look what you've survived so far. I don't know, Maxie. Just keep the chin up.'

He sighed. 'I better clear out now before the suits report me for interfering.' He put his hand on her forearm then left the room once the female officer came back in.

Brockie hung about the cell area and spoke to Logan, who was on a break from giving his statement. He spoke to the custody staff and was ready to leave when Maxine's phone rang. It was still on the counter with her other stuff, such as it was. The custody officer reached for it, but Brockie put up his hand and took the phone. He pressed the answer button and waited.

'Maxie?' It was a female voice and he knew it straight away.

'Connie?' He waited a moment. 'It's Charlie Brockie.'

'Charlie, what's happened? Where's Maxie?' There was tension in her voice – the first thing a working girl would think was that a punter had lost it.

'She's with us, Connie. There's been an incident but can't say too much.'

'An incident? What the fuck, Charlie? Is she hurt?'

'No, she's not hurt. Look, you can come here if you want.'

'Nae chance – Banjo would have a stroke if I went any-where near a cop shop. Fuckin' luck. Any chance you can let me know in the mornin' where I can find her?'

'Look, Connie... she'll be at court.'

'Fuck's sake! Listen, I need you to tell her somethin'.' Right?

'OK, but make it quick or I'm in the shite.'

'We've won the fuckin' Lotto.'

'The fuckin' Lotto?' Brockie repeated it because it didn't really make sense given the tragedy he'd just witnessed. It sunk in that she couldn't possibly be taking the piss and he stared at the door of the room where Maxie was. 'The jackpot?'

'Naw, no' the jackpot but five numbers an' the bonus number. Forty grand each. Forty fuckin' big ones! The poor cow's problems are over.'

Half the girls were locked up now and again, and Connie obviously thought Maxine had just sconed a punter or something that meant nothing in the great scheme of things. Most of the time they were sleazeballs anyway. Brockie looked down at the bags with her property and saw the ticket.

'You sure, Connie?'

'Course I'm fuckin' sure! Just tell her! I better go now.' She gave him her number and told him to call her in the morning about the court.

Brockie took ten minutes to work it all out in his head and decide whether it was good news or a tragic cosmic joke.

He opened the door to the cell they'd moved her to and hesitated.

'What is it, Charlie?' Maxine asked when she saw the look on his face.

He told her, struggling to deliver what should have been good news, and Maxine stared at him, trying to make sense of her newfound fortune.

Brockie left the cell a few minutes later and headed into the changing room, ignoring the other uniforms getting ready to go on duty or finish their shift and head off. He was weary; he just wanted to go home and put his feet up.

20

Maxine barely slept in the cold cell. She was exhausted and her thoughts were a mess. Sometimes she would slip into that half dream world, where she wasn't awake or asleep, then her imagination would fire up and she'd imagine Andy Dillon on top of her. So much hate in him and all directed at her.

Religion hadn't figured too much for her in this life, but she couldn't help wondering if she was being punished for some grievous sin committed in another. It was as if the gods had conspired against her in the previous year and she was being punished in stages. Was the lottery win good fortune or a last ironic twist delivered by some higher force intent on tormenting her endlessly?

The thought of court terrified her, and she was sure the jury would judge her as a prostitute before any defence was put to them. *They had to see the truth*, she thought over and over again, though never quite believing it.

Charlie Brockie had said that the way the van had been kitted out with restraints showed intent on Dillon's part, but she'd been in court before and knew it could be the cruellest place – the stand the loneliest platform on God's earth. The prosecution would attack her ruthlessly – that was a given. She was a fallen woman, and they'd hold all she had become up to the light, where the chosen citizens could sneer and pretend they had never sinned.

After he left the station during the early hours, Logan had got a hold of Connie and broken the full extent of Maxine's problems to her. Banjo had been lying beside her when she'd taken the call and had told her not to get involved. Normally she would have done exactly that, but she'd told him to shut the fuck up and go back to sleep, and he'd been snoring noisily by the time she'd pulled the front door closed behind her.

Logan and Connie had gone to work in the middle of the night and pulled together some decent clothes for Maxine. It had meant rattling a few doors, but the Campbells had come up trumps. They'd just taken possession of a fortune in women's gear knocked off in a job in Glasgow and traded through a gang they did business with from time to time.

Logan arrived at the station as the early shift workers were making their way to their jobs, cursing the freezing cold and wishing they didn't have to work in the still-dark hours. Connie drew the line at going into the station, but Logan was determined Maxine would look what she really was and not as the Crown would eventually paint her. He knew that appearances mattered. Although Maxine was only going to make a first appearance at court and all that would happen was a remand, he was determined that every person who saw her that day would at least not judge her on appearance.

Logan was torn by what had happened and blamed himself for not intervening. He'd known Maxine had never really been equipped for the street – if it hadn't been Andy Dillon then some other crazy would have hurt her or put her in the ground. He'd known what Dillon was the moment he'd walked through the boozer door, but it was too late for self-recriminations, and he was determined to do whatever he could for the girl now.

He still hadn't worked out what it was that she meant to him or why he suddenly cared what happened to someone else. It just seemed there had been a long dark period where he hadn't lived, just pretended to live – groundhog days, endlessly spinning round the same wheel – and now he was coming through the other side.

Charlie Brockie had made time to come and see him when he was back on duty. It was a no-no for a PC to go and see a name like Logan, who was too close to the case and, apart from that, had been pegged by Criminal Intelligence as an associate of gangsters all over the city. But Criminal Intelligence had never been able to recognise when someone took the decision to retire. As far as the force was concerned: once a bandit, always a bandit. But Brockie, though not the brightest intellect in the force, was blessed with street nous and saw what the advanced intel-gathering systems couldn't – that Big Tam Logan the enforcer was in the past.

When the door opened, Logan paused for a moment. Instinctively he didn't like cops, and if it had been anyone else they would have stayed on the doorstep, but he knew Brockie was straight enough and didn't piss people around for the hell of it.

'Can't be a social call, Charlie, and if you were lifting me, there'd be a team behind you.'

He pulled the door wide open and nodded him in. The policeman took a seat in the lounge and was as surprised as Maxine had been at what he saw there. Brockie had always just known Logan as a big hard man, and he'd presumed at the very best his living arrangements would be plain. He'd never have guessed that Logan would live in a place that radiated warmth. He'd heard the stories that the woman he'd married had changed him and here was the evidence.

'Drink, Charlie?'

'No thanks, Tam. Look, I shouldn't even be here, but I wanted to fill in a couple of things about Maxie's case.' He paused. 'Actually, I'll take that drink. Think I could use it, to be honest.'

Brockie swigged back a good mouthful of the malt. Although he was a beer drinker, the sweet warmth of the expensive booze ran over his throat like milk, and the effect was immediate. It was unusual for Brockie, but he'd been nervous going to Logan's door. The visit was absolutely unofficial, and if the suits knew what he was doing, they'd have his balls removed with a hacksaw. But he knew that Connie and the Big Man cared what happened to Maxine, and for some reason he wanted to give them something to hang on to.

He wondered why he was sticking his neck out, but sometimes just carrying out the letter of the law wasn't enough for him – he liked to introduce a bit of common sense into his work. Some would have called it humanity, and it had cost him in career terms, but Brockie had the job he'd always wanted, and he knew within himself that he would have been a disaster as anyone's boss.

'Just wanted to tell you that Maxie has a chance here.' He looked down into the remains of his drink, felt warm from its effects and wished he could lean back in the chair and chew the fat with Logan over the old days in Leith.

'The suits seem happy that Dillon was a bastard – they found that he'd put four rope restraints in the back of the van and no doubt what they were for. If he'd had the sense to tie Maxine up right away, she would have been in the mortuary and he'd be the accused. He was so doped up his brain was probably mince.'

Brockie swallowed the rest of the drink.

'There's a daft wee lassie, Kylie or somethin' – CID got a hold of her and apparently, she's off her trolley. Admits to all sort of stuff wi' Dillon, includin' comin' close to givin' Maxie a red card out in the county. Maxie had just got back here and must have been headin' for your place when Dillon got a hold of her. She's got a real chance, Tam.' He put the glass down on the coffee table between them.

'She's a working girl. You know they'll try and hurt her in court. Comes wi' the territory.'

Logan knew he was stating the obvious, but the man opposite had gone out on a limb just to tell him that the case wasn't hopeless. He wasn't sure why, but it didn't matter in that moment. They'd tangled years before but that was then, almost like another life for each of them, and they'd both learned that carrying grudges was pointless.

'But thanks, Charlie. Really appreciate you takin' the time. You want a refill?' He meant it, and it would have been good to exchange a few war stories, but that wasn't how it worked.

'Need to go, Tam. Another time.'

They both knew there wouldn't be another time, but that was fine with both of them. This moment was enough.

'Tell Maxie all the best when you see her.'

Brockie stood up and for a moment they considered shaking hands but left it there. No need. They'd both learned something in that short visit – they weren't really that different from each other.

21

When Maxine made her first appearance at the high court, the combination of shock and exhaustion left her in something of a dreamlike state. The people who inhabited the court were like ghosts who drifted past her vision, their voices muffled and unclear. Later the same night, she tried to remember what had happened and what her lawyer had told her, but it was like the remnants of a hallucination. Almost gone from her memory, only shreds drifted round the edge of her mind, worrying her, and despite her exhaustion, sleep wouldn't come.

The days on remand were much the same, and there was no sense of time passing. She withdrew into herself and barely spoke unless the screws insisted on a reaction. When she did speak, it was monosyllabic. Logan and Connie visited her whenever they could, and every time they left, they looked at each other, both thinking the same thought – that Maxine might not make it.

Prison did that. There was the tabloid impression of a taxpayer-funded holiday camp – then there was the shocking reality of being locked up, of living with the alien noises and smells that reminded you over and over again that you were alone, and all you could do was handle the fear or let it eat you from the inside. Tough men and women from the criminal world who knew and accepted the cost of their life choices might do time behind the doors – but they broke as well.

Maxine never slept for more than an hour at a time and woke more exhausted than when she'd put her head on the pillow. One night she got down on her knees and prayed, even though she wasn't a believer. She was so terrified in the half dark cell that God seemed all that was left.

There were nights she wished she could just go to sleep and not wake up, and there were moments that she believed it would have been so much better to have died under the hands of Andy Dillon. That way she would have been at peace and he would have been suffering years of what she was enduring now.

Logan had almost pleaded with her, and told her over and over again what Brockie had said – that there was hope – but Maxine wasn't hearing it. It was as if she'd given up, and Connie would wipe the tears away with the back of her hand and curse the world. They'd had a slice of luck with the lottery win, but it might just turn out to be life taking the piss where Maxine was involved.

'It's no' right, Tam. Just no' fuckin' right.'

Connie kept saying it over and over again because there was no way to explain the way the cards had been dealt. It was as if working the streets equated to a slow death sentence: you were allowed to occasionally think about another life but don't get ahead of yourself, girl – you're going absolutely nowhere. The good life? You're having a fucking laugh – someone has to do it for the punters!

Logan thought that at least Connie was lucky in that she could show such emotion. He felt exactly the same but had to keep it in till he was safely behind his door, where he would stare at the photographs of his wife and wonder why life could be such a bastard to deal with. He wished he was younger, he wished he was better looking and that he had a previous life that he could be proud of, and maybe in that other life Maxine could see the possibilities in him. It didn't matter – he'd decided that he'd keep his thoughts locked down, but whatever he could do for her, he do as far as it was possible. At the end of the day, for a few hours one night, he'd seen who she really was – and, like him, she was someone forced to live behind a facade they didn't want but struggled to shake off.

22

Things changed for Maxine the day her mother walked into the visiting area and fumbled nervously with her gloves. The daughter who she'd cherished since childhood had left her almost bereaved – the loss and the shock that someone else was inhabiting the identity of the girl they'd thought they knew was more than she could bear.

The first sight of Maxine in the visiting area nearly broke her there and then. The young woman looked so much older than the girl who'd been her pride and joy only a couple of years earlier. She'd had to steel herself to make the visit; her husband and sons remained unforgiving and had refused to join her.

Maxine's eyes filled as she stared at her mother and ached for her old life, when all her parents had lived for were their children. Her mother spoke to her and begged her to live. It was that simple.

'Your friend Tom came to see me, Maxine. He told me he was worried and that he thought you'd lost the will to live. He seems like a decent man and a good friend.'

'He is, Mum. A decent man in every way.' Maxine lost it there, sobbing uncontrollably, and her mother felt helpless, but the release was cathartic, and it was as if a poison was flowing from her in those tears. Just having her mother close was what she needed more than anything – someone from her old life who still cared.

'I'm sorry, so sorry for everything that happened,' her mother said. 'I regret it every day, and I hope you can forgive me.'

Admitting guilt was difficult for her. Her husband had said over and over again that they'd done nothing wrong, that it was all *her* fault.

In one respect he was right. But they had loved her too much, and the shock of discovering what Maxine had become had overwhelmed his idealised picture of what their lives should be. He'd lived a quiet life; his greatest risks were on the golf course, and his morals were shaped by the tabloids he read and believed every day.

But Maxine's mother knew guilt or innocence didn't matter – this was their flesh and blood in the worst of all places, she tried not to think of the world Maxine had inhabited because it was beyond her imagination. She ached to hold the young woman opposite, but it was impossible where they were, and it left her feeling old and tired.

At the end of the visit, Maxine walked back to her cell but all the weight had gone from her legs. She was drained, dark under the eyes with exhaustion, but the world had come back into focus. She had killed a man protecting herself and that was it, and she could either give up there or make her case.

That night she slept straight through for the first time in weeks.

When Logan and Connie came in the following week, they saw signs of life, and when Maxine explained that she'd spoken to her mother, the spark was back in her eye. She'd made the briefest connection with her old life and it had sparked that sense of hope once more. It was fragile, but the dark thoughts that had plagued her, the idea that dying wasn't such a bad option, had faded. Her situation was still terrible, but she had at least decided that she would face the court and see if there could be justice for a woman in her position.

23

When the judge was summing up, all Maxine could remember were two crucial points in the trial. The first was Kylie walking into the court chewing gum and staring down anyone who looked her way. It was almost as if telling a lie was too much bother for her. The girl just didn't care. Maxine had worried endlessly that Kylie would stick the knife into her and come up with some story that Dillon had been attacked earlier and that she was intent on ridding herself of the debt she owed him. It would have been a powerful line for the prosecution, but Kylie was no ordinary girl. She repeated the story she'd given the CID and no one, not least the jury, would forget her answer to one question by the defence.

'Andy wis a fuckin' wanker.'

The judge harrumphed and warned her, but Kylie didn't really do listening, and a few witnesses realised that they were looking at a girl who'd definitely be back in the high court at some stage as the accused. She described in absolute detail the blackmail plan, the fact that Dillon had been having sex with her, was her supplier and what had followed before Maxine had escaped.

The jury sat open-mouthed at her revelations. Maxine might have been the accused, but a teenage girl with a mouth like a sewer had stolen the show. Kylie was almost enjoying it and winked at the judge when she was excused. He harrumphed again, but a couple of the jury members would later swear there was something else in the way the elderly judge had looked at her.

The Advocate Depute tried manfully to discredit Maxine and paint her as a devious and scheming culprit in the death of Andy Dillon. He had some success, and when Maxine took the stand, he strutted like a hunter staring balefully at the prey clearly in his sights. Kylie had been a disaster for the prosecution, but the AD was intent on slaughtering Maxine in the box and felt he had a handful of aces.

But what surprised him was that when he fired off his first question, Maxine seemed to draw back her shoulders, grow another couple of inches and looked him squarely in the eye.

There were long exchanges where they batted the ball back and forth, and there were a couple of occasions where the defence counsel could have objected to the questioning, but they didn't intervene because they saw Maxine was defending herself better than they could. She was doing that rare thing of baring her soul, and if she was a liar, she was the best they'd seen.

So the battle was left between the two main protagonists, and at one point the AD watched one of the jury members brush away a tear at Maxine's revelations. It was the last two questions and answers that stuck in the jury's mind though – albeit for different reasons than the prosecution had intended.

'Did you kill Andrew Mason Dillon?' The AD swung round to face the jury before Maxine answered.

'Yes, I did.' Maxine was calm, and she looked straight at the jury when she said it.

'You killed him because you wanted to clear your debts. You planned it, you had regular sexual encounters with this man and you took your chance when he was vulnerable. Isn't that the case?' The AD looked at the jury again and waited for the trapdoor to open under the accused woman.

'I killed him because the bastard had hurt me over and over again. He was going to kill me – he nearly succeeded and I took my chance to live. He deserved it.'

The defence counsel winced at her answer, but the AD was watching the jury members' faces, saw exactly their reaction and leaned back in his seat. It was about more than her answers. They'd heard a tragedy unfold in the court – not the death of Andy Dillon but what could happen to an otherwise ordinary life and what falling into the gutter actually meant. They'd listened to Connie in the box, and Big Tam Logan, and had heard what living in the sewer of vice was like in real life. They'd watched Maxine defiant in the box, taking on a system that despised women like her, and saw only themselves and their children and how fate could rob people of their dignity. The AD saw it all and understood. He stared at the papers in front of him and wished it was time to head for one of the local boozers on the Royal Mile.

Maxine blinked several times when the jury came in and delivered a not guilty. It had been a close call, and her brief had warned her that it could go either way. Even after the judge had discharged her, she couldn't move till one of the officials touched her arm. She looked round and saw Connie on her feet, punching the air as if she was at a football match. Every day of the trial she'd scanned the court, hoping her mother would appear, but it had never happened. She accepted that it would just be too much for her, watching her daughter's life laid bare for public consumption. Still, she wished she could have seen her there, even just for a few moments. It was OK though and she understood – her mother had done enough just coming to the prison. It was what it was.

The advocate who'd defended her was a star – he walked her out of the court into broad daylight and freedom.

'There's the world, Maxine. Second chance, I think? Good luck.'

He shook her hand then swirled, his cape billowing dramatically in the light breeze, and he headed back to court to study the papers for his next case.

Connie ran the last few steps and almost did a nosedive trying to navigate the old cobbles in the ridiculous heels she'd picked for her day out at court. She looked great – different and dressed in the best. It was obvious that apart from the heels, her old working clothes had been left well behind.

Connie and Logan had both seen her often enough on remand, but this was different. During those visits, it had still been impossible to predict the outcome, and now they had the result, they seemed hardly able to accept what had already been decided. It seemed almost too simple. Someone in the jury stood up and said not guilty, the judge did his bit, you walked out of court with the brief and the trial was over. Maxine half expected a couple of uniforms to grab her – to say it was all a big mistake and that she was headed for some serious time inside.

Connie threw herself at Maxine and hugged her like a wrestler till they both heard Logan laughing out loud. It was an unusual sound – the Big Man hadn't laughed much in a long time.

'Tom' She said it quietly and saw his grin spread wide.

'Welcome back, Maxine.' Like Connie, he looked different, less stern, and some of the weight seemed to have lifted from those broad shoulders.

Connie and Logan took an arm each and together they all walked across Parliament Square. Although Maxine had no idea where they were headed, it didn't really matter – she was free. They never saw her smile slip for a moment when she remembered that this was no fairy tale; that the wolves were still out there somewhere in the shadows, but she put those thoughts away.

'What's the plan then, guys?'

'We've booked a posh wee place down the High Street, and we're drinkin' good wine like nice ordinary punters.'

They got to the edge of the square and then reality stepped out in front of them.

'Nice to see some fucker's havin' a good time.'

Bear Dillon seemed to appear out of the ground. Maxine recognised him from the court and wasn't surprised that he'd turned up. She'd heard the stories, and his late son had told her often enough who and what his old man represented.

She could see where his handle came from. He was built like a powerlifter, and it was years in the gym supported by steroids that had packed his six-foot frame with layers of muscle. He was a mean machine, no doubt about it. He had the bull head, tattoos and chunky necklace that would have spelled tosspot on most people, but not him. It kind of suited the whole package.

The girls stopped dead in their tracks, though Logan took one step forward and seemed absolutely calm. He knew how these things worked. Connie was frozen, but for Maxine there was no feeling of surprise. She knew the three of them couldn't just walk off along the yellow brick road and live happily ever after.

'What's the score, pal?' Logan said, and for Connie and Maxine, it was the voice of a man they'd heard about but never seen in action.

'The score is that ma fuckin' laddie's in the ground an' that slag wi' the smile on her puss put him there. Understood? Things will be sorted, hen. No' here, but it'll come, sometime when you're back on the street. Get the picture?'

Logan took another step forward and Maxine grabbed him by the arm.

'No, Tom. Please.' She looked at Dillon and told him she was sorry for everything that had happened and said, 'Let's go,' to her two friends.

Dillon was happy – he'd delivered his message. But as they walked past him, he and Logan locked eyes and passed several messages that didn't need words. The mood when she'd met her friends a few minutes earlier was gone, but Maxine had known it was just an illusion that came with the moment.

They tried hard in the restaurant. The food was a big improvement on her prison menu and the wine helped, but the notion of a happy ending was gone, and it only needed Maxine to cut up the self-delusion then toss it where it belonged. She waited till they were pretending to enjoy the sweet course.

'I'm leaving the city. It's no good – you saw what happened today.' She stared at the table and felt as if she'd betrayed them in some way. She wanted to take the words back the moment she said them, but it was done, and she was determined that she'd cause no more pain for the few people who cared about her.

Connie dropped her spoon next to her plate and rested her elbows on the table. She was a tough cookie – it was the only way she could have survived the life she'd been given. She tried her best to speak but couldn't find words because she knew that Maxine was right, and why she was right. She turned to Logan and saw his mouth tighten and strain with emotion. She shook her head and remembered life didn't have to hand out favours.

'I can take care of this, Maxine. He's second division and has no team behind him. Leave it with me.' Logan meant every word. He knew he was almost pleading but couldn't hold it back. He'd made the mistake of letting his imagination free after such a long hibernation.

'For Christ's sake, Tom.' Maxine's head snapped back, her eyes flaring with anger. It felt right – it was as if all those fears and nightmares she'd had in prison were given a release.

'Do you think I want this?' A tear rolled down her face, but she wasn't finished.

'I want to live, be happy, ordinary. Be a million miles from the life. Do you want me to be responsible for what would happen? More people hurt, killed? Jesus, Tom, get a grip.'

As soon as she finished she felt relief but saw the hurt in his eyes. His feelings were nothing to what would come if she let him a start a war with Bear Dillon though.

She tried to smile and put her hand on his.

'Please, Tom. I want peace and the same for you.'

She sighed and sat back.

'Who knows, if I can get through the next few months, stay off the dope, I might have a chance. But that just can't happen here.'

She waved to the waiter and grinned. 'Enough wine! Let's get a few vodis in like old times.'

24

Maxine had decided to travel in style and was sitting in first class for the first time in her life. She stuck a couple of aspirin in her mouth and washed them down with half a bottle of water. They'd done it in style the night before and the mood had lifted once she'd said what they all knew made sense. The drink had convinced them for a few hours that everything was alright. It was a necessary illusion. They were all pissed up at the end of the night, and their goodbyes avoided the truth that Maxine was determined to stick to.

The train picked up speed and ran past the small towns of East Lothian, and she stared at the space where the iconic landmark that had been the old Cockenzie power station used to stand. The great chimneys had been blown up, and the massive stacks that had towered over the Forth shores for years were gone. The world was changing fast and who knew what was coming next?

Maxine remembered promising Logan that if she could make it alone for a few months, she'd call him and tell him where she was. She fell asleep and dreamed of a new life where she'd hardly be noticed.

Maxine's mother came back in after a walk through the park with her dog, put the lead down and shook her head, trying to stop blaming herself for events she had no control over. Maxine's dad couldn't deal with it and had made her promise there would be no more contact. She'd been wrong again and was paying for it.

The light blinking on the phone caught her eye and she saw there was a voice message. It was short, but it was Maxine saying she loved them but she was going away, telling them to take care of each other and that she was going to try another life.

When it clicked off, her mother sat down in the kitchen and sobbed with grief at the loss of her child for the second time.

PART 2

25

In the days that followed, Connie decided she was finished with the street and that she was going to move to Ayr, where most of her family still lived. She'd hardly seen any of them for years but had kept in touch with the ones she'd forgiven mostly by phone. She'd never been happier apart from the situation with Maxine. Her friend meant so much to her and now she was gone, maybe for good, but it had been the right decision, and there was no doubt that if she'd stayed in Edinburgh it would have ended badly. Bear Dillon would have come for her at some point and that was no way to live. She was sure that Tam Logan would not have stood back and that would have led to him ending up in prison or dead himself.

Banjo went with her and they decided that getting married might be an idea – at the very least, it was an excuse for a good pish-up now they had a few notes in the bank. They both looked forward and actually believed that their lives had changed.

A few days later, Banjo was scanning the paper when he saw the article. He called Connie.

'Fuck's sake! Have a look at this, doll.'

Connie had become 'doll' now they had money – or at least more money than they'd ever had in the past.

Kylie the bam had been arrested a few days after Maxine left Edinburgh. It turned out when the old boy at the farm was sleeping after another session with her, he'd woken to find her emptying his wallet. He'd blown a gasket so Kylie had decided to take action and carved a couple of wounds on each of his arse cheeks. He'd thought he was going to bleed to death and called an ambulance and the police because he was sure she might finish the job. Kylie didn't even leg it. When the cavalry arrived, she was sitting in the living room watching Jeremy Kyle and smoking a joint while the old boy was barricaded in his room and bleeding heavily onto a new carpet. Apparently, she didn't give a fuck. It didn't get any better for the old boy either because the police were already on his case for sexual offences involving Kylie and, as it turned out, another couple of fourteen-year-olds.

Connie kept in regular touch with Logan, and although they kept talking about Maxine, she was gone, and every day they waited for a call that didn't come. Logan went into the pub at the same time every morning and kept checking the messages on his phone, quietly hoping while the world kept on spinning.

26

When Maxine left Edinburgh, she headed to Leeds. There was no particular reason for that city other than she'd been there for a couple of boozy weekends with friends back when she'd had a life. It seemed a place that few people from north of the border would visit. Newcastle was too close, London too expensive, and she knew from friends and visits that the Big Smoke could be a lonely city; she might end up in a worse position than she would in Edinburgh. Her memories of Leeds were of a young city – young in the sense that it had been redeveloped, felt confident and there were opportunities. If it didn't work out, she could move on and try something else.

The first days were desperate, and although she managed to rent a decent place quickly, the sense of being alone, unable to lift the phone for the reassurance of a friend or family member in case she put them at risk almost overwhelmed her. She spent her time wandering among streets full of people as if she was a ghost, not really existing except in her own mind, and the days felt almost dreamlike.

Then passing time worked its magic and she started to smile at the waitresses who served her coffee, who seemed interested because she wasn't a regular or a local. It dawned on her that they weren't engaging with a prostitute – they were talking to a young woman who had no past as far as they were concerned. Maxine could be what she liked, make up a past or pretend she was just a tourist recharging the batteries after a tough year at work. Then she started to wake up in the mornings from deep sleeps, free from booze, dope and nicotine. She was off the chemicals and found new reserves of energy as she walked around the city, the aching tiredness she used to feel in her legs gradually replaced by the buzz of raw energy pumping round her still-young body.

Leeds was a place full of surprises, vibrant – the old and the new structures in the city complementing each other. She found Roundhay Park, one of the biggest city parks in Europe, only three miles from the centre and spent hours there, walking, sitting and just letting her scars heal enough to move on. She loved the idle chance meetings with other people, usually women with children, though sometimes women with dogs would sit beside her on the benches and just talk for no other reason than to be pleasant.

There were no punters soiling her existence or threatening to mark her face. No one handing over the drugs she needed to get through the day without walking in front of a car. Leeds would have its own dark places, but she wasn't part of that and the darkness could stay wherever it was. She'd take her own life before going back to the street. She'd survived it once, and although few made it out, she was determined that she'd be one of them. The future was still an empty expanse that had no form, but at least she was alive and there was hope when she watched people being happy. There was a train station close to her flat, and she spent time there just watching people arrive and depart. Watching couples kiss, hold each other as if it was the last time, smile as children rushed to a parent who only been gone a short time but love drew them together like magnets.

For the first couple of months she soaked up the pleasure of no one knowing who she was or, more importantly, what she'd been. Money wasn't a problem for the time being; the lottery win had given her some breathing space, the freedom to at least make some choices that suited her. The small one-bedroom flat she rented became a haven that gave her time to heal, where she could listen to music and think in peace, and indulging herself in decent furniture made it feel like a home, something she'd only dreamed about on the streets of Leith. Eventually she found a job serving tables. For most people it would have been mind-numbing given the pay, but for Maxine it was the best job in the world. No more freezing nights, standing in doorways wondering if the next punter would be the one who'd leave her lying on waste ground with her skull caved in. Being an ordinary girl with a very ordinary life was like a gift from God.

Life managed to surprise her though. She made a real friend in one of the other waitresses called Jan, who was Welsh through to the souls of her feet. Nothing was sacred to her, and when they started to go out together, the first surprise was that she could make Maxine curl over laughing. It hadn't been that long ago that she'd thought that would never be possible again. But Jan was more than a sense of humour – she was savvy and saw enough in Maxine's eyes to know the girl had been through the wringer. She still didn't know what it was about but she knew to let it be; it would come out in time because Maxine was going to be a friend for life.

'Tell me a story, Jan,' Maxine said one night. 'One of those ones you pretend are true but just make up.' Maxine liked to just listen when Jan was in full flight.

'Just you sit an' listen, girl, an' I'll tell you the story about the night I pulled Tom Jones,' Jan replied. She told that one over and over again and each time changed the details to make it even more outrageous. None of it was true, of course, but that didn't matter.

27

Jan came up with more surprises – she was going to be a millionaire. This statement came right out of the blue one night after work over a coffee and a stale sandwich, but it didn't surprise Maxine – she always thought Jan was holding a lot in reserve. She grinned the first time she heard it and waited for a punchline that never came.

'OK, Jan, what's the big plan?'

'No, I *am* going to become a millionaire and I've definitely got a plan.' She smiled, watching the small lines scrunch on Maxine's forehead.

'Buying and selling.' Jan nodded, grinning as Maxine tried to work out whether she was serious or not.

'What, Jan? Buy and sell what exactly?' Maxine waited again for a punchline that refused to come.

'Stuff. I'm going to buy and sell stuff.'

She winked at her friend and tapped the side of her nose, then bit into the sandwich and grimaced at the effect on her palate.

'I'm not a career waitress, Max.' She'd shortened her friend's name right down. That was the way she was – wasting nothing, not even words.

'I took a good business degree – just been waiting for the day I kick off. Been buying and selling gear online for a while, first small time but been building it up. I just bought a thousand baseball caps from China at a couple of quid a shot, and I'm going to knock them on at six. All online.'

She sat back like the cat that got the clotted cream and seemed to be waiting for applause. Maxine looked a little stuck for a response; she'd taken to Jan from the off, but once again she'd failed to see what should have been obvious. For all she'd seen and the lessons she should have learned, she was still naïve. All that time on the street and what had she learned? Jan was the real deal in more ways than one – she'd sensed there was more to her than serving coffee and chatting to punters, and here she was, a force of nature just waiting to happen.

'God, Jan… good for you. I'm jealous.' Maxine sat back, lips parted, and felt a little sorry for herself, as if her friend was going to announce that her life was about to move on so ta-ta and see you around!

'What about you, Max? You're no mug, girl, but you're wrapped up tight. Thought you would have told me what it was… Has to be a something to do with a man – always is, eh?'

Jan put her mug to her lips and waited, hoping Maxine would give a little. If she'd had a face full of razor scars, it couldn't be more obvious that the girl had been damaged. Who hadn't, but it was clearly more than the average ditching by a married man. Jan looked at her beautiful face, those soulful eyes, something special about the shape and colour but lovely. She wondered what she would look like without that permanent air of hurt. Even when she made Maxine laugh out loud, it was still there in her eyes. She had asked herself time and time again what her friend was seeing in her dreams – or were they nightmares? There was the odd moment where she would startle when a door opened, as if the wrong person might walk in. At times, she acted like a nervous animal, always watching for a predator's approach.

Maxine stared across the table. She didn't want to lose Jan the way she'd lost everyone else in her life. All the people who mattered seemed to be in the past – there were no catch-up calls with friends and family bridging the miles to her home in Edinburgh. Every night she ran the images through her head. Family – even though her father and brothers had almost disowned her after she was caught stealing from the hospital where she worked. She hadn't disowned them and still imagined a world where the past had disappeared and her father would use the pet name he'd given her as soon as she'd learned to laugh at his efforts to entertain her as a child.

Reality would always gatecrash those dreams though, the cold memory of a career in nursing crashing in the shame of drug addiction then those nights on the streets selling herself to men who didn't care whether she lived or died as long as they got what they paid for. Every time she thought about it, she squirmed at how far and how fast she had fallen. Her mother still cared, and the need to speak to her was hard to bear, but the only way to protect them and herself was to leave and never turn back.

Sometimes she wished she'd just died when Andy Dillon had tried to kill her. It would have been over and everyone would have forgotten what she'd done. All sin washed away. But she'd survived and the waste of space she'd killed still had an old man with attitude – and Bear Dillon was one of those men who loved to watch the fear and blood pouring out of anyone who got in his way. It made no difference whether they were male or female, and he didn't pretend to have a code of honour like other men in his game. He'd sworn to take care of Maxine and that was part of the reason she'd stepped on a train and watched her old life disappear with the miles south.

Sometimes the situation would almost overwhelm her, but at least she was surviving; Leeds gave her all the cover she needed, but she ached to know what was happening with her friends, especially Connie, and Tom Logan was never far from her thoughts. That big hard man inspired such respect from all sorts of people, yet she knew there was more to him than the street legend. She'd seen the quiet tears, the way he'd treated Maxine as just another human being who'd been hurt along the way. Their world was as full of victims as it was of villains.

'I hope you can take the truth.'

Maxine leaned across the table and gripped Jan's hand, almost hurting her. Her lips twitched trying to contain the emotion of disclosure or part disclosure – her story would take too long to tell, and she still didn't have the strength to unload all of the burden she was carrying. She told Jan about the life she had right up to nursing and then the mistakes that had piled up so deep around her she had almost drowned in them.

She didn't intend to share so much truth, the horrors of street life, but then she couldn't stop – the words just kept on coming and it was like drawing poison from her system. Even if Jan walked away, she'd shared the guilt, and hearing the story from her own lips helped purge the terrible shame she carried with her every day. It was a story about a young woman who could have had a good life and had been foolish. If she was someone else hearing this story, she would have shaken her head but not rushed to judgement. There but for the grace of God.

Jan never interrupted, and the face that always seemed about to split into at least a grin was now blank and paler than normal; there was no way of knowing what was going on behind her almost inscrutable mask.

Maxine finished and felt exhausted, almost light-headed with relief. She'd been living like a fugitive and realised it couldn't go on. She waited while Jan stayed quiet, as if she was analysing what she'd heard. It had been a lot to take in.

'Jan?' Maxine bit her lip, waiting for anger, disgust, whatever it was that she thought she deserved.

'Think this warrants another drink. Jesus, Max.' Jan paused again as if the information download still wasn't completely forged into her hard drive. 'I'll get them in.' She got to her feet without asking what Maxine wanted. She was getting her another G&T whether she wanted it or not. It wasn't a problem and she definitely needed another drink.

Jan sat down and plonked the glasses on the table, pushing one towards Maxine with the other already at her own lips. 'Christ, I was going to admit doing a bit of shoplifting when I was a student. Just bits of food when I was starving. Gimme your hand, Max.' The colour had returned to Jan's face and her eyes were moist.

'I don't know what to say,' she added and shook her head. For someone never lost for words, she didn't know how to respond but realised that she hadn't a clue about life. Right up to hearing Maxine's story, she'd thought she was worldly, experienced and wiser than her years. Then this epiphany, the revelation that she'd only experienced drama on TV or at the movies. Sitting opposite her was reality, the awful truth of what could happen in this world because of the wrong place, wrong time, wrong man or, in Maxine's case, all of the above.

The worst experience Jan had faced was the natural, although premature, death of her father. Then the feeling that in some way she'd been treated badly by God or whoever the fuck. Maxine had been somewhere much darker – the other world, the other dimension where ordinary people existed side by side in total ignorance of what crawled about their streets at night when they were sliding into bed, safe from the world that lay outside their windows.

Finally, she said, 'We're off tomorrow so let's get pissed, Max. Come back to my place and stay the night. We can talk crap till we flake out. I'll cook you a full hangover breakfast in the morning. Right?'

Maxine squeezed her eyes closed, trying to hold in her relief that Jan wasn't angry. She sniffed wetly and grabbed a tissue, trying to stifle the flow.

They did it in style, and when they got back to Jan's tiny flat, they talked like teenagers, unscarred by the realities ahead. Maxine's confession couldn't be ignored, but there had been enough trauma for one night. They were locked in a safe little bubble for a few hours, the truth had freed up their relationship and it was as if they'd both discovered something good in themselves and their friend.

At the time, it seemed like they'd bought a ridiculous amount of wine, but when the clock hit two and most of the city slept, they realised that they only had empties and yet they were almost sober.

'Time for bed then, partner.' Jan said the word for the first time.

'Partner?' Maxine crushed her eyebrows together in an expression she used too often to supplement a question; it was leaving fine lines behind.

'I want you to share the business, Max. I need someone beside me if I'm going to be a millionaire.'

Her face showed only slight surprise that anyone could doubt what she regarded as merely a statement of fact.

'Fair enough,' Maxine said, though she didn't really believe it.

They slept, Jan in her seriously single bed and Maxine on the half-sized couch, her legs dangling over the edge. She woke after a couple of hours and moved to the floor, which seemed a more comfortable option. She'd slept in worse.

She said 'partner' just before she dropped off again and dreamed about a dark city. She didn't recognise it at first and then the buildings either side seemed to disappear into a bleak night sky. The place was deserted and she drifted upwards across shining cobbles as she realised it was Edinburgh and she was home. Despite the dark street full of shadows, she felt safe and woke again.

Maxine yearned to visit her home and found it strange that she felt this way – it was as if she'd left behind good memories, yet her life had almost been torn apart in the old city. Something had passed though. The girl who'd sold her dignity on the Leith streets was gone and Maxine wondered if anyone remembered her or cared what had happened to her.

There was one – she knew he'd wake up every day and ask himself the same question. She'd seen what was in his eyes, but she hadn't been able to give him what he really wanted. Then there was the guilt that she'd walked away from such a man and left him to care about her on his own. She forced herself to concentrate on Jan instead, and it dawned on her that her friend's level of confidence didn't fall out of the sky: she was talented, savvy and she had a plan.

'God what if it works?' She imagined good times and smiled just before the results of the wine came to visit. The hangover was going to be there in the morning, but she was OK with that. They deserved it, and they had a couple of days off to recover, so Maxine slept again.

28

Six months later Jan had proved her optimism was based on more than blind faith. The plan had worked, better than they could ever have imagined. It seemed to prove the point that there was money in muck – or in this case money in cheap goods turned over in volume. Maxine stood in the middle of the medium-sized industrial unit they'd taken over and if she didn't know better, she could have believed she was staring at piles of junk. She shook her head at the deal they'd done the previous day – it was a regular one that Jan had turned over time and time again. Thousands of baseball caps Jan had bought from a Chinese dealer. They'd gone up to three pound a shout and she'd just turned them over within twenty-four hours for six with barely any effort or expenditure. *God knows why people buy this crap*, she thought almost every day, but for Jan – who cared?

'Just understand your market, Max, and go with it.' Jan knew exactly what she was doing and they'd left waiting tables far behind. Maxine felt renewed, slept deeply at night and woke refreshed for each new day.

She'd restricted herself to booze one night a week and there was no ache now for the dope that had been all that had mattered on the streets – the drugs that had made the men who'd bought her just that bit more bearable; had helped her lock out the sound of their heaving efforts and her disgust at the ones who thought hygiene didn't matter for a street hooker.

They were making money, and despite her initial cynicism, Maxine had gone with it, and while she might not be a natural like her friend, she was good and realised that she enjoyed business and, most of all, the control of running their own thing. It wakened something else, the desire to do more. She hadn't died back there in Edinburgh; it was close but the day she'd stepped on the train at Waverley and left the few real friends she'd had behind, she'd been born again. Not to Christianity, for some faceless god who hadn't cared for her on the street, but as a survivor who should have died and had discovered the true gift of life. The gift nearly always taken for granted. Maxine would never make that mistake again; she could survive and carve out another life.

When she'd divulged her past to Jan, there had been another revelation – the sheer relief of disclosure, and she now thought often of that old saying that 'the truth will set you free'. It had; she'd sinned and paid a heavy price, but she'd decided that covering it up would be as much good as ignoring the symptoms of a disease that would eventually kill you. She wouldn't stand on a soapbox and shout it to the mob, but there would be no lies if the subject came up. People could accept who she was or she didn't need them. Tom Logan had and now Jan, who'd never lived on the dark side of a city. Maxine had paid in full for her sins and now it was time to move on.

29

Maxine and Jan reached a landmark when they realised they'd known each other for over a year and they were making money – real money. Most of what Maxine had taken from the lottery win was untouched and she was saving. Her needs were modest, and apart from membership of a good gym and perhaps indulging in quality clothes, that was about it as far as luxuries went. She had all she needed and could have more if she chose.

There were still those moments when Edinburgh drifted into her thoughts, the old city and people who been part of her life. The need to know what had happened to them since she'd left could feel like an ache at times, but she swore she would not put any of them at risk by reaching out.

Everything was changing for both of them. Jan glowed with the realisation that she was a success. Like the true businesswoman she was, she just kept upping the pace, and it was clear she was going to go all the way. It was time to stop and mark their achievement. If Maxine didn't realise it yet then Jan did – they needed a break. They'd worked almost non-stop to make the business a success. It was early days but they'd done all that, and they were tired and needed a distraction, even if it was just a short one.

'OK, Max. I've booked just about the best place to eat, we fill up on vino and then do the town. How's that?' Jan asked and grinned in that way she had.

Maxine loved it – the lopsided mouth that seemed to say *Happy Days* without her lips moving. She put aside her laptop and brushed a strand of hair behind her ear. She'd been lost in work and smiled back at her friend.

'Sounds the biso, Jan. Take it we need to get dressed then?'

The two of them tended to live in jeans and sweatshirts and the thought of dressing up sent a tingle sizzling along Maxine's spine. The sensation caught her like a stranger's hand; she hadn't felt that in a long time. The thought of painting up and going on the town hadn't crossed her mind, but as soon as it was suggested, she grabbed the idea. She was wise enough to know that the *all work* way of living couldn't go on or they'd both burn out and what they'd done with the business would have been a waste. Maxine wanted to live; she just needed someone to give her a prompt.

'Isn't it about time we tried to get some male company into the act, Max?' Jan replied. 'Christ, I can't remember what they're for but sure it's important and good for your health.'

She flashed that grin again but realised she'd just driven through a red light when she saw Maxine's eyes turn down to the floor as if they were digging up the evidence of a crime.

She walked across to her friend, put her hands on her shoulders and bent down at the waist to bring her face close.

'I'm sorry; I keep forgetting. Tell you what, you play Mother Teresa, but if I get a whiff of Old Spice I might just have to follow the spoor.'

Maxine looked up and snorted a laugh. 'OK, Jan. It's a deal.'

Back in the new flat she'd rented once business had taken off, Maxine stared at herself in the bathroom mirror. She was in her dressing gown and her hair was pulled back from her face, ready for the shower. Jan's words kept coming back. She'd never even considered being with a man again. Although she saw those looks often enough from guys who were interested, she never gave any green lights because she wasn't available. It might never happen again; there was no basic urge and she wondered how much damage had been done to her because she was still young and there should have been something. They met men all the time through the business, and just a few years earlier she would have imagined all sorts of possibilities, but there was nothing but a cold place where those instincts had once lived. Could she have this new life without a man by her side? Why not?

She leaned down and put her hands on the small dressing table and moved her face close to the mirror. Her eyes were crystal clear, and apart from a few tiny lines on her forehead, her skin was almost unblemished. She turned her face through a number of angles, looking for answers, signs that might tell her something. Her face was fuller; a good diet and a system not trying to cope with the effects of dope, adulterated with whatever shit the dealer decided to bulk it with, meant she looked good. A bit too serious perhaps – Jan kept telling her not to keep hiding the smile that could light up her face.

She went back into her bedroom, opened the bag on the bed and looked at the dress she'd bought for the night out, running the expensive fabric through her fingers.

'Who knows?' she whispered on her way to the shower.

Despite her reservations, Maxine felt the buzz as soon as she slipped the new dress over her head and felt the cool fabric slide down the length of her body. It sent another small shiver down her spine, and when she looked in the mirror, she almost cried at the reflection that seemed to be someone else or someone from the past. She couldn't rid herself of the thought that when she looked at her reflection, what she might see was the girl from the street who'd struggled just to stay alive. Could this be the same woman who'd fallen so far into what seemed like permanent night, sold herself to feed a habit and could have been all but forgotten – as if she'd never even existed?

She looked down and saw her hands were trembling, but this was another step along the road, and she realised just how much she owed Jan in the time they'd been together.

She took off the dress and laid it out for later. She had a few hours free before the night out, so she lay down on the bed and wondered again about Connie. She hoped the money she'd won had made her happy and she'd found a good life away from the street.

Sleep came like a warm blanket and she sank into its caress.

30

Connie stamped her feet and dragged on her cigarette, looking both ways before crossing the street at Leith Police Station and heading in the direction of the Links. She felt sick and tired, wondering how she was going to get through the night without stabbing a punter. Her world had collapsed. Like Maxine, she'd thought her old life was gone at last. Banjo had seemed happier that she'd ever seen him, and the clean break from their old life seemed to be working, but she'd come to learn the hard way that she'd been deluding herself – trying too hard to believe everything was possible.

Connie's roots were in Ayrshire, and she'd been brought up in Ayr itself, so they'd headed west and settled in the busy little port on the Clyde shore. It was probably the nearest thing to home for her and now she cursed herself for thinking that Banjo could change. She had every right to hate him, but she blamed herself for being so naïve. *Jesus Christ, how did that happen?* she'd thought time and time again since it had all fucked up.

It had been great for a while; she'd found a job in a cafe that just topped up what they had and Banjo had picked up some part-time work – the first for years as far as he was concerned. Unfortunately, Banjo was an arse and would always be an arse. She'd thought the money she'd won was safely stashed away, but it only took a few weeks before the old urges were too much for him and he'd started dipping into their savings. She'd asked herself a thousand times why she'd given a former junkie access to the money.

He'd managed to pick up a new bunch of pals who were even bigger arses than he was and only too pleased to help him self-destruct, but for a while he'd been the most popular guy on the block.

She shivered every time she thought about the day she'd come home knackered and realised he'd fucked off and the only thing left was a barely legible note saying he was sorry.

'That was so fuckin' nice o' him,' she whispered and her breath evaporated into the night air, a bit like the remains of her life.

She blew her nose again as a beat-up old Ford drew alongside the kerb and an overweight punter lowered the window. She leaned down and felt a blast of heat mixed up with cigarette smoke and body odour whack her round the face. Business had been light so she decided that at least the car was warm and what choice did she have? She got into the car and tried to pretend she was happy to see the creep.

An hour later she was back on her beat. All she wanted was to shower and scrub till her skin was red with the effort, as she did most days now, but it was impossible to wash those men away. Instead, she lit another cigarette and tried not to cry.

31

The restaurant was buzzing, the food and wine perfect and, as always, Jan was a hoot after the first couple of drinks. They finished their booze crawl in an upmarket bar full of pretence, and thankfully Jan told the guys who tried to make a move that they were committed lesbians and 'no thank you very much'. By the time they moved onto the third bottle, they'd lost interest in anyone else. That was the moment Jan got back to business.

'Why don't we expand, Max?' she said. 'We could take on some extra help and grow this thing. Doesn't mean we have to work harder – we can delegate now. What do you say?'

It was the moment Maxine had been trying to avoid but knew was coming. It focused her mind, even though the wine had dulled her senses a little. She leaned forward and put her hand over her friend's.

'Look, Jan, I love you to bits, you know that, but you're the driving force here. I just happened to be around when you took off. You don't need me, and at some stage I might want to do something else. I've never really travelled…' She paused; she was struggling to explain something she hadn't yet worked out herself.

'I'm still getting used to this new life. You know, sometimes it's as if all that back home was a bad dream, but I did have a life before that. Christ, I used to love nursing and never wanted to do anything else. I'm sorry, Jan.'

She paused, again searching for the words that wouldn't hurt her friend or spoil a good night.

'Look, I'm not running out; just not sure I can go all the way with you.' She grinned. 'Anyway, I'm not sure I could keep up with you – you work so damned hard, girl.'

The look on Jan's face suggested she'd almost expected this answer.

'I get it, Max, but we're good at this and don't undersell yourself. Look, this is nothing I'm going to do right now. Just planning ahead, so take your time and think about it. Now let's get this wine necked and see where it goes.'

An hour later, Maxine called for a taxi after Jan declared, 'I'm pulling, Max. Sure you don't want to join me?'

'How'd you manage that then, Jan? Anyway, I'm going back to the flat knackered and pissed, but you go ahead.'

'Watch this, girl – behold a master at work.'

Jan walked or rather swayed over to the bar and straight for a guy who'd been eyeing them all night. Maxine shook her head and grinned after about thirty seconds when Jan gave her the thumbs up and pouted her lips in mock lechery – or was it?

Maxine guessed the lesbian cover was ditched.

She almost dozed in the taxi, and when she got back into the flat she felt lost. There was a part of her that wished she could have just thrown caution to the wind like Jan. She was almost surprised when she realised what she was feeling – the need to be close to someone again. It had been so long, and she bit down on her lip as something almost forgotten surged through her. She took her dress off, slid into a bed that felt a little colder than normal and dreamed about home.

*

Maxine spent the next few days worrying about her reaction to Jan's proposal, but all her friend could talk about was the new man she'd 'selected' in the bar. Turned out he ticked a lot of boxes. She seemed surprised that she actually cared about a man; she'd had her own share of disappointments in the past, but unlike Maxine was occasionally still dipping her toe in the pool. There was almost no mention of business expansion so Maxine settled down and stopped worrying that they were standing at a crossroads rather than seeing one in the distance. She wanted more time to stabilise her life – as it was she was fine, and she didn't really want sudden change or a commitment that she might regret.

Since the night out, Maxine had taken a subconscious decision to free up her desires though. The need was there again and she allowed herself to imagine what it would be like to be with someone – feelings that had been locked away from the light, almost forgotten in those dark nights on the street. It would have been easy to give up on the human race, and in particular the males of the species, but her time recovering her life in Yorkshire and her relationship with Jan had shown her that she had to take control of her needs. She was a free woman who had every right just to feel human again.

The street had barely been an existence, where all control and personal choice had been taken away by the need for dope and the debt that had imprisoned her in a spiral of hopeless despair. But she was meeting people every day in the business world who made choices for themselves, and though it had taken time, she had finally accepted that she could do exactly the same.

Maxine was almost free of the past, though not completely, and as it stood, she couldn't go back to her home town without looking over her shoulder for a man who would try to kill her, given the chance. It was what it was and she'd settle for that, but she missed home and couldn't shake the questions that came to her constantly about her friends and family – and Tom Logan, always there but suspended, as if he was on the other side of a door that she wouldn't open. He was older than her and had connections to a life she wanted to leave behind, but even after all these months, he wasn't fading into the distance; instead he lingered, waiting in her imagination…

32

It was nearly two months after their night out that Maxine was staring at her laptop, reading the news as she ate a takeaway. It was the same routine most days – she caught up with the news when she came in from work. She was exhausted; the business was now probably beyond the point where they needed help and they would have to make the decisions Jan had discussed or risk losing trade, which wasn't an option for either of them.

Maxine always checked the local news in Edinburgh then the Scottish news. It was a lifeline to her old existence – she'd accepted that she couldn't separate herself from home despite everything that happened, but unlike most people who left to work south of the border or abroad, she had no active link to keep in touch.

There were so many times on the street when she'd cursed her existence and she'd thought she hated everything about Edinburgh, but of course with distance, she'd realised that it was her life and not the fault of the old city. It was strange how separation from her birthplace had made her pine to see the steep hills and streets of the capital once more.

The news from Edinburgh was pretty routine and the latest fallout from the Brexit referendum was still raining on political life north and south of the border.

She was halfway through a yawn when she froze and exhaled slowly at the little headline halfway down one of the inside pages. It wasn't a long report, but it made her chest heave as if the man it reported on had walked into the room. Bear Dillon, the father of the man she'd killed in Edinburgh, had been sentenced to fifteen years for drugs trafficking, firearms offences and attempted murder.

She went into the kitchen and poured a glass of water, unable to control her shaking. For the first time in months she craved something to take the edge off, and it reminded her that she was still a recovering addict.

She read the article again and her head spun trying to work out what it meant. If Bear Dillon really was gone from the scene then there might be a chance for her to go back, even briefly, to satisfy her need to know how things had moved on back home. For a moment she shuddered at the thought that her parents could be dead and she wouldn't know – what did that make her? Going home could be worse though. Dillon was in prison, but he might still be able to reach her through other people. Was it worth the risk – to her and those she loved?

She stared out of the window for a long time, wondering.

33

It had been one of those crazy nights on the streets of Leith. The Hibees had taken a painful beating from their old enemies at Tynecastle so it followed that there were a few skirmishes among the faithful. Charlie Brockie had finished locking up his last prisoner; he just wanted to sign off and walk across the road for a beer so he sighed wearily when he got the shout that there was a phone call for him. When he asked who it was, the young PC who handed him the phone told him that the caller had refused to give her name.

'Your bit on the side, Charlie!' he joked. 'Sounds nice though.'

The young PC smiled; he loved a bit of banter with Brockie, the man who was at the centre of so many legends about Leith Police. Half of them were spun wildly out of shape or just plain porkies, but Brockie used them to his own advantage as only the old hands knew how.

Banter was a staple diet in the muster room of any station and Brockie mouthed the words 'fuck off' as he took the phone.

'PC Brockie – who am I speaking to?'

146

There was no answer even after the second asking and he was about to put the phone down when he heard the voice; he recognised it straight away and was all ears.

'It's Maxine Welsh. Is it alright to talk?'

There was a pause as Brockie absorbed the words.

'Jesus, girl, where've you been hiding?'

There was another pause as she took it literally. Was there a reason to hide?

Brockie spoke again, realising she might have taken the wrong meaning from his words.

'Sorry, there's nobody after you, Maxine. Just surprised to hear from you. Is there a problem? Are you alright?' Brockie tended not to get too emotional or worked up about anything job related, but he knew that this girl was a puzzle in so many ways and he'd often wondered what had become of her or whether she'd just ended up in another rathole of a life.

'Yes, I'm good.' Her voice seemed small and timid. She cleared her throat and the nerves calmed.

'I'm really well actually, Charlie. Never got the chance to thank you properly for the way you treated me.'

'It's my job, hen. Always done it that way. What can I do for you?'

'Is it true Bear Dillon's inside?'

'Aye an' he's stayin' there. Took a flaky when he was arrested and tried to do one of the cops wi' a hammer. Ended up on the deck an' took a heart attack. Good enough for the man.' Brockie paused but it was quiet on the other end of the line.

'He'll no' harm you now, Maxine. He's history an' the thing is even the villains hated the bastard.'

He waited, trying to think of the right thing to say and not spook her.

'Thanks, Charlie.'

She remembered that there were people who cared about her. 'Have you seen Tom?'

'Tom.' Charlie Brockie had to think because to everyone in Leith and to everyone who knew him, Tom Logan was Big Tam. He worked it out though; he'd sensed at the time of her arrest that the man cared about her. What that meant was another thing. Logan tended to come to the aid of the underdogs, and maybe that was all it was, but Brockie thought there might be something more there – Logan had gone a long way to support Maxine after her arrest.

'Logan doesn't change, hen. Swear to God he's always been the same age and always will be. Freak o' nature if you know what I mean?'

He chuckled and even though he'd crossed swords with the Big Man over the years he respected him; it was an old-school thing and Brockie had been educated in the same arena.

'Will I tell him you called?'

'Yes, tell him, Charlie – tell him I'm well. Maybe I'll come home for a visit in a few months – really busy at the moment but yes, in a few months.' She surprised herself with the last sentence, but it had been there just below the surface and only needed a prompt. Saying it unlocked the emotion that had been straining for release. She cried softly but didn't put the phone down.

'Sorry, Charlie.'

'No need, Maxine. Have the occasional greet myself but don't tell a soul.'

'Do you ever see Connie? I think she was going to leave the city?'

Brockie realised that she must have cut herself off completely and hesitated.

'Seen her a couple of times, Maxine. You know what she's like, never changes.' He didn't want to tell her any more because he didn't know how.

'Need to go, Maxine,' he lied. 'Calls coming in and need to do my bit for Queen and country an' all that shite. Listen, take care an' I'll let Tam know.'

She said goodbye, wondering why he was so obviously holding back about Connie as he clicked the off button.

Home – she decided there and then that she'd go back and see what was there now. Would anyone care? She'd walked away after the trial and never contacted the people who'd stood by her side. It had been to keep them out of a war with Bear Dillon, but would they accept that after all this time? She decided to wait just a bit longer and not rush into a decision she might regret in case something went wrong with Dillon's sentence and he was released on some technical issue. It happened, and rushing could cost her, so against her instincts, she'd wait a bit longer and be sure.

34

As Maxine put down the phone, 160 miles north Patrick 'Bobo' McCartney banged fuck out of the Sally Army big drum and imagined what it must have been like for those bastards in the Orange Lodge on the parades. He was from the green-hooped side of the religious and football divide in the great city of Glasgow.

He was enjoying the sunshine that was helping the natives forget the weeks of regular pissing rain mixed up with low-pressure systems that had battered the country for weeks. Scotland had given the world so much but fortunately not its weather. Nature had a way of working its magic and only a few days of sustained rays had wiped the bad memories, making people feel there was still hope.

It felt like a long time since Bobo had walked away from his life as a failed criminal, picked up his Bible and joined up with God's army. He'd moved through to Edinburgh to get away from the city in the west that had made him what he was, but it tugged at his memories all the time. Rangers were back in the big league and he wouldn't be on those terraces screaming abuse at the team and the supporters in blue as he had in times past – those days when his gang was like his family, marching to Celtic Park, heart thumping from the adrenalin rush mixed with cheap booze and whatever dope they could lay their hands on.

Bobo was born a Hoop and had hated the Gers and their fans since he could speak. He sometimes missed those days; spitting venom at all that was blue and the battles which had broken out after the games were just fond memories now, but from another time that was gone for him. His gang were inside, junkie bastards or, in a couple of cases, exposed grasses for Glasgow detectives.

His life had moved on from the street gangs, and even though he'd failed at their level, he'd tried to move up a couple of rungs and had started working with real villains. For a while, his hopes of stardom in the criminal world had been rekindled, but that had all gone to rat shit as well.

He'd reached a low ebb in those days, when he might have been killed at the hands of the men he'd been associating with, but that hadn't been his real problem. Being killed was always a possibility when you signed up to join the gangsters, and at that time the question of reaching a mature age had never crossed his mind, aside from knowing that he didn't want to go there. He'd seen enough of the broken men, pissed out of their skulls on cider, who'd run with the gangs in their glory days. *Fuck that*, he'd thought at a very early age. The problem was reality – the simple fact that crime wasn't as easy as the telly and film dramas often depicted it. Kicking fuck out of a Hun supporter after a big game was one thing, but making a profit from dishonesty was quite another. The cops tried to lock you up, and worst of all, the gangster bosses were worse than the law. There was no such thing as the minimum wage and worker's rights didn't really interest the top men.

Bobo had just gone from one crisis to another, right up to a major fuck-up in Edinburgh when he'd been working with the McMartin gang and they'd tried to rip off another team transporting a shitload of dope from south of the border to Glasgow via the capital. The problem was that one of the couriers was 'Psycho' McManus and it was like planning to rip off the SAS – difficult to say the least. It had all gone belly up and so Bobo had gone into hiding. In the end, though, the people who were intent on hurting him were all with their maker or the devil now, so at least that one had gone away.

That near-death experience had brought about an epiphany, which in reality was just an escape route from his failures. He decided one day when he was keeping his head down that God had called to him, and after years of disappointments, he'd found a purpose in life. He hadn't spoken with God before but quite liked the man once he'd prayed a few times because he always got the answers he needed. Just like the Celtic, all you had to do was believe, and for a while Bobo was as passionate a believer as they came – no doubt about it.

It had been easier than he thought possible living without dope or booze, and the removal of the threat of prison or violence meant he could sleep at night. God had been a real pal, and taking it onto the street with the army band had given him a purpose for living again.

A real bonus was that a senior soldier had taken Bobo under his wing and taught him to play the drum like a pro, and to his own surprise he was good at it. He didn't exactly have a bulging social diary so a senior soldier of God actually liking him proved again that God was definitely on his side. He'd never been good at something in his life, but the Big Man had called him and it looked like he was a becoming a good soldier himself, with a purpose to save other sinners like himself.

Everything had gone smoothly enough since, although he found it difficult when wee neds who were almost carbon copies of what Bobo had been himself at one time delighted in ripping the pish out of the army band when it was doing its stuff. There was added salt rubbed into the wound because the tormentors weren't even Weegies and it was an outrage being wound up by Edinburgh bawbags who wouldn't have lasted five minutes on his old territory. His mentor saw Bobo's conflict in these moments, put a hand on the young man's shoulder and reminded him that Christ had recommended forgiveness in these testing moments.

'It's our faith that makes us stronger than them, Patrick.'

He always used his forename and Bobo could have sworn that he saw an aura round the man when he said these things. He bit his lip and accepted the teaching, so when the neds howled, he banged the drum just that bit louder because that's what the Lord wanted him to do. If it was good enough for Jesus and his old man, then it was good enough for Patrick 'Bobo' McCartney.

35

There are always moments that can dramatically change the course of lives, events and history – and Bobo had his on what had been another sun-filled day when God really did seem to be smiling down on his Scottish soldier. It was the night his mentor had invited him home for a meal and some Bible reading. Bobo saw this as yet another sign of progress in his life without crime, although he worried about the dark urges that still seemed to well up in him on a regular basis. He guessed these odd moments of temptation were just God testing his resolve, and he was determined to prove that he'd left sin behind him. He was walking towards the light and was glad he'd been saved.

'The Devil never stops his awful work, Patrick.' His mentor always seemed so wise and reassuring. 'This is how we prove ourselves to God. I have thoughts as well, and the Devil watches us all in our moments of weakness.'

That came as a surprise and a comfort to Bobo, that even a true soldier of God like his mentor still had to fight some brand of demons.

'The road ahead is hard, Patrick, but together, united as one, we can find comfort and joy.'

Bobo didn't quite understand all of what his mentor said but decided it was best just to smile and accept his words – whatever they meant.

The evening had started well and when Bobo arrived at his mentor's flat, he'd been surprised to find that he lived alone; he'd always presumed that such a man would be sharing his life with a good woman. It was a clean place but with only the bare essentials in furniture, which for Bobo was still better than anywhere he'd ever laid his head. There was a slightly unpleasant whiff of bleach in the air but he'd tolerated worse in his time, particularly in the pokey.

He often thought about his time in prison, the shock to his system when he realised that all the guff and bravado spouted by the neds outside the big hoose was just so much shite. Before it happened, the uninitiated would treat it as a necessary step along the way, and how many times when a sentence had been passed down on a mate would he hear the same old bollocks passed round in conversation as they toasted whoever was going inside over pints of crap lager?

'He'll dae it standin' on his fuckin' heid,' was the oft repeated lie.

Then there was the fantasy peddled when boys were released – the pretence necessary to avoid the harsh reality of what they'd experienced. When Bobo went inside BarL for the first time, he'd felt like a child in a nightmare. The slow, strangling days behind the doors; biting his hand at night trying to distract his attention from the noises that polluted the dark hours inside. He watched hard men seem to lose tone, shrink in the awful isolation of prison life. Bobo thanked God that he would never have to go back there.

There was food prepared and laid out like a buffet by Bobo's host, who seemed relaxed, although his eyes had taken on a slight glaze, but Bobo guessed that all came from being a happy soldier.

They ate, drank a couple of mugs of strong tea and discussed the glory to come for all believers. It had been a success right up to the point Bobo's mentor unzipped his trousers and tried to get him to perform a new kind of worship. Bobo froze in the face of yet another revelation and stared at what was on offer a few inches from his face. His mentor must have been pleased as he watched Bobo's gob open into an almost perfect circle. The shots of vodka he'd downed hidden away in the kitchen had given him a distorted confidence that the young man had exactly the same urges as he did and that God would forgive them.

A growl started deep in Bobo's throat and all the dark urges he'd been supressing surged up like water from a burst main. He pushed himself to his feet, his mouth changing shape, lips pulled back to expose his teeth like a cornered dog, and he whapped the nut on the bastard, who went down like the Titanic. Blood spurted from the old soldier's nose.

'Ya manky bastard,' was all Bobo got out before he ran into the night and kept running till his lungs burned with the effort; he threw up at the side of the road and walked home, a man undergoing yet another conversion.

That night, Bobo hardly slept, and when he did, the image of his mentor standing at absolute attention woke him as if someone had poked him in the ribs. He slipped out of his bed earlier than usual and got ready for his job in a city-centre coffee bar. His mind swam as he washed and shaved the irregular stubble from his face. The mirror had a film of condensation and he stared at his own reflection, wondering how many times his life could go wrong.

'Right side o' the law, wrong side, it's a' a fuckin' rip off,' he growled.

He'd avoided bad language since he was reborn but it felt good to curse again, although he was weary when he said it and he shook his head in confirmation of the words.

He was tempted to phone in sick, but he knew he'd just sit and brood then watch a bit of daytime telly that would just remind him of home. He'd avoided TV in his days in God's army because his mentor had said it poisoned the mind. He hadn't watched Jeremy Kyle for months and at one time it had been his favourite time of the day, laughing at the bams trying to knock fuck out of each other. He decided to go in. He liked the guys at work; although they did a bit of piss-taking, they were OK and just wound him up a bit about the Sally Army. *Well that's over*, he thought.

36

He walked to the line of shops in the centre of Craigmillar where he caught the number 30 bus into town each morning and watched the same weary faces he saw almost every day. Even in his short life, things were changing and there were features, skin colour and accents from across the globe in that line of commuters, all just trying to survive this wicked world. That melting pot of men and women reflected what certain parts of the city had become. Other parts wouldn't have changed that much, and if it was somewhere like the Grange, then who needed to get a bus? It was just the city anywhere, united by its name and divided by its wealth. He had ten minutes till the bus arrived and he looked at the shopfronts, sensing an old tingle. His mentor would have called it temptation and he would've been right on the money.

'Fuck it.'

Bobo pulled out his wallet and a couple of minutes later was back at the bus stop with a packet of twenty smokes in his mitt. He'd kicked the habit and he stared at the wrapping, wondering if he was doing the right thing. Though what was that after what had happened?

'Fuck it,' he said again, loud enough for a couple of the bored commuters to turn their faces towards him then flick away when he made eye contact.

He stuck the filter tip between his lips, clicked the cheap lighter a couple of times and sucked in the first lungful. It was a big hit on Bobo's cleaned-up lungs, and he almost staggered at the mini high as it washed through his brain, hitting the spots that mattered and sparking to life the dependency receptors that begged for more of the same. *We fuckin' love this stuff, Bobo. It's been too long, my son!* There was a moment of guilt but it soon passed, and after the third draw he settled down and felt OK.

A team of teenage radges arrived at the stop, high as fuck on something and started pissing everyone off. Bobo tried to ignore them and work out how the fuck he was going to handle the mentor situation.

When it arrived, the single-decker bus was stuffed with people and there was a weariness in everyone's faces even though it was just the start of the day. Bobo was forced to sit just a couple of rows in front of the teenagers, who just got louder, and it was like a chain reaction of noise. Everyone did what they normally did and tried to pretend they couldn't hear or see it, though a few prayed that there was a hard bastard somewhere who would do a Clint Eastwood on them – though that never happened. The Clint Eastwood types from Craigmillar didn't have to get this bus into town early in the morning. No one expected someone like Bobo McCartney to step into the breach, and a few of them had seen him in his Sally uniform so what were the chances? Bobo wondered what they could have been on at that time of the morning but who knew? There was enough dope both legal and illegal in the city to keep the junkies happy.

He was squirming in his seat, still thinking about his mentor and his sudden loss of confidence in God when the empty can hit him on the back of the head and made him jolt. It wasn't really painful but his nerves were frazzled and his tolerance levels low. The switch had been thrown and he stood up and turned to face them.

'What ye gonnae dae, ya fuckin' radge?' one of them asked. 'Gonnae read somethin' fae the Bible?'

The arsehole who'd opened his mouth dug one of his pals in the ribs and they pissed themselves at his line.

They'd recognised Bobo as the weirdo who always seemed to be on his own and occasionally wore God's uniform. That registered as no threat and therefore an absolute target for a piss-take because they all knew that he would turn the other cheek. Well, that was what Christians were supposed to do.

Bobo might have looked on the weedy side, although he had filled out a bit what with the clean living, but he'd trained on the east-end streets of Glasgow and definitely knew how to knock fuck out of the right target. Well, he had one right now and the target dropped his jaw in surprise as Bobo closed in, growling through clenched teeth. The boy's pals stared just as open-mouthed as Bobo grabbed the boy by the hair, pulled him upright then started to melt him with a perfect series of rights and lefts. When the boy went down in the aisle, Bobo sunk his toes into him a couple of times for good measure. It all happened in a matter of seconds and a woman held her hand to her mouth as the boy on the floor looked up at her with blood pouring from his nose.

'Come ahead then,' Bobo dared the boy's pals as he backed away towards the front of the bus, which had gone into a frozen silence.

A couple had their phones out, taking some pictures, and the bus driver had stopped to call the cavalry. Unfortunately for Bobo, and despite Police Scotland's diminished ranks, there was a car heading towards Craigmillar that took the call at almost the same time they spotted the bus parked at an angle at the side of the road.

The first uniform who stepped onto the bus was in a bad mood as it was and needed the call like a hole in the head. His wife had left him for a woman and every cop in the station thought it was open season for a piss-take. He saw Bobo's chest heaving, his face still blotched red with anger that hadn't yet subsided.

'Off the bus – now!'

The cop had spoken and that should have been enough, but Bobo needed to show the world how hacked off he really was. All he saw was a twat in a uniform setting him up to ruin another day.

'That wee shite on the flair deserved it. That boy done the right thing meltin' the wee bastard.' It was an elderly native of Niddrie Mains, brought up in the days when it had been more like the Wild West. She'd been raised the hard way but knew what was right and what was wrong.

'They boys were kickin' up fuck at the back o' the bus an' that boy' – she pointed at Bobo – 'belted him in the coupon. If I'd been twenty years younger, I wida helped the fella.'

There was a murmur of support from the other passengers and a couple of 'quite fuckin' right, missus' or words to that effect.

The PC nodded his partner onto the bus and pointed a beefy finger in Bobo's direction.

'Off the bus, you. Yer gettin' lifted – right?'

He stared round the bus, hating the passengers trying to make his life more complicated than it was already. The boy with the bleeding nose and sore face got to his feet and said the wrong thing.

'Ye better lift the bastard or the auld man'll kick up fuck.'

The PC saw something in the boy's features that rang an alarm bell and he hoped he was wrong.

'Who's the old man then, Rambo, as if I care?'

He got the answer he didn't want.

'Danny Beatson. You might have heard the name.'

Despite his pulped nose, the boy managed to grin and he poked Bobo in the ribs. 'You're fuckin' dead, pal. Once ma family get involved, ye'll get it tight.'

A number of people on the bus sank back into their seats when they heard the name Danny Beatson because that meant consequences.

'Danny fuckin' Beatson. Wanker! Him and his brothers. Ma man punched his puss in years ago an' he was an auld bugger at the time.'

It was the elderly woman again, proving she was definitely old-school Niddrie Mains stock. The PC squirmed because the involvement of the Beatsons meant real complications and he had to make all the right calls, but events forced his hand.

'Beatson? Never heard the name.'

It was Bobo who chipped in, his blood still boiling. He turned to face young Beatson, the PC watching it all as if it was happening in slow motion and he had no power to intervene. Bobo leaned back, then whipped his head forward in an almost perfect arc, cracking the head right on the bridge of what was left of young Beatson's hooter. Blood spattered a couple of the passengers for good luck. The boy hit the deck again and the PC drew his baton. He was too slow though and Bobo decided in that moment that he might as well go for broke. He owed the world a kicking so what the fuck?

He lowered his head and ran straight into the gut of the PC, who made a woofing sound as the wind was knocked out of his lungs. Beatson's pals had found their voice and started screaming what they were going to do to Bobo but not taking much action. The old Niddrie Mains lady got to her feet and, with a remarkable turn of speed and agility, started laying into them with her walking stick. Chaos broke out on the bus as it turned into a free-for-all though a few of the passengers had previous convictions and took the chance to take a couple of shots at the uniforms. The driver left the bus in a hurry and phoned the police again to send more cavalry because the first lot were under serious attack.

37

Bobo stared at the cell wall and every couple of minutes he shook his head, wondering how his life could have gone so wrong again. There was an occasional smile though, because when he took away the negatives, it was like old times, sticking the nut on the boy then doing one on the fanny in uniform.

The reinforcements had arrived too late to stop what had turned into a mini riot and the problems had spilled out onto the street. A few neds passing by had spotted the action and joined in by robbing a couple of the passengers of their bags while they were preoccupied trying to strangle each other. All in all, it had been a day to remember, and one uniform in the cell area had winked at him and said 'nice one' for sticking it on the cop on the bus, so it seemed the guy was a fanny after all.

He was startled when the cell door opened and it was time to head to court. He'd managed to sleep for a couple of hours and remarkably he felt calm but low. His life was shit; nothing worked for him, and for the first time he wondered if there was any point in going on. Thinking about an ending didn't frighten him anymore.

He sat in the van like a battery hen and decided that at least he would take this one on the chin at court. The last time he was before a judge it had been for a failed armed robbery and he had conducted his own defence, which had turned into chaos when he'd tried to attack one of the witnesses. He tensed the muscles in his face as emotion nearly overwhelmed him and his eyes stung with tears. He still had his pride, and he was fucked if he'd let anyone see him cry.

'Chin up, Bobo; chin up, son.' He wiped the back of his sleeves across his eyes.

A few hours later he was back in a van heading for Saughton and a few months behind the door. He could handle that but just couldn't work out or see a future. Bobo the eternal optimist was beaten and all his dreams were gone.

38

Maxine stared through the rain-splattered window of the train as it ran through the harvest fields of Yorkshire. The downpour was almost over, and the sun had thinned out and broken the clouds, letting the late autumn beams sparkle off the damp stubble left in the fields. Rolled-up bales flashed by, then white spots of sheep; in one field they were resting, in another they were all on their feet. *Why was that?* she wondered.

Winter was on the way again and the weather had chilled over the few days before Maxine finally stepped on the Edinburgh train. She'd almost turned around at the station and given up before she'd started. The idea of going back there, where all those dark memories were born, almost overwhelmed her, but she knew she had to do it and tried to remember her life before the streets. When she was young and daft and there seemed to be an ocean of possibilities ahead of her – the optimism of youth. Life had been good then, so normal and so uneventful.

Her eyes started to feel heavy – she relaxed and turned again to the world flashing past her view. Picture-postcard spires popped up over the hedgerows; above them, moving black dots – crows – flicked for no more than a moment over the tree lines.

She rested a corner of her forehead against the glass and enjoyed its cool touch – the carriage was too warm for some reason, even with the chilled air outside. In another couple of hours, she would set foot in Edinburgh again.

Edinburgh. She kept repeating the name of the old city over and over again in her mind. Staring through the glass, vague images of her friends tried to take form then vanished, so she said their names, her lips barely moving, as if she was trying to resurrect the dead. Sleep closed her thoughts down and her head dropped back as her lips opened a little. An old woman opposite smiled across the aisle and wished she was that young and that pretty again.

39

The train rolled into Waverley station and she watched the rest of the passengers go through the ordeal of pulling on their jackets and struggling with their bags while trying to avoid physical contact with everyone else in the carriage before starbursting to the next part of their journey. She stayed on her seat and, for a moment, felt the same cold panic grip her chest that she'd experienced in the station at Leeds. She considered going straight back to Yorkshire, but the little battle between the right and left hemispheres of her brain settled and she knew the alternative was more endless days of *what if* should she turn and run.

The station heaved with people negotiating a path as they moved in a hundred different directions crisscrossing the station concourse. Lives almost touching each other for the briefest moments. The train emptied as she stared out of the window, unable to move – it was as if she'd walked into a trap and leaving the train would expose her to her worst fears.

'You alright there, love?'

The words startled her and she looked up at the guard, who thought for a moment she might be another piss-head who'd had one too many miniatures. There was always one, and he hoped she wasn't getting ready to kick off, but she didn't look like the usual nutters they encountered who binged on miniatures as if they were non-alcoholic.

'Sorry.'

Maxine grappled with her bag, embarrassed; she just wanted to escape into the crowd where she could hide. She stepped onto the platform and felt the chill air that told her she was back in Scotland. Then the sound of the Scots tongue washed over her and there was a feeling of relief as the broad tones of home soothed her fears. It was mixed in there with accents and languages from countries all over the world, but that was what Edinburgh had become – the festivals and the Christmas market had made it a top destination for international travellers. The Scots voices were there though, rich and direct; they seemed to come from every direction and she checked the faces against the accent. Some Glasgow boys with their football colours laughed uproariously as they headed for the station bar. A policeman with a soft Highland voice directed a baffled Chinese tourist somewhere. She stopped for a moment, closed her eyes and said the word *home* to herself. Then she pulled on a woollen hat and dark glasses, hoping it was enough to make her invisible to anyone who might know her.

It seemed like such a long time since she'd stepped on the train to head south and leave her old life behind. It was all so different now. She'd rediscovered a reason to get up every morning and there was something else – she was proud again. Maxine had conquered so many demons and here she was: still young and healthy despite, exposing herself to so many risks, and there was an urge to build something again – maybe not the old career that had meant so much to her but something that had her own stamp.

She turned her collar up against the ever-present Edinburgh wind that whipped round her neck. Her hair was tied back and she had no make-up on. Anyone looking at her would have taken her for just another tourist taking advantage of the old city and the exchange rate helped by the value of the pound.

As the elevator moved her up towards the open air of the street, she felt the wind whoosh past her ears. That was proof enough that she was back on the east coast – the seemingly permanent wind whipping up off the Forth and rattling round the streets and closes as if it was chasing the citizens. Maxine realised she was invisible for the time being. Who would recognise her? Even the few people who'd cared would probably have to take a moment to compute her fuller shape, fresh colour and casual but expensive clothes. There was a flutter in her gut and she started to enjoy the opportunity to walk about in the city where once she had only seemed to inhabit the night. This was a chance to be just like anyone else or everyone else. She hadn't even booked a hotel so that had to be the first priority, and it took less than an hour to get checked in not far from the centre. There was a moment of hesitation when she saw how much it was costing, and then she grinned because she could afford it and she wasn't back in the city to torture herself. This Maxine Welsh could do exactly as she liked and for that night she intended to eat the best food and relax in her very expensive room.

Once she'd settled into the hotel and tested the bed, she ordered food, which was excellent – and should have been at the price – but she hardly noticed it, more intent on the view of the town from her room window. She showered and tried to sleep for a bit, but although she was tired, her mind was swirling with emotions and after a restless hour, she dressed and headed for the darkening streets.

She stood at the entrance to the hotel for a moment, testing her instincts, worried that there was someone there, watching and waiting, but she knew that was nonsense – Bear Dillon was gone so who would care that much? She tugged her collar up again to cut off the deepening chill as darkness settled on Scotland's capital with a freezing haze. The streets were still busy, and she loved the feeling of being anonymous again, how it allowed her to pick up the pulse of the town with all its dark places and memories. She wandered up The Mound and stopped halfway to look back towards the gardens, marvelling at the place as if she was a tourist on her first visit.

Later that night, the waiter showed her to her table in the half darkness of a restaurant not far from the castle walls. The flickering candlelight seemed to bring to life the ghosts that must have inhabited the old walls as dark shadows danced across the ancient stones. It was good to be home, but she would remain anonymous for another day or two then decide whether to look for her old friends.

She asked herself time and time again if this was the same city where she had almost been broken by the effects of failure, drugs and debt, where her life could have been snuffed out in the back of a filthy van by someone who'd thought he owned her. Maxine had found something so important out of all the debris of her past – that life was precious and there were possibilities for change if you looked hard enough.

She rested her chin on her upturned hand and thought about Tom Logan and that he was no more than a few miles from her. Before she'd left Yorkshire, she watched a James Cosmo film and realised that Logan could have passed for a younger version of the man. Such restrained power, iron-hard features and yet… and yet when he smiled there was a warm human being, concealed most of the time, but just there below the surface. He must have been fifteen years older than her and she was still confused as to what he meant to her. Her protector, but why? And why did she miss him so much?

40

Bobo McCartney stared at the cold cell walls. It was night in the prison – the worst time, although the days weren't exactly a walk in the park. It was never quite dark, the cramped cell was airless, damp, and although it stank, he hardly noticed that – it was a problem he'd just got used to. He sat with his legs over the edge of the lower bunk bed with his face in his hands. The nutter he shared a cell with slept like a baby, which was just as well because he drove Bobo crazy during the waking hours. The guy never stopped talking shite and acted as if he'd been overdosing on good quality speed, but it was just the effects of the legal highs that seemed to be available on tap inside.

Bobo was tempted to dull his own problems with the same product but decided that this time he'd give it a miss. His life was shit, but he didn't want to end up like the basket cases who were in a worse state than he was already. His senses were part dead anyway, and there were days he looked as spaced out as the junkies because he was fucked up inside, his brain scrambled and he couldn't find anything to dream about.

He was due for release and that seemed a frightening prospect – prison was bad, but he knew that the street might be even worse. He had no family that were interested in him, friends almost nil and he'd failed at crime and now religion. *Maybe not*, he thought, but religion had certainly failed him. Job chances zero unless he could find another coffee bar, but by the time he paid rent and bought the essentials, he'd be permanently broke. He'd always sworn he'd never end up like the cider bams, but that seemed like the only career path.

He snapped his head up when somewhere in the prison there was a scream. It was a place full of night terrors, nothing that was real, just awful reality and fucked-up lives. He put his hands over his ears as if it would help and heard his co-pilot snore even louder, so he squeezed his eyes closed and started humming to drown it all out. It was too much, only days to go till they opened the gate for him and he couldn't imagine where he would go.

Bobo got down on his knees, rolled over into the foetal position and wished he could sleep and just not wake up.

41

Maxine had agreed with Jan that she would take the week off, and they'd hired a full- and part-timer to ease the load. They hadn't had a proper day off since the business had started and she realised she needed a bit of space and the chance to sleep a little later in the morning.

After the shock of seeing the news that Bear Dillon was inside, she'd forced herself to take time before making the return journey to her home city. In fact, after the call to Charlie Brockie, she'd almost settled back into normal life in Leeds, letting the weeks and months pass before one morning, without any planning, she'd walked into the train station and booked her tickets. It had been time to go back – she was comfortable in her new life and had even gone out on a couple of dates with men she'd met through the business. She'd enjoyed it, but it hadn't gone further than that and she was being careful. Maxine didn't have to sell or give herself to anyone now unless she wanted to, and that's how it would be now.

She marvelled at her native city – its shapes and dark spaces, the tunnels and ghosts that inhabited the ancient town under her feet when she panted up Upper Bow and then onto the Lawnmarket and High Street. She'd always believed in ghosts as a child, and although she wasn't religious now, she was sure there was something called the spirit that still existed after death, just beyond sight of the living. Edinburgh seemed to be filled with those spirits from the past, and there were so many places for them to stay just out of sight: tunnels, chambers, the ancient closes that were still there under their feet.

Although she'd resolved not to think about it for a couple of days, the question gradually crept into the light until she couldn't ignore it any longer. Should she try to see her friends and family while she was here? It was natural to fear that they wouldn't have forgiven her for leaving in the first place and then cutting all contact.

She stepped into a cafe not far from the Tron and ordered a coffee she didn't really want, but it paid for her seat. There was a broad window and she could stare out onto the street and watch the endless lines of tourists and locals pass by in those moments where their lives touched before they travelled off to a different future. She chewed her lip and tried again to put all the options in a line where she could see them, but the answers she wanted didn't come.

It happened almost unconsciously in the end – she pulled out her phone, stared at the address file and keyed in a few letters which threw up Connie's number. The woman who had never judged or given up on her; the eternal optimist who, like Jan, believed it would be alright on the night. That's how it had turned out when she'd bought the lottery tickets.

'It's Connie. I'm probably on a fashion shoot so leave a message.'

The voicemail said all anyone needed to know about the pint-sized character who'd fallen into the game, but, unlike Maxine, had never had that cancerous self-loathing. Connie had been born and brought up in a family who'd offered little in the way of hope or love, so her expectations had never been that high anyway. As far as Connie was concerned, fate had put her where she was and that was that. 'Get the fuck on with it,' she used to say all the time. That was why she could live and almost love a loser like Banjo Rodgers, who had failure written into his bones but had treated her like the best thing that had ever happened to him – which she was. And Connie had thought it was a result going home to a man who'd never laid a glove on her.

Maxine pressed the end-call button and felt her heart race. It was stupid to panic because Connie didn't judge; she knew that better than anyone. Maxine was just applying her own hang-ups to someone who'd never been able to afford that luxury when she was dealing with other people. She pressed the call button again to leave a voicemail but Connie answered first.

'Hi, it's Connie – who's this then?'

There was nothing but her friend's voice and there was no mistaking who it was thanks to the *don't give a shit who you are* attitude.

'It's Maxine.'

She stopped there and the name hung on the line between them till Connie spoke.

'Jesus Christ.' There was another pause. 'Jesus Christ, Maxie, where you been?' Connie always shortened her name. 'I mean, what the fuck?' Another pause. 'How's it been, hen? Missed you like hell… Charlie Brockie said you'd called but then nothin'?'

For some reason, the form of words and questions were said in a way that made Maxine smile, and she knew her friend was at least the same in spirit – absolutely indomitable.

177

'I'm good, Connie, just good, an' can't believe I'm speaking to you. I missed you so much! I'm sorry but you know I had to stay away.'

Maxine felt as if all the conversations they hadn't had in the time since she'd left Edinburgh were queuing up for release. She started to breathe hard, as if she'd been running.

'Thought ye'd forgot your old pal.'

Connie started to blub, and that was a first because she didn't normally do tears; she'd used up her share as a child. It was too much and Maxine joined in, but it felt right and there was no trace of the anger she thought might come back down the phone at her.

'Where are you the now then, Maxie? Jesus, I worried my sweet arse off every day in case that bastard Dillon found you.'

Maxine heard Connie sniff wetly and blow her nose.

'You heard he's in the pokey?'

'Couldn't believe it. I always followed the news in Edinburgh. Nearly fell off the seat when I saw it. Phoned Charlie Brockie and he said he's in for the long haul and no one's upset, even on his side.'

She paused and felt her heart race at the thought of being able to revisit the parts of her old life that mattered.

'I'm in Edinburgh. Just been wandering about. You're the first person I've spoken to.'

'Jesus Christ. Where – when can I see you? Fuck's sake.'

'Think you're taking the Lord's name in vain a lot there. You're going to the burning fire, girl.'

The mood had lightened beyond anything Maxine could have expected, and she squeezed the phone as if it was her friend's hand.

'The burnin' fire's hee-haw compared wi' ma life, Maxie.'

Her tone flattened and Maxine realised the use of the present tense was intentional. The last time she'd seen

Connie her life had seemed to be heading in the right direction at long last.

'What about you, Connie? How's life and how's Banjo?'

The slight pause was enough to know that it was the wrong question and Maxine felt her heart sink. Connie'd had one stroke of luck in her life – the lottery win they'd shared – and that should have been enough to see her on a different path.

'We went to Ayr, probably the nearest thing to home for me. My fault, I guess.'

She stopped and Maxine heard her blow her nose again. 'Things were great for a while and I got a wee job that did for me. We had the dosh stashed away and, well… Banjo's an arse – can't be helped. He was dippin' it, an' his new pals in Ayr helped him spend it. Came back one day an' he'd fucked off an' left me wi' nothing but a note saying he wis sorry. Nice o' him, mind.'

She blew her nose again.

'What you doing with yourself?' Maxine asked, though she worried she already knew the answer to that one.

'You know me – a born survivor. When we meetin'?'

She was avoiding the subject, they both knew that, but avoided it for the moment because they were desperate to see each other and it wasn't time yet for the confessional.

42

They hugged each other as if it was the last time they'd ever meet rather than renewing a bond that few people could have understood.

'Jesus, Maxie.' Connie sniffed and pushed her friend to arm's length.

'You sure you're Maxie? Naw, it's no' you.' Her eyes glistened, happy to see the young, healthy woman smiling back at her. Clean, fresh, no trace of the street. Connie didn't shop expensively even when she had money but recognised quality when she saw it on Maxine.

'You look… I dunno, just… I dunno.'

Connie was tough because she had to be, but the contrast to what she knew her friend was seeing couldn't be more pronounced. She watched that little furrow scrunch up between her eyes, recognising that old giveaway that Maxie had seen something that bothered her. Connie imagined that she suddenly stank of the punters again, even though she'd showered and scrubbed till her skin hurt with the effort. But it was impossible to wash those men away, at least in the presence of someone else who'd been there.

'What's up, Connie? No – wait till we get a seat first.'

They were at the door of a cafe in Stockbridge that had all the feel of a little community, a community where there was money to spend not far from the heart of the city. They sat down and Connie reached over the table and grabbed both Maxine's hands, failing to hide her emotions. She'd always been good at that, and Maxine realised that even in the relatively short time she'd been away, the world had changed, and she hadn't been there to support a friend who'd made so much possible for her.

'Right, tell me. Everything was on the up when I left.' She looked at Connie's clothes and knew what they meant. The waitress looked bored and barely recognised the women's distress when she took their order.

The story was familiar to anyone who occupied the lower end of the criminal world. The tragedy of having nothing but the instinct to survive and consuming whatever was available when it was available because there were no rules. What she'd told Maxine on the phone was more or less it, and anything else was trivia. Banjo was a weak man who'd hated himself for years once he'd realised exactly what he was, what the past and future actually meant. He'd hated himself all the more when he'd stolen Connie's money and it had progressed from a quick dip to a gradual process required to feed what he thought he needed. It would have been incomprehensible to most people, but a few local low-level crooks showing him a bit of respect was just another drug he was unable to resist. Somewhere in his subconscious, he knew why they treated him like Jack the fucking Lad, but the high from both the smack and the boys was too much for him to resist. Connie sighed at some memory that touched her and looked at the table.

'Any idea where he is?'

Maxine felt helpless and angry.

'No idea, an' I don't want to find him. It's no' his fault – I shoulda known better. Banjo's just Banjo.'

'Where you working?' It was the question neither of them wanted Maxine to ask but it had to be answered.

'No' the street. Was for a while but in a sauna now… it's OK, an' the boy that runs it is fine wi' the girls. At least we're safe, an' if any punter kicks off, they get it tight.'

Connie filled in a few more details about her time in Ayr and what had seemed like a new life, and because it was her, there wasn't a moment of anger towards the man who should have gone down on his knees every day and thanked Connie for having him in her life. Once she'd explained what had happened, Maxine wasn't even that surprised when she thought about it. Banjo was a weak man. He'd been damaged to the point where they should have known that redemption was never going to be an option for him.

She remembered the story about how Banjo had lost his previous partner Maggie Smith, another sex worker who had taken her own life rather than living with the shame – not of her street life but being raped and abused by a team of Belfast gangsters who had tried to take over the west side of the city. She was collateral damage and what broke her was that Banjo had cared about her, a first for her but he'd had to stand by when she was assaulted and couldn't protect her when she was raped by the same men. What surprised Maxine was that Connie had let him near the money, but it just showed that for all her street nous, Connie was as vulnerable as the next one.

Maxine looked across at her friend's face, the eternal stoic who seemed to have found a way out of the dark only to be tossed straight back in. It was so typical of her to take the view that working in a sauna wasn't so bad. Well, to an extent she was right, but she deserved better, and Maxine realised exactly where her own ambition lay. That was the moment that she decided she was staying. She wasn't sure what she would do, but her instincts told her she had unfinished business in Edinburgh. Maybe she would cut ties again, but it would be on her terms, if there was a next time.

'Listen, Connie – listen carefully.

Jan had taught Maxine to believe again and she did. Now she had her own plan. When Connie headed for the Leith sauna to hand in her notice a couple of hours later, she tried not to get excited, but Maxine seemed to be offering her another chance at redemption. *Could it really happen again?* She shook her head every so often at the same thought doing a loop in her mind. An old punter drew alongside her. She'd been with him before; he was OK and had never caused her any bother in the past.

'Sorry, honey, I'm retired!' she called.

She turned around and headed for the bus stop – and hope. There was a moment where she thought of Banjo. She pitied him because she knew where he'd end up eventually. 'Poor bastard,' she said quietly and then moved back to thinking about her dreams.

43

About the same time Connie decided to retire from the game for the second time, Banjo was keeping his eyes fixed on the pavement. That was the advice – don't look at the punters. It makes you look beaten – like a hurt dog – and every so often one of them will take pity and weigh in with a few coins. If it was a bit of food, you had to look grateful when what you wanted was the fucking wonga. He was down and not quite out but getting there, and he knew that the time was coming when he'd be dancing about with the other space cadets off their tits on cheap cider or whatever did the job.

He thought about Connie every day and cursed himself for throwing away the best thing in his life. He'd spent what was left of her savings in record time and was astonished that in a matter of weeks he was on his arse and in a black hole with all the rest of the losers. *How the fuck did that happen?* he asked himself over and over, even though he knew the answer. He'd headed for Glasgow because he couldn't think of anywhere else to go where he was guaranteed to get a regular supply of his drug of choice. That had become just the odd luxury now, and he'd already started on the bargain booze, which was all that could take the edge off his days.

His lip still throbbed from the beating he'd taken just a couple of days earlier. His ribs hurt and he was still pissing blood after a young team of neds had decided that they'd break their boredom by kicking fuck out of him. Banjo hadn't fought back; he'd seen them coming, pissing themselves laughing at the opportunity for some sport, and he'd just curled up into a ball, trying his best to avoid major surgery.

They had taken turns to gob on him when they'd finished. He'd lain still for a while as if he was dead then uncurled, groaning at his various pain sites, before he'd managed to get himself to his feet and head for a nearby public toilet to clean himself up.

An hour later, he'd been begging again and the bruises on his coupon seemed to have attracted a bit of sympathy and thus a few extra donations. When he'd started to cry uncontrollably, it had brought in a bit more money, and a couple of kind souls had knelt down beside him and said some nice things before they'd fucked off and forgotten about him.

In the end, getting a cash boost was a kind of result. *Worth a sair puss, Banjo*, he thought and grinned at his own joke.

44

Maxine looked around the empty premises and nodded. The space was big enough and, more to the point, she could see what it *could* be. No more than a few minutes' walk from Edinburgh's Lawnmarket, the area swarmed summer and winter with tourists and spillover from the courts – lawyers and sometimes criminals, crossing their fingers for a result that didn't involve the pokey. Maxine had discussed it with Jan, told her what she thought and taken the advice she was given.

'Go for it, Max – you can do it. We're still partners so why don't we try this as a feeler in Edinburgh. It pays to diversify. If it works, you take that end of the business. Tell you what, I'll come up tomorrow and have a look.'

And that's exactly what she did.

At ten the next morning, Maxine picked up Jan from Waverley and they decided to cram in some early sightseeing. They walked the length of Princes Street and caught up with each other's gossip. They breathed hard as they negotiated the climb up Johnston Terrace on the south side of the castle. It was the quiet side – away from the throng of the High Street and the approaches from Princes Street. Jan stopped twice to crane her neck and stare skywards at the castle walls stretching high above them.

'Jesus, Max, that's some sight. I heard the stories but didn't imagine this.'

For a change, Jan seemed lost for words, but like so many before her, the old city was casting its spell over a first-time visitor.

'You've seen nothing yet – wait till you see the Old Town the other side of the castle. It'll take your breath away.'

Maxine felt that pride all natives have when showing off their home town and there was so much to show in Edinburgh.

Before they reached the top of the Royal Mile, Maxine decided on a detour down towards the Grassmarket and Jan began to forget why she was there. They walked past legendary pubs and the site of the old gallows where so many patriots, thieves and sometimes innocent men and women had taken their last breath. One named Maggie Dixon had even come back to life after the hanging and her name was immortalised in legend on the front of a nearby watering hole.

The next climb up the arc of the West Bow had Jan crowing and the ghosts that inhabited every stone reached out and touched her.

'God I'm in love! What a place.'

'Well, let's get to work and then I'll give you a full tour, including the city under the city!'

Maxine suddenly felt excited – Jan's enthusiasm for the town was infectious. They got to the front of the empty cafe premises and Maxine spread her arms and did a 'ta da', then spun round and said, 'Well, what do you think?'

Jan stood back and gripped her chin as if she was looking at a painting, trying to work out what the artist was trying to say.

'Let's go inside and you can tell me what the vision is. I've a good feeling here.'

Two hours later they were in a pub halfway down the High Street and Jan was nodding as Maxine told her the final part of what she had in mind. Jan had fired a string of questions for two purposes: to make sure that they'd thought of all the risks and to confirm they had a plan for future expansion. For Jan, there was no plan that didn't include expansion and she wanted to make sure that Maxine had that as settled.

'Never really thought of what might come next, Jan; I just want to make this a success,' Maxine said. 'You've seen it – there's no shortage of cafe and food outlets round here but quality sells, so I want to make it something that's a bit special and very Scottish. That might not make sense to you, but so much of what's around here is to con the visitors. The locals shy away from this area during the tourist season, which is just about all year round. I want something authentic that people will keep coming back to. Simple but I'm sure it can work.'

Jan nodded. 'OK, it's not exactly going to be the Ritz, small scale, but it could get us a foothold here. I've been doing my research and this city is booming, but we, or at least you, need to learn and get a feel for the business side here so maybe small is the idea.'

45

Across the city, no more than a few miles from where Maxine and Jan looked at the future, a man gripped his partner's face and squeezed till tears bubbled out between her eyelids. The pain was everywhere; he'd hit her more than usual and had seemed angrier than ever. Her gut had turned to hot water and she was afraid. Maybe this was it, the time he'd finish her for good. The panic came for the child she was carrying. The child that should have been a joy, but when she'd told him, his contempt had turned to blinding rage. She never understood what she'd done to make him like that, but then she didn't recognise him now – he was so different from the man she'd fallen for almost at first sight. How was it possible to get it so wrong?

He'd been everything she'd ever hoped for in a man – considerate, funny and he made her laugh. Then a short series of alarms that barely registered at the start, like the foreshocks that precede an earthquake long before the big event. At first it was anger for something she couldn't even remember now. The change in his facial expression, the smile gone, the eyes that seemed to belong to someone else suddenly full of rage. He'd apologised that first time; it was his job and she understood that. She couldn't do what he did or what she imagined he did, and so she started to forgive him until it became a habit. Even the first time he slapped her across the breakfast table, she'd felt guilt and shame and had done her best to please him, hoping the man she'd dreamed he was would re-emerge.

'You fucking slag. That thing inside you can't be mine. Is that it? Is that the truth?' He whacked her hard across the cheek and regretted it immediately because he didn't like to leave marks. He was better than that and didn't want the bitch to have proof.

'Tell you what, you're on your last warning, you hear me?' He screamed the question into her ear, making her double up and groan. She fell to her knees and sobbed like a beaten child.

Two days later she lost the baby, and when he came to visit her, he brought flowers. She stiffened as he took her in his arms and told her not to worry.

'It was meant to be. These things happen for a reason.'

He said it as if it had been an act of God rather than an act of hate. She made an attempt at smiling, trying as always not to offend him. He sat down and took both her hands in his.

'This is probably a good time to go our separate ways. It's never really worked and better to end it as friends.'

He squeezed her hands so hard she bit her lip rather than cry out and offend him. She looked at those hands that had hurt her so many times – the little thistle he had tattooed on the bridge between the thumb and forefinger of his right hand. He released the pressure and smiled.

'I'll need the flat so probably better that you go back and stay with your parents. They've a lovely big house and they'll be glad to have you. Never thought they quiet understood me.'

190

She cried again because she dreaded losing him; all she'd ever wanted was to make him happy, and if he'd asked her, she'd try again, even after all that had happened.

'I'm sorry I upset you,' she said and meant it. 'Can't you give me another chance?'

He looked at her as if she was an infant who needed the obvious explained to her in fine detail. He leaned close as if he was going to kiss her and whispered in her ear.

'I want you fucking gone. You disgust me.'

He gave her the kiss that she'd hoped would be the start of something new and she felt her chest squeeze tight at the thought that he wouldn't be in her life.

He smiled at the nurse who'd come into the room and told her to take good care of the patient. The nurse stared at him and didn't answer, holding back what she really wanted to say. She'd seen enough abused women in her time to know the score and this one was off the Richter scale, but there was no way the girl in the bed would make a complaint. It sickened the nurse the number of times she'd seen women suffer so much at the hands of cowards and still want to go back. The girl had been beaten into submission and the bastard would get away with it. She shook her head, straightened the bedclothes and wished she could make the girl understand, but she knew it would be wasted breath.

46

Big Tam Logan had almost the same feeling every morning when he opened up his bar in the heart of Leith. It kept him going; he needed it to avoid thinking about what he'd lost. His wife and his youth were gone, and the bar was the reason he still got up in the morning and went on living. Logan was every inch a product of the old Leith, a place that still had its own identity, even though the ancient port was joined at the hip with the city of Edinburgh and was starting to go all upmarket – *the place to be*.

The main artery to the city was Leith Walk; Logan walked it several times a week and had watched as it morphed, casting off its old image in stages. He would hear a dozen languages on the half-hour walk past cafes, restaurants and food retailers from all over the world. The local pish-heids and bams would still create a bit of noise and entertainment, but they were gradually blending into the new picture.

There was still a unique spirit in the place, though that came down through the legends and ghosts of the ages. Something to be proud of, being a Leither was a badge that came with its own bragging rights and usually an automatic loyalty card for Hibernian FC. Logan had been born there, discovered he was a hard bastard there – which had given him that all-important cred plus, in his younger days, permanent employment watching the backs of the local criminals who mattered.

But just being a hard man had never prepared him for the loss of his wife, and there were days when he wished he'd never met her. Love had come with a price that he'd never expected to pay. He'd bought the pub with her as their way out of the life and it had worked, combining a bit of his old world to the new. Cops and criminals used it because Logan kept the peace, and it had a kind of credibility for all sides.

After he lost his wife, he eventually adapted to life on his own by almost numbing himself, going onto autopilot and just getting through the days, until that cold winter night Maxine had walked through the door of his boozer. He'd met her a few times in his pub, but that night he'd discovered there was so much more to her, and against his own instincts, those feelings that had once been kindled by his wife had flickered again.

He was older than her, and pride and insecurity meant he couldn't tell her what he was keeping wrapped, so he'd played the friend and that was OK – it had filled a gap in his life. Then some fucking bampot had tried to kill her, died in the attempt and the end of the story was that she'd left the city for another life. He'd wanted her to stay so much but had been frightened to say in case it looked like he was pleading. Rejection terrified him so he'd watched her disappear, and it was as if she'd left with what remained of his dreams.

Life since she'd gone had reverted to a colourless treadmill and he only just made it through the long days. He always made the effort with the punters though; they bantered and he joined in, but it was all acting, and when he put his head on the pillow at night, he felt lost and afraid of the dark.

It had been months since Charlie Brockie had told him that Maxine had been in touch and she was fine. Every day he'd waited, hoping for a call that didn't come, and he felt like the unmarried half of an affair. Connie had arrived back on the scene rejecting all offers of help, and after a spell on the street, she was working in one of the saunas. He knew the owner, who occasionally dropped into his bar for a quick one before opening his own place.

Logan never involved himself in other's people's business unless he had to but he'd stepped in for Connie, inviting the sauna owner through the back for a drink. The guy had been pleased. Being a friend of Logan carried a fair bit of cred – he was the man who knew everyone that mattered. Logan had been courteous but delivered the message that if Connie was mistreated in any way, the sauna business would have to be run from a wheelchair. There was no argument – Connie got the best punters and was treated like the owner's second in command. She never knew why; she'd just grabbed the privilege with both hands.

Each morning Logan polished the glasses religiously and this one had been quiet apart from the regulars – a cross section of hard drinkers who did their stuff before noon, a couple of night-shift workers who needed the booze to pretend they had a social life and the odd character. Mick Harkins was certainly a character, and one of the few who still made Logan pay attention.

'You'll polish the glasses away, Tam,' he said. 'I'm tellin' you, I saw this programme that we're all too clean now. We need germs and muck – strengthens the immune system. Pubs are supposed to be a bit manky. I mean, they've stopped us smokin' – a disgrace for the ordinary punter by the way. So help us stay heathy, Tam, and stop cleanin' so much.' Harkins put the fresh pint to his lips and winked over the rim at Logan while he waited for a response.

'Thing is, Mick, you don't have to worry 'cause you can't be killed. I mean, that boy run you over wi' a car and failed. Stake through the heart – only thing'll kill you, boy.'

Harkins missed his police career every day but would never admit it. He was as much a part of the furniture in Logan's boozer as the bar itself; he lent a kind of colour to the place and was a daily reminder of those days when they had been in opposing camps. The drinkers told a lot of stories about Logan and Harkins crossing swords, and some of them were even true.

Like Harkins, Logan missed the buzz sometimes, the occasional super high when he could have lost his life protecting his employers. He knew that there were more bad days than good though, a lot of bad days, but those highs had been something else before his wife had shown him another way to live.

He was lost in his memories and didn't even see her walk into the bar and stop for a moment as she remembered the woman she'd been the last time she was there. It looked much the same and, as always, the place was spotless, just like the man who took such a pride in his bar.

Harkins looked round and his eyes widened, just before he nodded. Maxine felt her chest tighten as she stared at Logan, who was side-on to her behind the bar and, as always, polishing the glasses. Before Jan had left to go back to Leeds, Maxine had admitted that seeing Logan again worried her more than anything else.

He seemed lost in his thoughts but looked the same. Big, powerful and gentle all at the same time. She knew his reputation as a younger version, but he was the kindest man she'd ever met, though she was unsure how he'd react after she'd walked out of his life after all he'd done for her.

'Hi, Tom.'

Her voice seemed so small; it trembled when she spoke and she felt awkward.

Logan reacted slowly, as if he needed time to absorb the sound of it. He'd heard that voice often enough in his imagination so there was no great surprise till he turned his head and saw her standing there. He stopped polishing the glass, blinked as if it was just his imagination again and then accepted it was her. It took a little time because this wasn't the same Maxine who'd left Edinburgh in fear of her life, exhausted by the street then a trial that could have put her away till middle age. It was Maxine alright but the one he knew she'd been once and could be again. He'd just never seen this version in the flesh.

Logan knew how to do reserve; he'd spent his life controlling his emotions. He caught the lump in his throat and remembered that his place was as her friend – nothing more. He half smiled, which was a lot for him.

'Jesus, Maxine, you look… well… really well.'

He put the dish towel and glass on the bar then didn't know what to do next. Maxine did – that half smile had signalled to her that he was another one who wasn't angry, or if he had been, he wasn't showing it. She relaxed, then walked round the bar and hugged him. He was more than a head taller than her and he looked over her at Harkins, who raised his glass, winked and headed out of the bar.

47

Logan's regular dayshift barmaid came in and took over and the two of them headed down to the Shore, the sky clear as they walked the roads that held so many memories for both of therm. For Maxine, it was different – when she'd worked the street, she had almost hated the place because it had always seemed grey and hostile, and so much of that life had been spent in the dark hours. Now she was a tourist and she took in the old buildings around the Shore like any other visitor, and it felt as if she was seeing some of them for the first time.

Logan hardly spoke. His head swam with words, but he couldn't find the right combination, and he thought whatever he did say might seem foolish, so he let her talk while he listened. He nodded to a passing couple who came into the pub from time to time and he wondered if they thought that Maxine was his partner. The idea made him feel warm and he wished that it was true.

They walked into one of the old watering holes that at one time had been more like battlegrounds but were now part of the developing transformation of the old port and found a table where they could talk without an audience.

Logan was as quiet as ever, happy just to listen to her story, so he continued to let her talk, finding it hard to take in the way she'd changed her life and put it back on course. To cap it all, she looked like she'd stepped out of an advert for expensive perfume.

Maxine seemed full of ideas, and he felt his heart quicken when she said if things worked out, she might stay permanently. She missed home – always had during the time she was away – and he wondered what she meant by home. It was wonderful to sit and listen to her hopes for the future, and he wanted it all to happen, but Logan had survived because he was a realist and so he eventually offered his advice. He didn't want to dampen the mood but he knew it was better to be prepared than caught defence-less. The world could be a cruel place, and if Maxine had a fault that ran through her story it was that for all she'd seen and endured, she could still be naïve. He pushed his glass to the side and she saw from his non-verbals that he had something to say. She stopped and waited, watching those serious eyes reinforce his message.

'Remember, Maxine – the past will come back. You could get away from it down south, but in this city, you'll have to face it at some stage. Edinburgh isn't that big, still a bit of a village in many ways and I don't know if you've realised it but your story is interesting – you'll attract people and not all of them for the right reasons. As long as you're prepared and have a way of responding, then who knows – you might just survive till the day you're just someone with a colourful past. Just go into this with your eyes wide open – but there'll probably be days when you'll wish you were back in Leeds.'

He leaned forward and the half smile broke the serious expression on his face. 'You know what though, girl? We're all happy you're back, and I'll help in any way I can.'

He leaned back and watched her absorb his warning, nodding because he was right, but she knew it all already.

'I know, Tom, but I decided I'm not going to hide from it. I did what I did, and if I could go back and speak to that stupid young girl with all that promise in front of her, I'd tell her just what can happen. I can't though. That's the thing, Tom – we do what we do and spend our lives worrying about it. I'm just going to make the most of it. You know, there are nights I still think I'm there, in the cars with the punters. It's awful but it's starting to fade a bit, and I want to put something else in place of those thoughts. I'd change the past but I can't. I've forgiven myself and just hope the people I care about can do the same.'

Logan nodded – she was on the right lines with reality.

'The people that care are sorted though, Maxine. Bear Dillon's out the way, thank Christ, so you can forget him. Anyway, you're back an' that's all that matters.' He felt like a lead weight had lifted just being near her, and that would do. He just hoped she'd never work out what he really felt for her. Sometimes it made him ashamed, as if he was needy. Logan being needy was unacceptable, and he realised that the premature death of his wife had made him vulnerable in more ways than he'd first thought.

Maxine sighed happily. 'It's just so good to see you, Tom, and you look great.'

She sat back, all smiles and he watched her eyes water up, remembering just what she'd been through, but emotions were raw all round. She was happy to see him, happy to spend time with him. *Friends*, he thought. Had he ever had any close friends apart from his wife? Logan was beginning to examine his own life in a way he'd never done before.

'Let me take you out for something to eat later this week.' Maxine's offer took him by surprise.

'We can catch up properly.'

He couldn't refuse and he wasn't going to. The days when Logan did more than exist, wondering where his life was going were over. They exchanged numbers and Maxine left to take care of her last piece of reconnection.

48

She needed to try to see her mother, but when she called, it was her brother Billy who answered. Later the same evening, Maxine wondered why she'd believed that everything in Edinburgh would just be frozen in time, that the city and its people wouldn't move on till she made a return appearance. What a fool she'd been. It had all gone so well up to that point – Connie and Logan had acted as if she'd never been away, the business was in gear and so she'd deluded herself into thinking that all the pieces of her life would just fall nicely into place and she'd live happily ever after.

But her mother had suffered a stroke and was now in a care home. Her father, who would have nothing to do with her anyway, was still at home and in poor health. Her brother had been cold with her since her problems with addiction and descent into prostitution, but when he spoke to her on the phone, he seemed tired of the past and knew for all her faults that she would be upset.

'She's not suffering, Maxine, apart from barely knowing she's in the world or who anyone is. Look, if you want to see her, carry on. What's the difference now? God knows where you've been or what you've been up to but the past is where it is. I'd stay away from Dad if I was you though.'

Maxine explained to him that she was back in Edinburgh and hoping to run a business. There was surprise in his voice – he'd never expected that – and there was a long silence. He'd once expected to hear that she'd had died of an overdose or been killed in some rathole by a client. They'd been so close at one time, but the revelation that his wee sister was a thief, a junkie and a hooker had killed part of him, robbed something from his youth and dreams. He'd never thought he would forgive, her but his mother's illness and Maxine's voice had made him ache for another reality. Life was too short to hate.

49

Maxine stared at her mother and choked back the tears as she watched the woman who'd brought her into the world staring at something only she could see. A line of saliva ran in a tiny clear strand from the left side of her mouth then down to her chin, where it paused before forming into a larger droplet and heading down onto the breast area of her cardigan.

All her training as a nurse didn't prepare Maxine for the thought that the woman who'd given her life was only partly in this world. Her mother's face was expressionless and she noticed her hands trembling as she tugged at something on her cardigan that wasn't there. Maxine had been full of optimism since coming back to Edinburgh, but the meeting with Tom Logan and now the sight of her mother had put her feet back on terra firma. For a moment, she wished she'd stayed in Leeds again with her dreams rather than facing the truth that the clock always moved forward and certainty only existed for death and taxes.

One of the carers put a chair next to her mother and touched her shoulder gently. She'd seen the expression on Maxine's face so many times – the bewilderment at what life had cruelly inflicted on a loved one. Maxine sat down slowly then remembered she was there to visit a sick woman and not wallow in her own regrets. She put her hand on her mother's forearm, bent forward and touched the back of her hand with her lips.

'Mum?' Maxine said for the third time, though she knew there was no chance of a coherent reply. The second time, her mother's eyes had flicked towards her as if the sound of her voice had connected with the circuits that had survived in her brain. It was only a moment though, and if there had been a flash of clarity, it was gone just as quickly – her eyes switching off again as she went back to that place where only she existed.

Maxine bit her bottom lip and felt a single tear escape down her cheek. She knew she had to keep a hold of herself. Her mother's smile seemed to broaden a little, but it was like a polite gesture to a stranger who was in her physical space.

'I've come home, Mum. And I'm staying.'

Maxine remembered the meeting she'd had with her mother before the trial, what her forgiveness had meant to her at the time. Her mother's love had not been destroyed completely – a link to the past still intact.

Maxine spent a couple of hours telling her mother all about Leeds, her friend Jan and all the good things that she'd done. Her mother said nothing, and if anything registered it was impossible to tell, but she had to try.

Later that night, she opened the door of the flat she was now renting. She walked into the kitchen and stared out of the window, trying to gather her thoughts. So much was the same in Edinburgh and so much had changed.

'It's just life, Maxine – just life,' she said quietly to her reflection in the kitchen window.

She called her brother again and could barely keep the emotion out of her voice. She promised to visit her mother whenever she could and felt her heart squeeze with hurt at her brother's words.

'Just let me know when you're going so I can keep Dad away from you. Don't want to upset him any more than he's been already. He'll never forgive you, Maxine. You have to know that. What's done is done, and you seem to have got your life back on track, but just know that about Dad.'

The words cut through her like a knife, but then she'd taken more than her fair share of emotional wounds in her time and this wasn't unexpected. Billy had only spoken the truth, and could she really blame him or her father for the way they felt? She'd fought through so many problems and this was just another one she'd have to face and resolve, one way or the other. She was responsible for so much of the pain her family had suffered, and if there was even the slightest chance of making something up to them then she'd do it.

All she could do was visit her mother. It wouldn't achieve much, and she couldn't even be sure her mother knew what was going on or who she was, but she would visit no matter what – and maybe, just maybe, it would make a difference. If nothing else, and in a small way, it helped ease the burden of guilt she would be forced to carry no matter how her life changed.

50

The business had worked out better than Maxine could have hoped for and they'd kept the profit margin tight to draw in the customers. It was a success, and every couple of days Jan was on the phone to her friend with all the advice she could offer, Maxine wondered what she'd done to deserve someone like her – it was a minor miracle to run from Edinburgh and find this guardian angel who she felt she'd known all her life.

Like the start of the business in Leeds, the hours were endless, and most nights she fell into her bed in the old flat she'd rented just off the Royal Mile. It was small but beautiful, and the ancient walls seemed to tell her stories from other ages. People would often talk about character in a building, but for Maxine it was the touches from other lives long gone. She had always loved the supernatural tales her father had told her. There was one about the spirit of a child who haunted Fa'side Castle near Musselburgh, and she'd been so disappointed when she'd visited it and failed to find any trace of the little ghost girl called Mary.

The city had begun to matter to her in a way she'd never appreciated before. Living in the heart of the Old Town seemed to connect her to the past, to those other lives long forgotten and the endless legends of the men and women who'd left their mark on the city's history.

After six weeks, she knew she was heading for burnout and forced herself to take a couple of days off and trust the place to Connie and the other girls she'd employed, who'd worked almost as hard as her to make the place a success. They were a team and she realised she had to start delegating to them.

'I'm not going anywhere,' she told them when they asked. 'Bed and walking about the city is all I want.'

She waved to Eva and Karolina who, although they weren't related, could have been taken for sisters. They were part of the growing Polish community who propped up so many businesses in the area. Karolina, the younger of the two, made Maxine smile every day because within a few years she'd perfected an almost flawless and very broad Scots accent. It was remarkable when Maxine remembered her struggles learning French at school. The great British flaw – complaining about immigrants failing to learn English and at the same time almost ignoring every other language on earth as worthy of study.

Connie was in charge when Maxine wasn't there and she'd surprised herself at how quickly she'd adapted to her new life. The other girls knew nothing about Maxine or Connie's past life, but they both knew and accepted it might raise its ugly head at some point. Logan was right that Edinburgh wasn't big enough to hide in, but they'd agreed between them that if it happened, then they should face it head-on. Denials would have been pointless and self-defeating.

'I'm not ashamed anymore, Connie. We did what we did and it cost us more than anyone could understand unless they'd been on the street themselves.'

Maxine said it over and over again, trying to convince herself that it would make things easier when the time finally did come.

51

As soon as she started her break, it dawned on Maxine just how tired she was, but there was something else she needed to do. It was time to really start exploring the town, get to know it again, learn its history – like so many natives of great cities she realised that there was so much that she'd heard about, even boasted about, but had never seen or experienced.

She decided to start acting like a tourist herself and explore the place, including the sometimes-beautiful country areas outside the city borders.

Maxine walked along the old west pier at Musselburgh harbour and breathed in cool, salty air. There was a breeze in the grey dark of early evening; she felt cold and pulled her woollen scarf just a little tighter round her neck. She'd caught the bus down to Musselburgh to see the place where so many of her family had been born and raised. Her parents had both been natives before moving into the Edinburgh suburbs as a kind of mark of success, and she'd spent the day wandering around the town, then through the beautiful old village of Inveresk and the wooded area along the banks of the river Esk.

It was nearly time to head home but she wanted to look at the harbour and the house looking onto the Promenade where her mother had been born. Her father's birthplace on the other side of the river had been torn down in the sixties and replaced by concrete boxes which looked like a diseased growth in the heart of the ancient place that had witnessed so much in Scotland's story because of the strategic bridge that spanned the river Esk.

The harbour was quiet, and the moored cruisers bobbed erratically on the short waves whipping across the water on the variable winds. The clear artic air blowing down from the northern wastes made the lights on the Fife side of the Firth glitter like jewels and Maxine felt like she could almost touch them. She just wanted to walk to the end of the pier, stand for a moment then head home. Then her little pilgrimage would be done.

She breathed deeply again and watched the pier end light spin rhythmically, telling sailors where they were and which port they were seeing, each light like a fingerprint exposed by the sequence of flashes.

Maxine was about to turn and head for home when she noticed a shadow on the opposite pier. It was almost dark but she could see it was a young man. That shouldn't have been unusual, but he was sitting with his legs over the harbour wall, his shoulders slumped and he was looking straight down into the water. It didn't feel right, but she turned and walked back towards the town lights. It was nothing to do with her and what was she seeing anyway?

She was passing the south end of the harbour and should have kept going, but she'd spent a long time on the street living on the small signs and non-verbals that might protect her, never mind anyone else, and so she stopped.

'Don't do this, Maxine.' She whispered it into the breeze and ignored it, all at the same time.

Walking slowly down one side then turning along the east pier, she gradually picked up the shape of the guy, who hadn't moved as far as she could see. Maybe he was pissed but that was still enough for concern, the way he was sitting.

Her steps slowed down again as she became nervous that he might have a go at her if he was drunk or just hacked off at something. This was Scotland and violence could come out of nowhere.

The urge to turn for home again was powerful, but she already carried enough guilt for one life and she couldn't help imagining a headline where a young man had been found drowned and apparently ignored by an unidentified woman who just didn't care. She shook her head and walked the last few steps towards the end of the pier and stood below the flashing light. The guy had his back to her on the harbour wall and was facing onto the open sea.

Bobo McCartney had just had enough. He'd spent the day wandering the streets of Edinburgh like a ghost – no one seemed to notice him, and why should they? He was still a young man, yet he felt old before his time, a spent force even though he'd achieved nothing but failure. All those dreams of being a gangster had given way to the reality that he didn't count. It was the same when he'd been released from prison – the screws hardly seemed to notice him, and there were no dramatic words or threats that might have been handed out to the real hard men. Hard words from a screw when you walked out the door were a mark of respect. Bobo got none of that, just the feeling that even in prison he lacked cred. The only relationships he forged were with other losers.

As the day wore on, he was drawn to the idea of heading towards water or the sea. At first it made no sense for someone who thought water was for brushing his teeth; the nearest he'd been to the sea was as an away fan when Celtic played Inverness. That place was the pits for a Glasgow man and the coldest fucking ground he'd ever been to. He'd jumped on a bus and intended heading for Portobello then just sat where he was till he saw the old harbour at Musselburgh on his left and walked off at the next stop. The town meant nothing to him and it was getting dark, but that was what he wanted – darkness where no one could see him. It was bitterly cold but he didn't notice. He bought some chips smothered in sauce with a can of the Bru before heading for the harbour, which was almost deserted apart from a couple of dog walkers who passed him, no doubt heading towards the warmth of a home he could only dream of.

He sat on the wall at the end of the east pier and worked his way through the chips without really tasting them. The heat as they passed down into his gut was a momentary pleasure before he drank half the can then tossed it into the little waves being swept across the Forth by a wind that had turned and settled from the cold north.

When the can bobbed then sank into the darkness of the water, he knew what he had to do. The pain of living was too much even for him and he just wanted it all to be over. He'd given up trying to think ahead because there was nothing he could conjure on the horizon of his imagination. Only darkness. He'd begun to dread the moment he put his head on the pillow at night because all he felt was emptiness and dread of the next day – and the next. They were all the same.

He seemed to drift off into a kind of daydream, as if he'd taken a hit from a luxury piece of weed. Once he'd made his mind up, it was as if everything was OK and he didn't need to take any more of the daily prescription of shit. Slipping into the water wasn't an end but a beginning of something better – it was almost inviting. Bobo wasn't afraid of anything anymore because he had an answer: just switch off.

'You OK there?'

Maxine waited, thinking she should have just left this alone. The guy remained still and didn't seem to hear her, but she'd reached out and couldn't turn away now without at least a 'Fuck off, hen!' Which is exactly what she'd do if he gave the order.

'You OK there?' she asked again.

She decided that would be her last try – her flight instincts were jangling, telling her to get out of it. It was getting dark, they were at the end of a harbour wall, the tide was in and the guy could be a bam.

Bobo had been so lost in his thoughts that he hadn't registered the first words Maxine had spoken. Her second attempt gradually sank in and he turned, as if he was coming out of a light sleep. He shivered and suddenly felt cold – very cold. He hadn't had much female contact recently and the concern in her voice was food to a starving man. The only problem was that he didn't know what to say to someone who was just trying to be friendly. What could he say? *Sorry but life's shite an' thought it would be an idea just to jump in the sea. Apart from that I'm fine.*

'I'm OK, hen. No probs.' He turned back to look into the darkness and hoped she'd just go.

But Maxine knew exactly what being lost felt like. She didn't know this guy, but it was all there in the flat tones of his voice. Her defence instincts told her again that it was probably just some punter who'd fallen out with his other half, or lost at the bookies or was pissed off with the whole debate about Brexit. The world was full of anger so why not? But it was more than that – she just knew it.

213

'You a local boy then?'

As soon as she asked the question she wanted to boot her own arse. Was that the best she could do? Apart from anything else, he was clearly a Weegie.

He turned again and saw the concern in her face. She was a beautiful girl and Bobo didn't get many like that asking after his health. He raised his eyebrows and grinned.

'Long way from home, darlin'. Long way from home. Just a bad time, know what I mean?'

'Been there,' she said, nodding. 'It's rough. I remember when I used to think there was nothing else. What was the point? Nearly ended it at one stage.'

She shrugged, surprised she'd made such a frank disclosure to a stranger.

Bobo was still pissed off at life, but she'd touched the curiosity button and so he swung his legs round and faced her, still sitting on the harbour wall. He stared and Maxine felt awkward; she hadn't a clue what to do next, so she just opened her mouth and spoke. Let the words flow in streams. Five minutes later, Bobo was down beside her and he talked back as if she was an old friend. In a way, they were old friends – at different times, they'd looked at the same place within themselves and despised what they found.

An hour later they were in a bar only a few minutes from the harbour and Maxine realised that she'd probably stopped a young man from killing himself. There was something quite overwhelming in that idea although the boy seemed revived – born again. He was open enough about it and she could see why. It was another story of a life that had started out as hopeless and then just plain flatlined. She knew what it was, but there was something vulnerable in the guy – he'd already told her about his time inside, but she knew from her own experience that there was always a chance of a way back. She excused herself, stepped out on the street and phoned Connie. She didn't bother with prevarication and got straight to the point, telling her friend what her big idea was for the day.

'You what, Maxie? You're takin' in strays now. Thought I'd be enough for you.'

'Just need to find this boy somewhere safe for a couple of nights,' Maxine almost whispered. 'We need another pair of hands for the business anyway, and we could do with someone to do odd jobs and driving. It's just a feeling – I need to do this, Connie, just don't ask why.'

She heard Connie sigh on the end of the phone, then there was a little double click and exhalation signalling that a smoke had just been fired up.

'OK. There's two o' us in this flat but there's a box room he could use. We've got sleepin' bags here. That's the best I can do, Maxie. Swear to God if he makes a wrong move we'll rip him up. The lassie I stay with is into bodybuildin' an' I can kick off wi' the best.'

After she'd hung up, Maxine sat down beside Bobo again; his hands were clasped tight together and his eyes looked down into his drink. She put her hand on his shoulder and saw the lost soul exposed. She knew exactly how he felt.

'My friend has a place you could stay for a few days. It's not the Balmoral but it'll be warm and safe till you get something better.

He looked sideways at her and only just avoided breaking down. He wanted to take her hands and kiss them. Thank her for realising he was in the world with her.

'Look, I run a small business. We need someone to do odd jobs and a bit of driving – any chance, Patrick?' She didn't know him as Bobo.

'The money wouldn't be much. Anyhow, what do you think?'

He blinked, trying to compute the messages firing through his circuits telling him to run, stay and continue trying to kill himself all at the same time. He sniffed a couple of times and she handed him a tissue.

'Suppose so. Aye, right.'

He tried a half smile, wondering if this was all just another wind-up by some cruel bastard who'd let him down, just another kick in the balls from life. If this woman was at it though, she was the best actress he'd ever seen.

They headed for the bus together then on to Connie's flat on Leith Walk.

52

Life seemed to slip into a kind of normality far quicker than Maxine could ever have hoped for. The business was in profit and she looked forward to going in every day, and loving work was a gift that rubbed off on the girls who worked there. Connie was equally content with her new life and, remarkably, had taken to Bobo – she'd adopted a kind of big support role which she loved, and he lapped up every moment of something he'd never had. In fact, Bobo started to feel something new in his life; it was a bit scary because he began to look and think about Connie in a way he'd only ever read about and sneered at in front of his mates. He did his best to hide it though, because the thought that he might fuck up this last chance terrified him and kept his feelings in check.

In a way, it felt like the business belonged to all of them and it was attracting new regulars every day. A real bonus was that there was a stream of customers from the Faculty of Advocates, who started to regard it as their territory and a place to meet and talk cases.

The days passed and it almost felt like this had always been Maxine's life, her old existence no more than a bad dream. Logan was there whenever she needed him, or when they would all meet up for a drink or a meal. He kept his feelings close, but Connie had seen it time and time again – the look in his eyes that said it all. She knew the best course of action was to stay out of it, but she cared for them both and wished the world would find a way for them. It almost annoyed her that her friend didn't see what she saw in the Big Man's eyes.

53

In the end, it was all just too straightforward – God didn't give away free passages. The day Danny Beatson walked into the cafe, it was as if an alarm had gone off, reminding them that life could be a bastard. He breezed in with an ugly little fucker called Mike Duran who had to stand on his tiptoes to get to 5'6" but was a nasty bastard with a reputation for unnecessary violence – and Danny Beatson's favourite attack dog when he wasn't doing the business himself.

'Two plates o' stovies, love, and make it snappy.'

He winked at Connie, who had no idea who he was, but it didn't matter. He was clearly there to cause bother; she'd seen it all before and read the signs. Maxine was out with Bobo, picking up some new equipment, and Connie was there with the two other girls, who knew that trouble had walked in the door but that they weren't equipped for it. Connie was though and had already decided that if the two radges wanted to play then she wasn't going anywhere. The place hadn't opened yet, but the door had been unlocked, although the closed sign was still on view. She looked round slowly at the daily specials and took her time pretending to examine them before turning back and smiling at the two men.

'I was sure we don't do stovies an' right enough, they're no' there. You must have got us mixed up wi' some place else.'

She crossed her arms in the gesture that signalled 'Get to fuck'.

Beatson grinned and kept his eyes fixed on Connie when he spoke.

'Hear that, Mikey? No fuckin' stovies.'

Beatson's problem was that he'd never actually got in touch with reality – he was widely recognised as a menace or a 'fuckin' eejit' as most cops and criminals would have described him. He was a Z-lister who kept imagining that he was further up the greasy pole than he was. For the police he was trouble, but mostly small time, and he took as many second prizes as first when it came to a knuckle contest. Connie knew the type: let him walk over you and you were in trouble, but go eye to eye and he might blink first. She gave him eye contact but said nothing and waited for his next move.

It took a minute for Beatson to work out that the wee burd behind the counter wasn't going to bend over and that pushed his red button because now he had to think up a smart-arsed reply. He hadn't expected that and it threw him. The colour ran into his cheeks like he'd over rouged, and the side of his left eye started to tic as it always did when he was put under pressure.

'I want stovies. Me an' my pal here want stovies. I hope you're no refusin' tae serve me? If ye are then I'll take that as an insult.' He turned to Duran and winked.

'I don't like stovies, Danny. Can I get somethin' else?'

Mike Duran was good at violence but he was a halfwit who pissed off his employer whenever he failed to get a line of banter or threats. The circles of red spread out on Beatson's cheeks; they looked like they were about to burst into flames.

'Shut the fuck up, muppet,' Beatson snapped at Duran, who could have taken him apart with one hand tied up, but Beatson paid the wages that allowed him to hand out snash to the staff so he did nothing.

Connie grinned and Beatson realised he was clearly on the back foot – almost on his arse in fact.

The door opened behind them then and Maxine walked in with Bobo, who immediately picked up the scent of trouble. He'd never met Beatson but he'd always known at some stage they'd have to cross paths after the nutjob he'd done on the bus. Of course it was him in here now, causing trouble.

Bobo waited for Beatson's next move. He considered legging it to take the problem away from Maxine and the girls who had made him believe again. That might not work though, and the freaky-looking minder with Beatson seemed like he could run down a greyhound, so better to see who made what move, but if it kicked off, he'd go down fighting. Bobo had belief in himself again. He might be a failure, but he was a Glasgow man and knew how to use his hands.

'Whoa.'

Beatson seemed pleased with the new arrivals and he had enough of a description to know he'd found who he'd been looking for. He'd been trying for months to find Bobo, and a couple of the idiots who'd been on the bus the day Bobo had been arrested had spotted him working in Maxine's place. It was one of those opportunities to show he was a main man. Spill some blood and claim it was to honour the family name. He turned to face Bobo, who just waited, placing the box he was carrying on the floor.

'You McCartney?'

Beatson pulled his shoulders back, expecting Bobo to crumble, but it didn't happen. Duran became edgy as adrenalin started to pump through him in pre-violence mode, while Connie stepped out from behind the counter.

'Aye. That's me. Who's askin?' Bobo didn't waver and his first thought was to make sure none of the women were hurt.

Maxine stepped forward directly between Bobo and Beatson. She knew exactly what was happening – Bobo had told her every detail of the fight on the bus and who was involved. He'd warned her that this could happen, but like everything else, Maxine seemed to take the load as if she owned all their demons.

'You.' She looked straight at Beatson. 'Leave the past where it is. You hear me?'

Beatson didn't like women who talked back and now he was faced with two of them. That pissed him off for a start.

'The lassies had nothin' to do wi' this. I'll take it outside,' Bobo said. He felt absolutely calm, no fear, almost happy that he could show Maxine and the girls what they meant to him. He'd take what was coming because it was the right thing to do. He put his hand on Maxine's shoulder and said, 'It's fine. I'll take the two o' them. I'm a Glasgow man, for Christ's sake.'

He grinned from one ear to the other as Beatson's red patches spread down onto his neck, Duran almost pogoing on the spot with the adrenalin rush. They were at the point of no return and it was just a case of who lashed out first when the door swung open and two uniforms walked in. It wasn't an intrusion after a call, just a couple of hungry cops who'd heard that the scran was the business in Maxine's place. They were both young men, but while one was Mr Average in looks and size, the other was something else at over six foot, his half-covered upper arms indicating regular curl sessions at the gym. He was the one with three stripes, clean good looks and was definitely no pushover.

Everyone was surprised for a moment, including the cops, who saw battle lines drawn up and needed a few seconds to compute. The big sergeant opened his mouth first.

'Someone going to explain what the problem is here, or am I wrong? If so, I need some eats.'

He locked eyes with Beatson, who seemed to take a half step back.

'Danny boy, hope you're no causin' a problem wi' these good people. I warned you the last time.'

The uniform glared at Beatson and waited for an answer, but Connie came in first.

'These boys wanted stovies an' we don't have stovies,' she said through her teeth. 'They seemed to be annoyed about it.'

'You.' The sergeant pointed at Beatson. 'Outside.' He turned to his colleague. 'Keep the rest here till I have a word wi' Danny.'

Beatson followed the uniform out onto the street and the cop nodded to a lane running between the buildings. They walked into the lane and then into the corner of a disused exit that stank of piss from the winos who used it. The uniform turned and grabbed Beatson by the throat, then put his face as close as possible without contact. Beatson didn't resist because he knew what this particular cop could do even when he was in a good mood.

'Now you listen to me, Danny. Just nod whenever I ask a question.'

He pressed a bit harder and watched Beatson's eyes start to bulge with a mixture of fear and pressure.

'This is my area. Whatever the fuck you're up to, it stops here. Understand?'

Beatson didn't even blink.

'That was a question, Danny.'

'Esss.' Beatson couldn't say yes with the vice on his throat, but it was close enough.

'Now I can either use physical violence, or worse still I can put it around the scum that you've been a registered grass for years and let them deal with it.'

The uniform grabbed his captive's chuckies with his free hand and squeezed hard enough to enjoy the long groan that escaped Beatson's lips with a trickle of spit.

'You wouldn't want that, Danny, now would you?'

He grinned as he watched Beatson try to shake his head. He started to release the pressure gradually, let go and then took a steep back.

'Now I need to wash my hands, Danny, 'cause I'm guessing with your personal hygiene problem you haven't washed the old goolies this week, eh?'

He nodded, pleased that he'd injected just the right level of fear into Beatson, who looked like a frightened school-boy. They walked back into the cafe together and Beatson nodded to his attack dog, signalling that it was time to go.

'You forgot something, Danny.' The uniform nodded in the direction of Connie.

'Sorry for any misunderstandin', hen.'

Beatson looked at the sergeant, who nodded back, then headed for the exit. They heard Duran ask, 'What the fuck, Danny?' before the door closed behind them.

The sergeant grinned and shrugged. 'We aim to please. Now, any chance of getting something to eat?'

Connie looked like she was in love and said, 'Comin' up, handsome – what would you like?' She hoped it was her.

Maxine offered them a booth and anything on the house.

'Thanks. We'll take you up the next time we're off the clock and pay now. Freebies are frowned on in Police Scotland.

You OK, pal?'

He directed the question at Bobo, who felt like he'd just crashed back to earth face first. Beatson was gone for the time being, but he knew that was not how these things ended.

'Fine, thanks.'

He'd never liked the law but he wondered why he didn't like this cop a bit more.

'You must tell me what that was about sometime but need to go once we get the scran.'

He pulled out a card and handed it to Maxine.

'Any bother from him again, just ring that number and I'll take care of it.'

She watched him leave a few minutes later and looked at the name on the card. *Sergeant Jamie Marshall*. It had his work and personal number. She stuffed it into her pocket and sat down with Bobo to make sure he was OK. It was as if a cold hand from the past had touched her shoulder. Here it was again – Bear Dillon was away but here was another problem they didn't need.

Bobo felt guilty and offered to leave, and he saw her anger for the first time. It wasn't going to happen – she told him they were friends and it would all be OK. Neither of them believed that, but he nodded anyway and tried not to think what might visit them again.

54

It all happened quicker than Maxine could have imagined with Jamie Marshall – the attraction was almost instantaneous. She knew she was interested, but it confused her again. He looked good, strong and she guessed he wouldn't have a problem attracting women, but she knew nothing about him. After everything she'd been through, there was always that nagging doubt, but condemning all men on the evidence of her life to date was just wrong and she knew it. She'd gone from almost no experience as a young woman to abuse in one way or another. She sometimes found it hard to believe that she hadn't had one relationship of any kind where there was care and love. It had to be possible because she saw it and read about it all the time – or were all the stories of romance just so much pulp? Then there was Logan, who asked for nothing and treated her the way she'd dreamed of, but she kept her feelings locked up because of his connections to the old life. For all he'd been to her, his links to gangland meant she'd already convicted him, even though he was the most honest man she'd ever met.

The policeman was just there, available unless she was mistaken, and she ached for the thrill of a relationship with as few complications as possible. She kept reminding herself that she was human and part of her had been dead since the time before her days in Leith.

At least with a cop she felt there was a degree of safety if she let herself go. Most of her experience with the law had been positive. There was the odd bastard, of course, but then there were people like Charlie Brockie – he was the business, and though he could be hard, he was fair and never judged the working girls.

Marshall started to appear every few days and it was clear he was always looking for Maxine, although he made half-hearted attempts to pretend otherwise. She'd held herself back for so long and it seemed as if this knight in blue armour had walked in at just the right moment. Everything was going well, her life seemed to be taking shape for all the right reasons and he looked too good to be true. She kept reminding herself that there had to be problems ahead, but she couldn't dampen down her optimism – right up to the point Connie gave her a reality check.

'You have to tell the boy, Maxie. He's polis, for Christ's sake – sooner or later he'll twig, an' I wonder he hasn't worked it out already. I mean, there were enough headlines at the time.'

She put her hand on her friend's shoulder.

'He'll probably run a mile, but better that than somethi worse in the future.'

'You're right, Connie; I've been putting it off. Go talking like we're in a relationship. It's been so lo I thought that part of my life was over, but no stop thinking about him. A cop of all things! W guessed it back then?'

'Not me, honey. Mind you, when I was f off trying to get a punter I'd never imagir noon tea to lawyers. There you go.'

Connie hugged her and told her to get on with it but thought again about Logan. She wished Maxine could see what she saw. In fact, she wished the man looked at her the way he looked at her friend. Unfortunately, Logan was a stubborn bastard and would never take the initiative so speaking to him would have been a waste of time.

She was nervous about speaking to Maxine about it because, at the end of the day, maybe Jamie Marshall was just what she needed. God knows he had looks, presence and the way he'd sorted out the two bams meant he was the real deal on the street.

That's where the little maggot of doubt irritated her. Something about the series of events with Danny Beatson just didn't feel right. She knew good cops and she knew a few bad ones, and she couldn't work out why Beatson had backed off so easily after he'd gone outside with Marshall – or why Marshall hadn't taken his partner with him. In fact, the other cop had hardly opened his mouth, and when she thought about it now, he'd looked like he hadn't wanted to be there.

She shook her head and decided she was overthinking e whole thing. Maxine deserved a bit of relief and she better to let it be and allow her friend to make her own es rather than lose a friendship that meant so much

55

Marshall started to come in every time he was on duty, then it was a coffee together, then he finally asked Maxine out. They sat in one of the booths, which gave them at least a degree of privacy, although Connie was working and doing her best to overhear what was being said. Maxine had dreamt of this moment then felt her heart sink a little, knowing the question had to be followed by her own disclosure. She bit her lip and found it difficult to look him in the eye.

'Jamie.'

She froze and couldn't find the next words she'd rehearsed so many times. She tried again.

'Jamie.'

'That's me.' He grinned and his eyes scrunched up at the sides. The smile was real.

'Look, I'm flattered, honestly flattered and well… I'd be up for that in a minute, but there's a problem.'

She looked down at the table and struggled to get the words out. She looked up again.

'Thing is, I've built up an awful lot of baggage for one life and some of it's not good. No, it's worse than that.'

She pulled out a tissue and dabbed her eyes and nose.

'Anyway, here goes and I'm not going to be offended if you just turn and walk after this. It's fine.'

He reached across the table and grabbed her free hand.

'Listen, Maxine. If you're going to tell me about your time on the street and the trial, forget it. I have more details than you about that case. To be fair, I didn't twig at the time, but the cop I was with the day Beatson was here recognised you and told me on the way back to the station. My first reaction was to let it lie and forget what I was feeling. But I hardly stop thinking about the woman sitting across the table from me today who just couldn't be that other person.'

'Wait.'

Maxine stopped him and sat back, half surprised but needing to have her say.

'I am that person, Jamie. That's the point, whatever way you put it. I was down as low as I could get and now I'm in a different place, but it's still me, and you can't separate who I was and who I am. I decided that I'm not going to hide from that part of my life.'

'Bad choice of words then, Maxine. I meant, I spent a lot of time thinking about it and well… I just thought we could go out and find out a bit more about each other. Nothing rushed. At the end of the day, it's boy meets girl, boys likes girl and girl likes boy. Simple really.'

He gave her that grin that made him look like a boy again.

Connie watched it happening, still wondering why she didn't feel better for her friend. She convinced herself it was just her lifelong mistrust of the police. What else could it be? He was a charmer, maybe that was it – just too much of a charmer, but Connie admitted to herself that the problem might be that she just hadn't had many dealings with charming men. Her type tended to come from the arsehole junkie end of the spectrum. She shrugged – it was Maxine's choice.

Things just took their course: Maxine and Marshall met up and confirmed that they were attracted to each other, and for the first time Maxine thought she might just have a chance of sharing some personal moments with a man who ticked most of the right boxes. She hadn't lost her head and there were doubts, but the desire for intimacy had been suppressed for too long and it was time for that to change.

56

What they couldn't know was that while Danny Beatson might have been humiliated and forced to back off his mission to make up for the assault on his boy, it was still an unacceptable situation he had to do something about. Mike Duran kept nipping his head over what had happened and it ate at his mind.

He knew how it worked – if someone like Bobo McCartney could get away with banjoing his boy, he'd pay a price. His credibility, whatever that was, was damaged already, though Beatson's idea of his credibility was something different from that of the people that knew him and the police. For the locals in Craigmillar, he was a dangerous nuisance; for the other criminals, second division – decent second division but he lacked the grey matter to be promoted to the premier league. For the cops, he was a pain in the arse who caused more bother than he was worth, but he was also someone who could give them severe grief if he was on a mission.

He seethed with hurt and his rage grew and spread like terminal cancer – whatever Jamie Marshall could do to him was put aside and all that mattered was his reputation, which in his delusional mind was something precious.

It ate him up and the faces in the cafe that day came back to him in his dreams. He tried popping more dope than usual but it only made him worse. He started to double up on the bevvy and raged to Duran, who wondered if he was working for the right team. He had his own reputation as a violent fucker to think of, and he was growing edgy listening to the ramblings of Beatson, who seemed frozen into inaction, although there was an abundance of talk. The uniform's actions with Beatson that day bothered him and wore away at the back of his damaged brain. Duran didn't know but was beginning to suspect that his employer was a paid informant, and if he'd had proof he would have killed him before he could beg for mercy. The subsequent train of events were set in motion when Duran sipped his beer and listened to Beatson, again pissed out of his skull.

'Somebody has to pay, Mikey. Somebody has to pay, mate.'

He swigged back on the cheap whisky.

Duran had heard enough.

'Well what the fuck we doin' then, Danny? Sitting here and talking shite again a' night? We're a fuckin' laughin' stock!'

Duran was past deferring to his employer and on the point of pissing off to another team.

'Right then, Mikey. Fuck Jamie Marshall! We're gettin' that wee Weegie shite McCartney. That's it, that's the order. The bastard gets a good cuttin'.'

Duran nodded, stood up and wondered again how the fuck the uniform sergeant had managed to put Beatson right in his box. It stank but that was for another day – he had the nod to go for Bobo McCartney and that was that.

Beatson couldn't even remember the conversation the next morning but it was too late by then – as far as Duran was concerned, the job had a green light so it was going to happen. He was high with the thought of a bit of blood and had spent the night snorting a decent bit of Charlie and watching his favourite films, usually involving American special forces wasting hundreds of terrorists.

57

Big Tam Logan had taken Bobo under his wing and liked the boy, although he sometimes wondered why because he ticked all the wrong boxes – a Weegie, no class as a criminal and a Celtic supporter. Back in the day, Logan wouldn't even have given him a second look and would have treated him as a second-class citizen. At first, he only did it for Maxine, and although he didn't show it to her, it was grudged at first, but she'd told him what had happened at Musselburgh harbour so he'd given the boy a break.

Maxine knew that Logan was the kind of man Bobo needed to listen to and learn from – the older head that seemed to have been missing from his life. There was enough work in the cafe to keep Bobo fully occupied, but when he had time off, Logan gave him some casual work. It took a bit of time – Bobo definitely wasn't a quick learner – but Logan saw that the boy was doing his best and just wanted a new start. For all the problems in his life, there was something endearing about Bobo; Logan warmed to him and saw he might be worth saving.

When Logan was no more than a boy, he'd seen so many young men like the Glasgow boy pop their clogs long before their time – drugs, violence and the scourge of the AIDS epidemic back in the *Trainspotting* days. Those days when the drugs squad decided that taking the junkies' needles away from them was a good thing. They forgot that addicts don't give a fuck when the brown's cooking, and who cared if there was just the one needle left available in a room full of other junkies? Logan never forgot those days and the friends who were no more than kids themselves lost to the virus.

The locals in Logan's boozer took to Bobo as well and liked to pull his leg about his Glasgow roots, but he enjoyed the banter and learned to give as much as he got. Mick Harkins warmed to him as well, though he remembered when Bobo had tried to pull off a robbery in Edinburgh while grassed up to the eyeballs. He kept that to himself when Logan told him how Maxine had met him though. Harkins had seen as much as Logan and more – his days of all-out war against neds were over, and anyway he had his own share of skeletons that he preferred stayed away from the light.

Bobo had just finished an afternoon job for Logan and was heading for the cinema at Ocean Terminal. He went there every week; there was something warming in sitting there in the dark, watching alternative lives that he could pretend were his own, even if it was just for a couple of hours. He'd started to feel good about life again and some of his old optimism had returned, but he'd given up the idea of ever returning to crime. It was all down to Maxine, and she'd given him more affection in the short time he'd known her than his family had given him all his life. All he wanted to do was make her proud of him, so as far as he was concerned, the past could lie where it was.

He still worried about Danny Beatson, and there was always the likelihood that he'd just walk into him someday, but hopefully whatever Jamie Marshall had on him would keep the peace. He knew that was probably overly optimistic, but he hadn't any other choice apart from heading back to Glasgow, and he knew exactly where that would end up. He wouldn't last five minutes, and he needed what Maxine and Logan were giving him in abundance. He felt he mattered again, and the fact that people cared was something of a revelation to him.

He zipped up his coat when he walked quickly back out onto the street. It was cold, the wind whipping around the streets, and he watched a chip paper tumble along the pavement in front of him as if it was racing to get home as well. Normally he would have stopped for chips but he felt a bit queasy, which he guessed was down to the inordinate amount of juice, popcorn and ice cream he'd consumed during the film. It was only a ten-minute walk to his flat, and he just wanted to get there and warm up. A storm was on its way and the gales that had blown all day were dying down a little before the big event arrived the next day. It was like winter after a warm spell that had lulled Edinburgh's citizens into a false sense of security once again.

Bobo saw the door to his block of flats like a friend waving him home. The nausea had worn off and he wished he had bought some chips, but it was too late now and he wanted to catch what had happened at Easter Road. Hibs had been locked in a Scottish Cup tie, and while he was a Celtic supporter through and through, as an immigrant to the capital, he'd started following the green side of Edinburgh's football divide.

He pursed his hands and blew warm breath into his cupped fingers, trying to get some heat into them. He started to fumble for his keys, took the last step towards the door and couldn't stop shivering. A lorry sloshed its way through the wet street behind him and the headlights painted his shadow on the door to his stair, drawing his eyes up after opening the lock.

It happened in a moment – Bobo saw the second shadow right behind him, and he'd been in enough battles in his time to know this wasn't a pal on a surprise visit. Attacking a target at their door was a favourite because nine times out of ten you could guarantee finding the guy there at some point. Danny Beatson had still been hanging about in the back of Bobo's mind, and although he knew the bastard had backed off, he wouldn't have forgotten. Bobo tended to be careful in his habits, but he was cold, tired and had just wanted to get home. Any other night he would have spotted the car where his attacker had waited for the right moment, but not this night – it was just Sod's Law yet again.

Mike Duran was fired up; he'd only been waiting a couple of hours in his car which was no great hardship. He'd seen Bobo a long way off and had plenty of time to get into place. It wasn't a killing; the boy was to be sliced up a bit. Enough to get the message out that no one fucked with their team and ensure Duran kept his reputation intact, although doubt still gnawed in his gut about Danny Beatson. What the fuck did the cop have on him?

If a bizzie had something, they normally wanted pay-back. Duran had started to piece together a few situations where punters they knew had been taken out and they all stank of a rat. That could wait, but slicing up this Weegie fucker would have to have an effect on whatever was going on between the uniform sergeant and Beatson. Apart from anything else, Duran was like an animal needing a kill, or at least some blood – and Bobo was supper as far as he was concerned.

Bobo spun round and surprised Duran, forcing him on to the back foot, but he still managed to swing his blade in an overhead motion. Bobo had crossed his arms in the

238

classic defensive stance and took the cut on his left forearm. It was deep enough to hurt, but although the pain was sickening, his survival instinct kicked in – he wanted to live.

Duran raised the blade again, his face a mixture of rage and bloodlust, lips drawn back from his teeth like a dog, his eyes no more than black holes with the street lights behind him. Bobo tried to grab the knife with his right hand but missed and got the blade instead, and he screamed as the metal sank into the palm of his right hand, severing muscle and tendon. He gasped as he let it go, sinking to the ground and spinning round with his back to Duran, who took a step away and grinned. He watched Bobo curl over, trying to nurse his wounds and waiting for what came next. Duran leaned down and whispered in Bobo's ear.

'Think yer a wide boy, eh? I'm no finished wi' you yet, boy.'

Duran was pumped full of adrenalin, anger and dope. He needed to finish what he'd started and he wished he could kill the bastard. He wondered whether he should ignore Beatson and go for the high of a kill.

He slashed the blade across Bobo's right buttock and stood back again, admiring his work as blood drained onto the slabs. That's when his attention was distracted by pure chance. He saw the blues and twos flashing along Commercial Street from the Leith direction – the patrol car was burning rubber.

Duran presumed wrongly that the bizzies had been alerted by some nosey punter and he was caught in two minds. He was high with the taste of blood but in that frozen moment he gave Bobo a chance to survive. He'd heard the two-tones as well, swung his head round and saw Duran staring towards the source of the sound. He was in severe pain and didn't want to bleed to death, but he was angry, wanted some payback and saw his chance.

Gritting his teeth, he forced the pain into the back of his mind and pushed himself up with all the force he could muster, keeping side-on to Duran, and drove the back of his elbow into Duran's face as he turned back to look at Bobo. The flashing blue lights turned the blood that spurted from Duran's nose into a momentary black spray. His nose was mashed and he staggered backwards onto the main road, but the police car was already past them and heading towards whatever their call involved.

'Ma huckin nose, ya bastard.' The pumping blood and damaged cartilage meant he couldn't speak properly. Duran bent forward and let the blood flow onto the pavement. A couple of neighbours were at the windows now, already on the phone to Police Scotland, while a drunk weaved past Duran and stopped to peer at him with just the one eye open.

'Ye awright there, pal?' The drunk patted his pockets, looking for his fags, even though he didn't have any left. That was his plan – be nice to the punter with the burst hooter and he could mump a fag off him.

Duran looked up and snarled just before he hoofed the drunk up in the chuckies and watched the guy flip arse up over a hedge into a rubbish-strewn garden. He snapped his head round and Bobo was gone. He stared at the blood splattered over the path and saw there were dark smudges over the door. Bobo had got into the stair and behind the safety of the heavy entrance door.

'Huck it.' There was another blue light approaching from Leith and he couldn't be sure if it was following the other one or coming for him. He headed towards the main street and legged it into the darkness then stopped for a moment as he remembered the wheels he'd used were parked in sight of Bobo's front door. It would have to wait – he'd come back the next day. It shouldn't attract too much attention unless the bizzies started checking all the parked cars and it came up as police interest.

'Huck it.' He walked off towards the town, blood still streaming down onto his jacket.

The police arrived and were confronted with the drunk, who was holding his knackers and claiming that he'd been assaulted. The uniforms were under pressure – all over the division things seemed to be kicking off and they didn't need this drunk tying them up for a couple of hours. They told him to go home and sleep it off.

The drunk didn't like that one bit and took a swing at one of the cops, who were then stuck at the station for the next couple of hours processing the guy. They'd seen all the blood at the locus, but it was Leith and there was always a rammy somewhere. There was no sign of an injured punter so the piss-head's arrest was the only result of the call.

58

Bobo had barely managed to crawl up the flight of stairs to his flat. The guy he shared with was away with his squeeze for a couple of days so the place was empty. He toiled to find the keys with his uninjured left hand but Sod's Law meant he had to struggle to retrieve them from the right pocket of his jeans. The effort and pain were just too much – he was sure he was going to pass out when he threw up at his door.

He pushed the door open, almost fell inside and took a few moments leaning against the wall there before pushing the door closed in case Duran came back and found a way in. He looked down, saw he was standing in a pool of blood and wondered if he was going to die. Bobo had been brought up in one of the toughest schemes in east Glasgow where so many members of the community ended up scarred for life and occasionally just plain dead, so why not him? He wanted to live though, more than ever, and he was afraid, groaning in reaction to the fear pumping adrenalin round his body.

'No fuckin' way,' he hissed through clenched teeth before making his way to the bathroom He grabbed a towel and wrapped it around his damaged hand. The pain from his wounds had become excruciating and beads of sweat rolled down his face, though he felt cold. He had no idea how to control the bleeding for the huge wound on his buttock so he took a bath towel, headed into his bedroom, planked it on his bed then sat down gingerly. He wanted to scream but just panted through his distress. There was no way he could just sit there and expect the wounds to magically heal. He pulled his phone from his shirt pocket and called Logan. When the Big Man answered, Bobo just couldn't help it and broke down in tears.

'Tam,' was all he got out before he choked on the tears.

Logan knew right away that there was a situation and he tried to calm the boy.

'Take it easy, son. Just breathe and tell me what's up.'

'I'm in the flat, bleeding, Tam. Stabbed.'

That's when Bobo slid off the bed onto the floor; he was unconscious in seconds.

Logan was there a few minutes later. He got one of the neighbours on the entry phone and they let him into the close. He went up the stairs two at a time, and when Bobo didn't answer after the second knock, he broke the door open with one kick. Logan had enough experience to know exactly what it took to put the door in.

He got to work on Bobo right away and didn't hesitate to call an ambulance. There was just too much blood and no chance they could sort this quietly.

Bobo came around and tried to speak, but the words were barely a whisper.

'Who did this, son?'

Logan put his face close to Bobo's, holding him like a child.

'Beatson's mate at the cafe.'

That was all Bobo had the strength for, and he closed his eyes again. It was enough though. Logan felt the anger close his throat, but he controlled it. This wasn't the time for action – the first priority was to get the boy into the hospital.

'We'll talk later, Pat. Just take it easy, son.'

He wasn't sure that Bobo could hear him. He didn't want to step into his old life again but there were times when you just couldn't walk away.

The paramedics arrived quickly and Logan forgot about where this might end up and all the consequences that might result from the attack on the Bobo McCartney.

'Right, we need to get you to a hospital as soon as, pal.'

The paramedic looked like a cheerful soul despite his work and had finished the actions needed to stabilise Bobo, who looked to be asleep.

Logan called Maxine, who'd been away for a few days. No one had told him but he guessed that she was away with the cop. Connie seemed to avoid talking about Maxine's relationship, and he thought he knew why. It was strange what could be communicated without a word being spoken. Connie knew what he was feeling, and a couple of times she'd given him a slight non-verbal nudge towards Maxine, but he just couldn't make that move.

He knew Connie was becoming involved with Bobo and that they probably wouldn't be able to see him for a few hours, so he decided that Connie could wait till the morning to start worrying.

He headed for the hospital, pulling the door to Bobo's flat as near to closed as possible, but there was little or nothing worth stealing in the flat so they could worry about that problem later. The one thing that was certain was that the situation with Beatson and his minder wouldn't go away on its own. It was the old problem that dogged him. Maybe there was a God after all and this was his burden – the price of his sins.

59

Maxine lay in the darkness. She hadn't slept since Jamie Marshall had thrown his arm round her a couple of hours earlier and she chewed her lip till it hurt. She'd so looked forward to their short break away to St Andrews, but now her old doubts had come back with interest.

She'd felt like a teenager again when she'd said yes to going away together for a couple of days, giddy with nervous excitement at the thought of a new beginning, of discovering another person, then intimacy and just good old pleasure in the most human of ways. She'd been shocked that it hadn't happened in the way she'd imagined. She hadn't expected a miracle, knew that it might not be like a true romance story, but beginnings could lead to better things, couldn't they? It just hadn't happened though – not even close.

When they'd arrived at the hotel, there had been something almost delightful in the nervous tension between them and the knowledge that they would soon move past that point together. They'd unpacked, and it was strange because she'd wanted him right there and then but instead he'd suggested they should go for a walk along the beach and 'not waste the day'. She'd decided that she knew so little about proper relationships that she should let him take the lead. *What was the rush?* she'd asked herself – there was time for anything.

Marshall was just so confident, and that assurance had become almost overwhelming – he seemed to be certain about everything. He assumed control very quickly, but it was as if he was going through a series of moves. Maxine had wanted spontaneity, just like the books, and to be lost in her emotions, but it wasn't like that.

She'd managed to shake off her doubts during the walk along the beach, blaming her past again, and when he'd finally said, 'Think it's time we went back to the room, Maxine. I can't wait,' she'd relaxed fully, feeling that tremor of anticipation again.

She'd taken his hand on the way back. It was strange because she'd never noticed the little thistle tattooed between his thumb and forefinger. She'd always thought it was just a birthmark but there it was – so insignificant compared with the body art she saw every day in the gym.

'Never asked you about that little tattoo, Jamie. Most men seem to be half covered nowadays; did you lose your nerve about getting a proper one?'

She'd squeezed his hand and almost winced as, just for a moment, his eyes had seemed to fill with dark shadows – then they were gone and he'd grinned.

'Too much to drink one day and a gang I was hanging around with all decided to get this thing to show together-ness, for want of a better word.'

He'd looked straight at Maxine and reconnected with her eyes. Then he'd changed tack so suddenly it had thrown her for a moment.

'Listen, I know you must think I'll have taken cold feet but the truth is I'm thinking of packing the job in. Police

Scotland isn't exactly filling me with corporate pride and I can't stand the bullshit anymore. Always fancied my own business, so your past and my uniform wouldn't clash.'

He'd squeezed her hand a little too hard and she'd tightened her lips. She'd seen it again then – as if something had flown past his eyes and cut the light just for a second.

'Jesus, Jamie, take it easy – you're forgetting I'm a mere woman.'

She'd been surprised by his declaration; she'd thought he was one of those cops addicted to the job.

'Never saw that one coming,' she'd said, 'but it's your decision as long as you're not just giving it up for me.'

She had been puzzled by the abrupt change of subject, and his disclosure had reminded her that she knew so little about him – and it was beginning to bother her.

She knew there was no chance of sleep. He moaned, and she wondered what he was dreaming and who he really was. There had been passion, but she'd had that same feeling that it was controlled. She'd kept trying to look into his eyes, to connect, but Jamie Marshall had been somewhere else. She had desperately wanted that connection but there was nothing there. He'd made no effort to satisfy her and when he was exhausted, he'd lain back without a word.

Maxine suddenly felt cold and all her old doubts came flooding back. Was something wrong with her? she wondered over and over again as she waited for the night to pass. Her first instinct was always to blame herself when things went wrong, and she sometimes believed she had a curse on her that she'd never really cast off. It was always the same line of thought. She'd made the wrong choice again and her mind drifted to Tom Logan, a single tear wandering down her cheek and falling onto the pillow.

60

When Maxine received the call about Bobo, she was back in Edinburgh within a couple of hours and had almost welcomed an excuse to cut the break short. Marshall had said he'd come with her, but she'd put him off and said she'd call as soon as she had news.

'Don't get involved, Jamie. Might cause you a problem – conflict of interest and all that.'

She hadn't felt convinced by her own words and she'd noticed something flicker again in his eyes.

'Just let me know if I can help,' he'd replied, though it didn't sound convincing. He'd picked up her tension; the fact that there was no warm afterglow from their time in bed, and she could tell he was angry, though he was kept it controlled. When she'd left him and stepped outside the hotel, she'd breathed deeply, as if she'd escaped from something noxious, and thanked her stars that they'd brought their own cars because she had been in Inverness the previous day on business.

When she arrived at the hospital, her face tight with strain, Logan was waiting in the cafe area for her.

'Jesus, Tom, what happened? Did you talk to him?'

Maxine sat down opposite Logan and saw that, tough as he was, the attack on Bobo had upset him. She knew how protective he was of all of them; that's how he was, and he'd feel guilty for something he had no control over. It occurred to her that this little band of friends – all damaged in one way or another – had become so important to all of them. It was strange how life and circumstances had thrown them together.

Logan explained as much as he knew and that it had been Mike Duran.

'Is he going to be OK, Tom?' she asked, her voice breaking with emotion; she felt her own share of guilt that she'd found Bobo on the edge of despair and now he was on an operating table. Those emotions were mixed up with the confusion of Jamie Marshall, and disappointment seemed to hit her in waves, knocking the confidence she'd managed to rebuild since she left Edinburgh.

'He's lost a lot of blood, but he'll survive. Lucky to be alive – must be cause he's a Weegie.' He tried a shot of humour and Maxine nodded, but her smile hardly registered.

'That bastard Duran wasn't worried about killing him. When you do that much damage, it can go either way.'

'Is there anything we can do? What about the police?' Maxine was struggling to find a way to be useful and, like Logan, she felt the past reaching out to hurt her again.

'No sign of the law so far but I can handle this one. I'll sort Beatson and Duran. Don't worry.'

'What do you mean, you'll sort it? Christ, Tom, is that what I've come back to?' Maxine's eyes flashed with anger and her mouth was tight with raw emotion.

'That seems to be the only answer you ever come up with. Hurt the other guy even harder than he hurt you. Escalate till everyone is dragged in. I'm fucked if I'll let that happen.'

She let her anger subside – the man opposite her didn't deserve it. But her rage wasn't only directed at Logan; it was at herself, Jamie Marshall and what was happening to them all. She took a deep breath and steadied herself.

'Look, Tom, I'll phone the police if they don't know already. We do it right. No arguments.'

She tried to smile across the table and watched the tiny changes in his face as he struggled to contain his reaction to her words.

'I'm sorry, Tom I didn't mean to be angry at you… it's just that things are a bit difficult for me at the moment.'

That's when she broke down completely, tears washing down her cheeks. She took her face in her hands and couldn't control it.

Logan was startled by the raw emotion and he came round the table and put his arm round her shoulders.

'It's fine, Maxine. He'll be OK and this'll go away. I promise you.'

He felt the words were all wrong but he needed to say something. It wasn't the way he would act with anyone else, but no one else touched him the way she did. He felt his throat close and realised that he was close to tears himself, shocked again. Logan didn't do tears – or hadn't done since his wife had died and that evening with Maxine. He stiffened his back and gripped his own feelings.

'Come on, girl – I'll get you something to drink.'

She didn't speak, just put her head on his shoulder and let her tears run their course. Logan was frightened to move, didn't want to move – and just stayed close to her for as long as possible.

61

Maxine walked in the door of the cafe and saw Connie look up from the till, watching for a sign that said good or bad news from the hospital. Maxine had avoided calling her during the night and let her sleep but rang her first thing. The main message was that Bobo was alright – hurt badly but he would survive.

Although there had never been a full-on discussion on the subject, Maxine knew her friend had developed feelings for Bobo, and given Connie's previous relationships, she thought why not? He'd turned out to be thoughtful and kind. He seemed to have made a habit of telling them what a bastard he'd been in the past, but Maxine, Connie and Logan carried their share of sin so there was no judgement on their part and Bobo had found a home at last.

Logan was behind Maxine when they walked into the cafe and they both looked washed out and grey. There were no half smiles and Connie wiped her hands then headed to the back office. The other two girls were working and the morning rush had settled down, the office workers, lawyers and tourists heading back out into the drizzle that had soaked the Old Town since the early hours. Maxine shivered and pulled her jacket off, following Connie into the office. Logan told them he'd get a couple of brews and bring them in.

'How's he doing, Maxie?'

Connie looked worn and her heart thumped with the strain of worrying that she might lose someone else before anything had even started. She'd been given the same chance as Bobo, all through Maxine, and taken it, and why would she deny herself another shot at finding a man who cared? She didn't want a movie star, just someone who'd stay – someone she could count on to be there when things were tough.

Once she'd lowered that ice wall and let Bobo in, she hadn't been able to resist his almost childish vulnerability. The stories of his gangster days and failures hadn't surprised her too much – in fact, sometimes they made her laugh. She'd lived so much of her life with failure – failed people who thought they were the norm and failed systems playing lip service to caring.

'He'll survive,' Maxine replied, 'but he was badly hurt and lost a lot of blood – apparently the cut on his backside wasn't far off a killer. It was the freak who came in here with Beatson. No doubt about it – Pat got as close a look as he needed to be sure. He's weak but we got in to speak to him this morning. Charlie Brockie came and they think they've found the car he was in – one of the neighbours saw someone like him waiting in there for ages before Pat was stabbed.'

She shook her head and sat down, weary.

Connie asked the obvious question. 'What about Beatson?'

'No sign of him. Strange he leaves it to someone else.'

Maxine looked up and smiled as Logan came with the tea. He put the cups on the desk and played mum, pouring the tea, before handing them over to the two women. He looked every bit as knackered as Maxine; his face was set and there was something in his eyes she was too tired to notice, but Connie knew exactly what it was.

'What do we do now, Tom?'

Maxine had turned to the Big Man; they'd hardly exchanged a word coming back in the taxi.

'First thing is we wait and see what happens next. I'll make some enquires through friends.'

He put his hand up to signal caution.

'I won't do anything myself. I'll just find out who gave the order, or whether this lunatic was acting on his own. Hard to see that but can't understand why Beatson wasn't there.'

He pulled on his tea and tilted his head back for a moment to ease the tension in his neck and shoulders. He felt too old for going to war; Maxine was right that for the time being they could leave it to the police and see what happened. However, he knew that the cops might decide it was just a minor dust-up among the neds and let them get on with it. If that happened, he could still step in, and if Maxine didn't like it then he'd have to cross that bridge when they came to it. She couldn't know how these things worked, but he'd let her have her way for the time being while he kept a lid on the anger burning a hole inside him. Senseless violence again. He'd seen so much of it – the wasted, wounded and dead. What was the point? There was a time when he would have carried out a job involving extreme violence then ate his fish supper afterwards without a thought for the man in hospital. Now it didn't make sense to him.

'What then?' Maxine asked, imagining a worst-case scenario that involved tit for tat with the people she cared about so much.

'Let's see what happens.'

There was enough in his eyes to say he knew exactly what came next. 'Do you want Jamie Marshall involved?' he asked. 'You guys told me he seemed to know Beatson.'

Logan hated bringing Marshall's name into it because he was still under the impression that something was developing between Maxine and the cop.

'No, definitely not.'

It was said too quickly and Connie frowned. They left it at that but Logan picked up the same message that there was a problem, though he was smart enough to leave it at that.

'Fair enough. I've plenty contacts inside the force and can find out if anything's developing. They're taking a statement from Bobo as soon as he's compos mentis, so let's just wait and see after that. I'll be back and forward here but just be careful for the time being till these guys are locked up or out of the way.'

62

Logan didn't want to say too much because he knew that all the options were bad. Do nothing in response and it might all go away, but men like Beatson and Duran were scavengers, and once they had a taste of easy blood, they tended to come back for more. He didn't know them personally but had heard the names, and he'd already made a couple of phone calls to men who would know. One was to CC Campbell – a gangster by trade who knew the community better than most.

'He's a wanker, Tam. Danny Beatson thinks he's a name but it's all in his wee brain. Dangerous wee radge though if he thinks he's on top. Mikey Duran is mad as fuck but thick as shite. Just put on this earth tae draw blood – typical wee man. Story is they met inside and Duran wis caught playing Beatson's trombone when they were co-pilots. Need any help?'

Campbell meant it. Logan was one of the few men he trusted in this life and he owed him more than he could repay.

'Fine, pal – I'll call if I need some cavalry an' the cops are on this as well, so better you stay back.'

He stared at the wall but already had a picture of Beatson and Duran forming in his mind. He scrolled down his contacts list and called Mick Harkins.

'Need a wee favour, Mick. You know I'd never ask normally.'

It was true, and he knew that if he ever tried to give Harkins a using then the ex-detective would tell him where to stick it. But they liked each other now after years on opposite sides of the battlefield and that counted for something.

'Heard what happened to Bobo, Tam. Not acceptable. What do you want and I'll say yes or no, my friend. That OK?'

He fired up a cigarette and waited.

'Nothin' that'll put you at risk, Mick. Just what the polis assessment of these two bandits is. I'll take care of it after that.'

He wondered if he'd made the right call. Maybe he should have left it with Campbell. But criminal assessments of an enemy tended to be subjective, depending on who was telling the story. A cold police analysis wouldn't do any harm.

'No addresses or where they'll be kind of thing, Tam. If they're found in the canal, I don't want a trail back to me. Too old for the pokey now. That OK?'

'Perfect. If I need to give them a visit, I just don't want any unexpected surprises, like a sudden appearance of shooters or Rottweilers that'll bite my face off. Maybe it'll die down but I'm just being careful. You know me.'

'I know you, Tam, and remember you're too long in the tooth for the pokey as well. Tell Bobo I wis askin' for him. Laddie didn't deserve that.'

'Cheers, Mick; I hear you.'

63

Maxine sipped a coffee she barely tasted and thought how quickly things could change. She had always known that so why was she so surprised?

Jamie Marshall sat opposite her. He was off duty, and although they'd talked it over, he'd found it hard to reassure her, though he'd certainly tried his best. They'd stopped pretending that their trip away had been a romantic success though, and as far as Maxine was concerned, all the signals she was picking up were negative. She worried that maybe she was just too damaged by past events to have a proper relationship with a man, but it really didn't matter why. What she felt was what she felt – and it wasn't changing. He was trying to patch up whatever had gone wrong, but the more he tried, the more non-verbals she picked up that she didn't like. He became angry, then personal, then it was as if a different character took his place. That's when the poison seeped out into the open and Maxine almost froze in the face of it.

'Maybe too may punters in the past, eh?' he said. 'That it? Maybe you prefer payment for the business.'

He smiled at his own words, but his eyes were like dead pools.

His venom frightened Maxine, but only for a moment – then she remembered who she was and what she'd survived. She'd promised herself she wouldn't avoid the past or wear it like a permanent reminder of her shame. The words only cooled Maxine, and she decided as his anger rose that she'd do cold and precise. She waited till he was finished, watching his chest heave slightly with the rush of energy and rage.

'It's fine, Jamie, say whatever you like – it won't make a bit of difference. I've no idea who you are, and thank God it didn't go further. Now go or I swear to God I'll call your boss.'

He stood up and nodded. 'Truth is you were crap anyway. If I'd been one of your punters, I'd want my money back.'

He leaned forward, hands on the table, his face close to hers.

'Just watch your back, girl, because I might just creep up behind you.'

'GTF!' Connie had half heard what was going on and was now behind Marshall, who looked round in surprise.

'What the fuck?'

He glared at Connie, who stood her ground.

'GTF, officer, or just get tae fuck. You move yer arse or I'll start a breach of the peace here and see how your pals in the job like that one.'

'Another fucking slag with big ideas.'

He grabbed his jacket and left without looking back.

'You OK, Maxie?' Connie sat down and took hold of her friend's hands. They were cold and she'd started to shake with the aftershock of Marshall's words.

'Fine, Connie. How did I get that so wrong?'

She shook her head, bewildered by it all.

'Men, my friend. All bastards… apart from Big Tam Logan.'

She smiled and winked at Maxine, hoping the reference to Logan had the desired effect.

Almost on cue, Logan walked through the door and sat down beside them.

'You two OK? You look a bit frazzled.'

'God, you know how to charm a girl, Tam,' Connie said. 'Just worried about our boy.'

He nodded; he knew there was more but left it there. He'd picked up some information from his own contacts both inside the force and the criminal world.

'The CID are all over this case now and keen to get both Beatson and Duran. There's enough cops out there who want to put them away so make no mistake: if they show their ugly mugs, they'll be there. Beatson seems to have gone off the radar, but he'll not be far from home territory and likely he'll be with one of his mad sisters.'

'Mad sisters?' Maxine looked up, interested in the word 'mad'.

'Honestly, they're worse than him – complete nutjobs – and the cops hope to God they don't find him with one of them because we're talking World War 3. They've all got records for violence and serious crime.'

He shook his head involuntarily. Logan still had the old-fashioned idea that women shouldn't be involved in crime.

'Apparently the last time they tried to lift the eldest sister – or Bam as she's known – she grabbed one of the uniforms by the undercarriage and they had to baton her hand to get her off the poor guy.'

They were distracted by the door opening again and Logan recognised the woman who walked in, although he didn't know her personally. Maxine knew her but couldn't work out where they'd crossed paths.

64

Jacquie Bell walked over to the table and stuck out her hand, which Maxine shook cautiously.

'I'm Jacquie Bell. I'm a reporter, Maxine; I covered your trial. Don't know if you remember me?'

She smiled. She was an attractive, almost glamorous woman, but she was from the press, and for different reasons, Logan, Connie and Maxine went on high alert.

'Can I talk to you alone?' Bell came right to the point, which was exactly her style. She was high profile in crime reporting, and if she wanted something, it had to matter.

Logan looked round at Maxine and saw her lips were tight. It was the old story: when it came to crime, problems never came alone and never from the same angle.

'It's alright, Tom. Go and have a coffee with Connie.'

She squeezed his hand, a small but intimate gesture in front of the reporter. He felt his heart constrict; she knew him well enough to have noticed the nervous flicker in his eyes. He did as she suggested and moved across the cafe with Connie.

Bell raised her eyebrows at Maxine. 'Tom Logan? Bit of a legend.' She waited for a reply but Maxine ignored it.

'Coffee?' She gestured to the seat opposite and Bell dropped into it and sighed. She sounded weary although she looked fresh, as if she'd just stepped out of the shower, though the truth was she'd been up all night on a story that had come to nothing – or rather couldn't be printed without another source.

'God, my feet are killing me. All-nighter. Tell the truth, I could do with a drink even at this hour. However, coffee's probably a wise choice…'

She smiled, and it was warm and genuine because her eyes did it as well. The mouth can lie but the eyes can't.

'What can I do for you?' Maxine asked after she'd returned to the table with two steaming cups and pushed one over to the reporter. She sat down, tried a little sip of her fresh coffee and stared over the rim, wondering what was coming next. Connie waved to her on her way out – she'd decided to head home then visit Bobo in hospital.

'Heard about the problem you had with Danny Beatson.' At the expression on Maxine's face, Bell half raised her hand but not enough to be rude – just reassuring.

'Look, don't worry about who told me because it's my job to pick up this kind of stuff. It's you I'm interested in, Maxine. Is it OK to call you by your first name?'

Maxine nodded and waited.

'You're a real human-interest story – the previous life, what happened at the trial, then you reinvent yourself and now this. Does the old life go away though?'

'Wait.' Maxine stopped her and wondered how many times she'd have to hand out the same caution.

'I didn't reinvent myself. People keep saying that but this is who I am – it's just different times.'

'Fair enough, but listen to me: the press are going to start sniffing around this place, and no matter what you think, you can't avoid the past. My advice is to take it on, use it, go on the front foot and I think it could work out for you. That's my pitch anyway. But have a think about it, check me out and see what you decide. You always have control if we talk.'

She pushed a plain business card across the table and stood up.

'Thanks for the coffee,' she added, though she hadn't had any. 'It would be good to talk to you regardless. I like talking to people who've lived a bit.'

She stuck out her hand and Maxine took it again. It was warm and dry with an easy grip that didn't intimidate. She tried not to but she liked the reporter; there was something in her manner – confidence but not arrogance. She always thought reporters were born without hearts, but she'd been wrong before about people. *Too often*, she thought as Bell walked out of the door, already lifting her phone to her ear about another story.

Maxine turned to Logan, who was now back sitting opposite her. He was trying his best to mask something he didn't want to share, avoiding eye contact, so she reached across the table and took his right hand, looking at the thick, powerful wrists and forearms that must have taken years in the gym to develop.

'What do you think, Tom? The reporter wants to make me a celeb – fallen woman climbs out of the pit, makes good and lives happily ever after. What's the chance I'll live happily ever after?' She felt her eyes well up but she wasn't going to break down, not this time.

'I think everything's possible, Maxine. You want something enough then who knows? I think you deserve to be happy. Maybe telling your story is no bad thing and might even help a few people along the way.'

She looked deep into those sometimes-sad eyes and nodded.

'God, Tom, what would I do without you?'

He tried to think of a reply but nothing sounded right. Instead he kept quiet and wondered how it would all end.

65

When Jamie Marshall left the café, missing Logan by a couple of minutes, he walked towards the old Lawnmarket then decided on a quick drink to calm him down. He was going to be late for work but didn't hurry his steps – there was too much on his mind and the job could wait.

After the first half of the drink went over his neck, he decided to call in sick; he was in no state to work.

His time was up whether he liked it or not. The rubber-heel squad were on his back and he needed to jump before he was pushed. He could have won an Oscar for some of his performances yet he hadn't quite managed to convince Maxine. He seethed with the rejection. It had always been the same – the need to control burned in him and ate his guts like a cancer. He didn't really need another relationship, but it was important for him to have someone under his power – it made up for the contempt people had for him once they worked out what he really was. Class acting worked for a while but eventually people saw through the performance. Maxine would have been that little bit different; the fact that she'd been a hooker had excited him at first but now he wanted to hurt her. A reformed hooker giving him the elbow was not acceptable. Once he was clear of the job, he would put her in her place.

He finished his drink and decided against another one; he needed air and his chest felt tight with anxiety as he headed for the High Street.

'Fucking bitch!' he muttered every couple of minutes, his thoughts like fire in his head. 'A fucking pro.' He said it again, ignoring the looks of the two silks who passed him near the High Court.

He felt his hands shaking and wondered what the rubber heels had dug up on him. Had someone talked? The women he'd disciplined in his time had deserved it, and the thought that one of them might have complained infuriated him. If he found out who it was, they'd get a house call and he'd do it properly.

He didn't notice Connie waiting at the bus stop – watching the world go by and worrying how things would pan out with Bobo. She wanted to shower and change before going to see him. She looked up, alerted by the familiar sound of Marshall's voice as he walked past, but it took a second for her to realise who it was. There was a change in his face and expression; it was even darker and angrier than it had been when he'd left the cafe, which didn't seem possible but there it was. He seemed absorbed in his own thoughts and was talking to himself. She decided to have a few more words with him now they were both away from the cafe and there were enough witnesses at the stop to put him off doing anything more than giving her a few verbals.

'Jamie!'

She took a step forward but he didn't hear her, so she took another few steps to catch him and touched his shoulder.

'Jamie!'

The hand on his back acted like a fire alarm and he swung round, teeth bared.

'What the fuck?'

He paused when he saw who it was. He was breathing too hard and there was a film of sweat on his brow.'

Connie had been around enough bams in her time to recognise when someone was ready to kick off. Without a word from him, she knew exactly what was going on in his mind – another slag sticking her nose in where it wasn't wanted. He looked round and saw that a few of the citizens waiting at the bus stop were showing an interest.

'Whoa, boy, just asking so keep the heid,' Connie said, holding her palms up and backing off, and he realised he'd let his cover slip too far. He'd spent a lifetime acting different parts and realised he didn't need this little incident on record so he pulled his face back on.

'Sorry, Connie, just had a bit of aggro with a driver there who nearly ran me down. Gave me a bit of a scare to be honest.'

He was back in character.

Connie was streetwise and although she nodded and told him it was fine, she'd recognised the non-verbals as well as the blindingly obvious, and she'd seen something she didn't like one bit. She decided this wasn't a guy she wanted to take on just as her bus drew in and saved the moment for her. He frightened her too much.

'Need to go.'

She jumped onto the crowded bus and watched Marshall through the window. He hadn't moved and was staring at her in a way that made her hands shake.

66

Danny Beatson raged every time he called Mike Duran's number and got no answer while the bizzies were all over the Craigmillar area trying to dig him out. He'd heard what Duran had done to Bobo McCartney and while he had no objection to the damage inflicted on the Weegie, the mad bastard had left enough evidence to convict ten men. Apparently the Weegie had identified Duran, who had been damaged in the skirmish and left enough blood at the scene to make sure the cops could DNA him. And because it was Duran, it was assumed that Beatson had given his minder the order to go ahead. But Beatson had only a half memory of being pished and maybe saying something that could have been interpreted by Duran as a nod to do the business. It was the drink again – it wasn't what he would have said if he'd been sober, and it was a fuck-up of major proportions.

The police would get him eventually, but he was sure he just needed to deny it because they'd toil to prove he was involved. That wasn't the only issue though. Jamie Marshall would assume that he *was* involved and that particular uniform was a fucking psycho who'd not let a little problem like evidence get in his road.

Then there was the latest information that Bobo was buddies with Big Tam Logan, the barman from Leith. Beatson didn't know him personally but the reputation was enough. Apparently in his younger days, he was known as Tam the Bam – a machine when it came to knuckle competitions. OK, he was retired, but these gangsters could be a handful, and this one seemed to have allies all over the place, including the Campbells from Leith. They were premier league and definitely operating in a different world from Beatson, who suddenly felt exactly what he was – small time –because whatever allies he had were not answering the phone.

He tried Duran's mobile again and again and swore every time it rang out.

'Answer the fuckin' thing!'

He said it again and again, as if Duran could hear the order.

'What?'

The sudden sound of Duran's voice threw Beatson, who was lost for a moment.

'What is it, Danny? I'm fuckin' busy.'

Duran was his usual 'don't give a fuck' self.

'What is it? For fuck's sake, Mikey! The bizzies are rakin' the bins for us or have you been sleepin' through this fuckin' mess? You should've taken a video an' stuck it online just tae make doubly sure every fucker knew it was you that sliced that Weegie up.'

'An' your point is, Danny? You gave me the nod, so tough tattie.' Duran didn't seem the least bit fazed, but then why would he when he was a complete radge?

'You're goin' inside for a long time, Mikey, an' they'll get you eventually… right?'

He waited but knew already it was a lost cause. It was one of those moments in gangland when someone was in serious shit, but all that came was a shrug of the shoulders and an acceptance that it was what it was. Some men didn't mind the pokey, and in Mike Duran's case, he was pissed off with Beatson anyway – he'd had enough of a gangster who lacked balls and the other issues that had troubled him since they'd visited the cafe.

'Shit happens, Danny. By the way, think I might give they burds in the cafe a visit. Then I'm comin' for you, my friend. Been runnin' this shite through the napper an' I think you grass tae that fuckin' uniform wi' the stripes. No other explanation for what happened in that cafe. You're fuckin' rat, Danny – worst thing, an' I'm fucked if I'll be tarred wi' the same brush. Be seein' you.'

The phone died in Beatson's hand. All he could do was gulp a couple of times as his mouth had dried up.

Beatson stared at the phone as if it was covered in dog shit. He'd always lived with a set of delusional certainties that were collapsing round about his arse. All because his idiot son and his halfwit pals had acted the galoot on an early-morning bus. Life had been OK up to that point and now there were only bad options. A crazy like Duran on the case plus Jamie Marshall to come was a nightmare, and he didn't have an answer. If it got out onto the street that he was confirmed as a grass, then the people he'd helped put away would line up to put him in the ground or cremate him themselves – probably while he was still alive.

'Fuck's sake.'

Beatson was still staring at the phone in his hand and dropped onto the sofa, which was stained with an amazing variety of fluids from over the years – including bodily ones. He was keeping his head down in his sister Vera's house in Newcraighall. She was the toughest nut in the family – in fact the sisters were the real lunatics; the male siblings just pretenders. Vera Beatson had done some heavy time for a variety of crimes of dishonesty, with a couple of serious assaults just to polish off her CV.

'I'll fuckin' kill that bastard,' he mumbled. 'Swear to God, I'll do time for Mikey.'

He fumbled with a cigarette packet, and his hand shook as he stuffed the filter between his lips and flicked the plastic lighter. He heaved in a lungful and held it there for a moment to get the maximum level of poisons into his blood.

'Who you killin', Danny boy?'

Vera had walked into the living room as her younger brother was talking on the phone. She'd rolled a joint that looked long enough to buzz half the street and was grinning with the effects of the heavy-duty skunk.

'Here – take a wee puff, Danny. That'll put ye right, son.'

She grinned, showing her stained yellow teeth, her eyelids drooping in the mellow warmth of the dope.

Vera Beatson was the eldest of the siblings and the one who everyone, including her family, agreed was the most cracked. She's been trouble since the day she could walk and disobey her mother. She could barely remember her old man, who'd legged it after the birth of her siblings; Danny had apparently been the last straw for a man who believed he'd helped give life to the Scottish version of the Addams family. He saw more of their social workers than his wife, who supplemented her benefit money in Cockburn Street, where she had to wear half a ton of make-up and dark glasses to hide the truth.

Even by her sibling's standards, it was hard to find a redeeming factor in Vera's nature or looks. She just didn't give a fuck and fought like a cat when she had to. She was tall, too thin and her eyes seemed to be narrow slits; it was almost impossible to see the dark pupils behind the eyelids. When she used dope, they looked closed, and it seemed a wonder that she could see at all. Her nose ran slightly to the right, the legacy of a break when someone had whacked her coupon with a beer bottle, and her tight lips and almost milk-white skin meant the men in her life were few and far between – and mostly pissed.

She offered the joint to Danny and turned up the volume on the telly so they could better hear a couple of loonies abusing each other – someone had shagged some other loonie's sister or mother or something. Vera didn't really give a fuck – it was just fun watching how the other half lived. It never occurred to her that she inhabited that half of life as well.

'Who you killin', Danny boy?' she asked again and noticed his hand trembling.

He told her about the conversation he'd just had with Mikey Duran. She shook her head and wondered why her brother had ever tried being a gangster; he was never really equipped for it, and it annoyed her that she hadn't been born with a set of balls because she definitely had the mind-set for the game. Danny was a tosser – that was all there was to it, and it was a pain in the arse having to let him bed down in her place while the bizzies were active.

Beatson even told her that Duran thought he was a grass. Her lip twitched at the word; that would be the final insult to the family name, as if it wasn't bad enough already.

'A fuckin' grass…' She stared at him, wondering. He was essentially a weakling and weaklings talked to the bizzies – it was a well-known fact. 'You're no' a grass, Danny, are you?'

She'd never considered it, but as soon as the word left his lips, it seemed to strike a chord. So many numpties the Beatsons had dealt with seemed to have had sudden and very unexplained visits from the law.

'Course I'm no', Vera. Fuck's sake.'

271

He looked down at the carpet and the burn mark where Vera had left a hot iron too long. She saw the lie – he couldn't look at her.

She stood up, the mellow touch of dope overpowered by a sudden rush of adrenalin and anger, took two short steps towards him, grabbed his face in her long bony fingers and squeezed. She was incredibly strong for someone of her build and she pulled his face up to hers.

'Tell me again, Danny. Are you a fuckin' grass? Don't lie 'cause I'll see it an' smell it.'

He was beaten, and staring into those narrow slits, he knew she could see into his soul.

'The polis had me by the knackers, Vera. Honest fuckin' truth.'

He blubbed as she pushed his face away and sat back opposite him, pondering what it all might mean for her and the family. They'd all be tarred with the same brush and that was unacceptable because it would mean her moving from her territory, and that wasn't going to happen. She could do without the answer, but it was obvious. She didn't do pondering; she was a sharp thinker and decisive in a way her useless brother never could be.

'First things first, Danny – I should fuckin' cut your balls off, you hear me?'

She delivered the words with so much venom a line of spit left alongside them. He nodded and kept his eyes on the floor, rocking slowly as if he was in mourning.

'We need to make this problem go away… now!

'If Mikey goes anywhere near these two women at the cafe then it just gets worse. The question is: will he go for them first or you? Either way, we need to get tae him pronto.'

She leaned back in the seat then tilted her head back and drew in more smoke, holding it, before she sighed and let it out into the room again.

'Fuck's sake,' she wheezed. 'This stuff is the biso.'

She went quiet for a minute and Danny looked up at her. She looked like she was sleeping, but it was hard to tell with those eyes. When she spoke, her head still resting on the back of the seat, he blinked at the words that made his skin chill.

'We do Mikey and he disappears forever. No body to find and the cops' just write it off as a missin' person. They'll issue a warrant an' forget it in a couple o' weeks. Job done.'

She smiled and sat up, opening up those eyes so he could see part of the dark pupils that seemed to glint with menace.

'Just have to find the fucker though. That sound like a plan?'

'Aye sure, Vera. Sounds like a plan,' he said, but he knew it was all going to end badly, no matter what permutation came to the surface of this pool of shite.

'Here, take this – finish the bastard.'

She stood up and offered him the rest of the joint.

'I need tae go for a bit. Put some feelers around for Mikey. There's a baseball bat behind the front door if you need it.'

She pulled on her denim jacket – summer and winter she wore nothing else on top.

She walked out the front door with purpose; she'd already made up her mind that the situation required urgent action. Danny had brought a kilo of smack from his flat in case he needed to turn it into cash and that would do nicely for what she had in mind.

She caught the bus into the city and called the local suit she'd been grassing to for years. She talked to him because he was a looker and she'd fantasised over him a thousand times. She would never have talked to the bizzies normally but she made an exception for him.

'So my brother was a grass,' she told him when he picked up. 'Fuck's sake, man – that takes the biscuit. Anyhoo, he's sittin' in the flat wi' a big fat bag o' smack covered in his prints. All yours, lover.'

The detective was over the moon and did his best to hide the fact that he thought she was a reptile.

After she'd hung up the phone, Vera walked into the nearest boozer, ordered a double vodka and blackcurrant, and grinned at the thought of what was to come. Her younger sister Donna had still been in bed, recovering from the mother of all benders. She'd lost it completely after being dumped by the world's biggest waster, who she'd claimed had been the love of her life. Vera was pissed off with her; she was supposed to take care of a bit of local dealing that brought in good money, but she'd lost the gear and the money and was leaving herself open to a visit from the law or another dealer who fancied taking over their business.

Fuck her! Vera thought. It was time to get rid of both her and Danny. Donna had a hair-trigger temper and was possibly becoming even more of a radge than Vera.

When the bizzies arrived, Donna would just be emerging from Zombieland and would kick off. It was a nap.

Vera threw the double vodka down her throat and imagined a romantic weekend away with her favourite detective.

67

Connie pushed open the door of the boozer and scanned the bar. It was busy, but she knew where to look for the regulars. Mick Harkins was at the corner of the bar he'd claimed as his own, with the best view of the telly in the shop. She looked for Logan, but he wasn't behind the bar.

'He's in the back, Connie,' Harkins called over, then raised his glass and turned back to the screen showing Donald Trump telling the American public that good times were back and America was to come first.

'President of the United States. God help us all.'

Harkins said it to no one and everyone. A couple of the old regulars nodded but actually believed Trump was right about everything.

Connie knocked on the door of Logan's den, the place where he would sit quietly and relax during the day. He'd become a creature of habit and had his regular times for these breaks. He was tuned into Radio Scotland, having become interested in politics for the first time in his life. He'd even started to debate a bit with Harkins, who hated almost all politicians but at the same time was incredibly knowledgeable about the subject. The question of whether to have another referendum or not was keeping the bar-room lawyers in business, and Logan felt quite stimulated by the whole thing. He sat up when he heard the knock and grinned when he saw who it was. Logan grinning wasn't a common sight and Connie wished again that Maxine could see what she did in this man. He stood up and gestured with his mug of tea to see if she wanted one.

'I'm fine, Tam – just wanted a word. How you doin'?'

'Fine, Connie.'

He'd been deep in thought about his wife and Maxine all at the same time. His wife had been more than just enough; he'd never expected someone like her to love him and real-ity had been restored when she'd died. Somewhere deep in his subconscious he believed that he was responsible for her cancer. It was foolish but he'd been a gangster when they'd met, and in some way, he was sure he'd contaminat-ed her with the violent pathogens that infect the players in that life.

Connie didn't know where to start or how to say it, because she knew he could be both the right and wrong person to share her concerns with. It didn't matter though, because as far as she was concerned, Logan was the wisest of men – he'd lived on the dark side, survived and come out the other end knowing what actually mattered, and she could trust him.

'It's this cop, Tam. Maxie's been deep wi' him, but there's been a separation of the ways, if you know what I mean.'

She watched him, knowing what the words would mean. It must have hurt when he'd found out that Maxine was involved with the cop, but once again he'd kept it tight. She decided to take a risk and say what she was thinking.

'Look, Tam, I know what she means to you so for God's sake stop tryin' to pretend in front of me. She needs her head looked at as far as I'm concerned… right?'

He didn't have an answer and realised lying to Connie was a waste of breath so he just nodded. Connie remembered why she was there and carried on.

'There's just somethin' bothers me about him. I can't put my finger on it but there's bad vibes. Maybe I'm bein' an arse but I don't want to see her hurt again. Christ knows she's had enough.'

She bit her lip, wondering if she was just jealous that her friend would always find someone if she really wanted it. Maxine had been dealt better hands all through her life while Connie had never had a break.

'Hope it's no' me bein' stupid, Tam. She's fallen out wi' the guy, but I've a feelin' that he's no' finished wi' her, if you know what I mean? What do you think?'

'What's the problem, Connie? They've fallen out – it happens.'

'There's just somethin' about the guy. Aye he's a bizzie, but there's been some bad bastards in the job. Right? An' I don't like him, Tam.'

Logan rubbed his chin then stood up. 'I'll get some coffee. Sit, relax and I'll be back in five minutes.'

He came back into the room dead on time and had Mick Harkins with him. Connie stayed quiet and chewed her lip a bit more. Logan offered Harkins some coffee but he'd carried his beer through from the bar area.

'Naw, Tam. Coffee's bad for the stomach; I'll stick to the beer.' Harkins sat down and smiled at Connie, who regretted ever opening her mouth. Logan poured her coffee without asking because Connie never refused the stuff.

'Right, Connie, Mick's the boy with the contacts in the job an' it'll go no further than us. Let him have the details.'

He turned to Harkins and nodded; the ex-detective nodded back.'

'Sound as a pound, Tam.' He turned to Connie. 'What's the Jackanory, hen?'

Connie told him and Harkins scribbled a few details on a piece of paper Logan had pushed over the table. He knew cops, even the retired ones always needed a pencil and paper.

'This won't come back on me, Mick, will it? Don't need any hassle wi' the law.'

Connie was nervous and it showed.

Harkins smiled and told her not to worry. He stuffed the piece of paper in his pocket, told Logan he'd see what he could do and headed back into the bar.

Logan topped Connie's coffee up and changed the subject, but his mind was somewhere else. He'd been to visit Bobo in the morning and knew that this attack had left too many loose ends. He had the Campbells looking for Mike Duran now, and if anyone could find him before the police, it would be them. When they did, he'd decided he'd do the job himself. Bobo had been trying to get the life he'd never known, an' some radge had come along and taken it away. Bobo's body would recover but the boy would hardly talk, and his eyes seemed far away – as if he'd decided there was no escaping his old existence. Maxine had told Logan about the night she'd met Bobo and he wondered if the boy was thinking that idea was his only way of avoiding the next car crash in his life.

'What you thinkin', Tam?' Connie asked.

'Nothin' really, hen. Feel sorry for the boy. He's just one of those souls who can't win – doesn't matter what he does. We need to keep an eye on him – make sure he's OK.'

He grinned at her as if it would all be right on the night, but he knew this one would only be resolved by action.

'I'll go in and see him, Tam. You're busy enough here. Maybe I was just worryin' about nothin' over the cop.'

She massaged the sides of her forehead and hoped to God it would all turn out peacefully so they could get back to the good life they'd been enjoying.

'By the way, Connie, when it comes to feelin's, I think you need to make a move on yours.' He grinned at her again and gave her wrist the lightest squeeze.

'I'll see what I can do, Tam.' She let herself smile back and decided it was time to get on with her life.

68

Despite her decision to grab life by the short and curlies, Connie sat on the bus and worried all the way to the Royal Infirmary. She was worried about everything: Maxine, Bobo, herself. Was it possible just to achieve a normal, boring existence where the weather was the main theme of the day's discussions. She even wondered where Banjo was. Probably in a bad place, but although she wouldn't have taken him back, she hoped the poor bastard was OK and still in the land of the living.

She bought some grapes that looked a bit past their sell-by date, but Bobo wasn't a fussy eater and five a day still meant nothing to him, although Connie had been trying to convince him about the benefits of a heathy diet.

When she walked into the ward, he looked up weakly, but he made a good attempt at a smile, which lifted her mood again. She bit her lip and suddenly had a strong urge to hold him.

'How's the patient?' She sat down and plonked the grapes on the cabinet beside him.

'Lot better, Connie.'

He looked like he meant it.

Connie suddenly seemed to be lost for words and the swirl of emotions inside her meant she struggled with what to say next.

'Want a grape?' She lifted the bag and put it on the bed next to him.

'Aye right. Starving in this place, to be honest. Could you bring a sanny the next time?

'Sure thing. What would you like on it?'

'What about vinegar crisps an' maybe a bit of pickle?'

'Jesus, Pat, you're as common as muck. They'll be like wet rags if I put pickle on them.'

The idea and the innocent request made her snort a laugh. She smiled broadly as he thought about it for a moment and then laughed himself.

'Aye right, Connie. Common as muck an' proud.'

He lifted his good hand and punched the air. Bobo McCartney was OK and once again had refused to give in. It drew a tear from Connie, and she felt happy in a way she just couldn't rationalise. It was as if they'd just shared something very personal.

She stood up and just let her feelings go, putting her arms round Bobo, who was startled by the gesture, though only for a second. It only took moments for cheek to cheek to go to lips to lips. There was another moment where neither of them had any idea what to say or do next, and they were almost afraid to give up on the contact. When they did, they both looked embarrassed until Connie broke the ice.

'Well, how was that for you then?' She swallowed and hoped it wasn't all a huge mistake.

'Fuckin' Barry.'

He grinned from ear to ear as if it had been much more than a kiss.

'Jesus, Pat, you ever heard of romance?'

'What?'

'Just eat the grapes.'

She took his free hand and he squeezed, confirming that the kiss hadn't been a mistake. That was good enough for both of them, and in their own ways they both swore they wouldn't let this one get away.

Connie headed back to the cafe an hour later, lost in thought – all was good for a change and maybe it would even stay like that. Wee Connie was happy.

69

Jacquie Bell smiled when she sat down opposite Maxine again; Maxine had closed up the cafe for the night and hoped she was doing the right thing. She'd thought carefully about the offer the reporter had made. Her first instinct was to ignore the press completely, but she was savvy enough to know the problem wouldn't just disappear because she ignored it. She'd talked to Connie and Jan often enough about the risk that her trial and life would come back to haunt her and here it was.

The reporter was right though – her choices were limited. She could ignore it and let it fester through rumours, fake news and the loonies who inhabited so much of cyberspace. She could lie about it, though that would stand for about five minutes, or she could do what she'd tried to do in her private life and not hide from what had happened. Put her hands up and accept the truth, show the positives, that redemption was possible and lives *could* change for the better. There were other women out there on the streets and worse who might, just might, take something from her story. She'd thought about it and surprised herself by phoning the reporter and telling her she'd do the interview.

'Where do you want me to start, Jacquie? Tell the truth, I led a pretty boring life up to the fall from grace.'

Maxine sipped some apple juice; her mouth felt paper dry.

'That's the point, Maxine – an ordinary life ripped up by addiction, the fall and rise. Trust me, people will get this story, and all those ordinary families will know the same could happen to their own. Start at the beginning and I'll cut out what we don't need later. I won't publish anything till you give it the nod. OK?'

She smiled and clicked on the record function on her phone. 'Is it OK to record?'

'Sure, no problem,' Maxine replied. 'Do you want something to drink before we start?

'You don't have any good whisky, do you? I don't get embarrassed about asking – it's the reporter in me.'

'I do, as a matter of fact. Think I'll join you.'

Maxine came back to the table and opened up a fresh bottle of malt, poured two extra-generous shots and started to tell her life story. Bell hardly interrupted because she didn't have to.

Two hours later, they decided to call it a night and the reporter arranged to come back the following day. Connie had come in the door while they were talking but had just nodded and headed into the back office to chill and think about Bobo. She'd come back from another hospital visit and there was more than a spring in her step – the girl was bouncing, and Maxine looked forward to her daily report on their flowering romance. Bobo was going to be released in a couple of days, and for a brief spell they almost forgot that mad Mikey Duran and Danny Beatson were still out there somewhere.

When the reporter left, they shared a nightcap and relaxed. Connie was worried about Maxine revealing all to the press but, in her heart of hearts, knew it was probably the least bad choice. What was the worst that could happen?

70

Jacquie Bell walked away from the cafe door into the cool night air and felt just the lightest touch of damp against her face. It felt good – tiredness had made her skin feel tight and dry, so a touch of natural moisturiser gave her some relief, and pushing her legs into action eased off the aches.

She shook her head. Years in the business never quite prepared her for the next set of revelations she investigated. Maxine was ordinary and extraordinary all at the same time. Hardly anyone would have ever noticed her life if she hadn't taken the same fall so many others had. There was something exhilarating in her story – moments from being just another murdered sex worker then famous for a couple of lurid headlines then dropping out of sight for ever. *Well not now*, she thought. It was so much easier to remember the murderers than the victims when they worked the street. Just look at the Yorkshire Ripper or his predecessor, Jack. Bell pulled out a smoke and decided she needed to sleep, but that was easier said than done.

Mike Duran watched the reporter walk away from the cafe. He had no idea who she was but she looked the business, though he put that aside. He then made a mistake that would cost him later. He thought Bell worked in the cafe, and because the lights had gone out at the same time she'd left, he assumed she must have closed the place up. He hadn't worked out that Maxine and Connie had closed down and gone into the back office. He'd arrived after Connie had come back from the hospital, but before Bell left the cafe.

That little moment would save a life. If Connie had left on her own, Duran would have taken her out. That was his plan – no logic, just his demented idea of the way ahead. He swore under his breath and blew into his hands to warm them as the evening chill turned into near zero temperatures. He walked off towards the university area where he'd stashed a stolen car. He was determined to get the mouthy wee cow who'd wound them up in the café, then it would be Danny Beatson.

'Fuckin' rat,' he growled. He knew it was true – so much that he'd only suspected about Beatson now made sense.

And when it was all done, the pigs could do their best and he'd go down fighting. Honour restored.

71

'Tell Connie what you told me, Mick.' Logan was in the back room of his pub and nodded to Harkins and Connie to sit down. Harkins had a beer in his hand again and looked serious enough for Connie to guess her gut feeling might have been right.

'This guy Jamie...'

He hesitated and scratched the stubble on his chin, choosing his words carefully. 'Guy's a psycho, bad news and the rubber-heel squad are on his case. He's got a record of prisoners with unexplained injuries. He might have survived all that but he hands out the same lessons to the women in his life.'

He took a mouthful of beer and watched Connie sit forward and grip her chin in a stress gesture. She said 'fuck' before he spoke again.

'Police Scotland have a zero-tolerance position on domestic violence so one of their own handing it out is bad karma. The problem is that he seems to dominate the women completely so there've been no formal complaints but plenty circumstantial. Anyway, the bottom line is that they're going for it – he's under investigation and knows it. Seems he's put in his ticket and jumping ship before the knock at the door.'

'You sure about this, Mick?' Logan had to be certain.

'Absolutely, Tam – you know I've got friends in the job and this is straight from the people involved. They were interested that he was involved with someone else and were concerned that she might be next. I told them I'd get word to her. Can you do that, Connie?'

Harkins had said as much as he wanted to. Getting inside gen from the job was becoming a serious business and could cost his sources their job, but it was in everyone's interest that Maxine didn't become the next one in hospital.

'Jesus, she's going to take this hard. The first guy she's been involved with since she was on the street. Maxie's struggled with trust.'

Connie glanced at Logan, saw his frozen, contained expression and knew her words would have an effect on him. She wished to God that Maxine had put her trust in him – she knew Tam would have cut off his thumbs to take care of her.

'I'll do it, Mick, and let you know it's done.'

'He's dangerous,' Harkins told her, 'and he knows there's going to be an early mornin' knock, an' if the Fiscal has her way he'll do time. That means he's unpredictable. Thing is, he seems to enjoy hurting women – can't control it.'

'What you thinkin', Tam?' Connie chewed a nail, feeling like she was back in the old life.

'Think we need to take care of Maxine,' he replied. 'Let me know when you've spoken to her and leave the rest to me.'

Harkins had seen the look on his face before, but it had been back in the days when Logan had been the enforcer's enforcer, almost unstoppable when he was told to go to war. He knew there was no point in giving advice to a man like Tam Logan, at least not serious advice – banter was OK but not what he decided to say anyway.

'Tam, there's still people in my old mob who think boys from your side of the game don't change. They'd think it would be justice done if they could lock up a guy with your pedigree. You hear me?'

'I hear you, Mick.' Harkins was right and Logan appreciated the gesture but he'd already ignored the warning as his phone rang.

It was CC Campbell. 'We've tracked down Mikey Duran's rathole. Want us to take care of anythin', Tam? Free service – consider it done if you say the word.

'Just keep an eye on it and I'll get back to you in a bit. I'm with people.'

He looked at Harkins and Connie, who were both staring at him wishing they knew what message he was getting. They both picked up that the wheels were turning and no one could stop it now. Logan put the phone down.

'Let me know when you've told her, Connie, and you take care. Duran's still out there and remember you gave him a mouthful – he's loose and mad so take care.'

He turned to Harkins. 'Mick, drinks are on the house tonight so fill your boots. No one will know about the info you got.'

He smiled but there was a sadness in his eyes as he pulled on his jacket and left the pub without another word.

72

Danny Beatson slipped another smoke between his lips and lit it off the fag still burning between his fingers. He was on his fourth packet that day and between regular black coffees, no food and the nicotine, he felt like shit. His hands shook like a wino and he hadn't slept since he'd walked in the door of Vera's house. His sister Donna padded into the kitchen to put the kettle on after having slept most of the day. The dark circles under her eyes and lank hair made her look like an extra in a zombie film.

'Where the fuck is Vera?' Beatson almost shouted at his sister.

'Fuck knows, Danny. Been sleepin' all day. How? What's the problem?' She rasped the words through a throat that felt like the beach. Donna was pissed off with her sister anyway, and the bitch was on her back all day about bringing in some money. Donna just didn't have the energy for dealing – between alcohol and dope she was a wreck, barely getting through the days.

'She was supposed tae be bringin' me some fresh smokes. You'll need to go for them.' Beatson was fired up to melting point with the mixture of fear and chemicals.

'Fuck you, Danny,' Donna slurred as she poured water over an old teabag in a cup missing a handle. She put the cup to her lips and realised the water was cold – she'd forgotten to switch the kettle on.

'Shit.'

That was all she got out as Danny came up behind her and grabbed a handful of her hair, pulling her head back while his free hand wrapped around her skinny neck. The cold tea soaked the front of her top.

'Did you say "fuck you"?'

It almost felt like relief, squeezing her throat and seeing her fear.

'That woke ye up, ya fuckin' junkie cow.'

Beatson had lost it completely and didn't even hear her squeeze out the word *please* as he killed her. He just couldn't stop until he saw the white of her eyes bulge and start to dot with tiny red pinpricks. When he let her go, she slid to the floor and didn't move. Beatson tried to absorb it, and as reality took over again, he waited for her to roll over and curse him – but she couldn't. He'd slapped her about more times than either of them could have counted and it always worked out – a bit of aggro then they'd get pissed or smoke a joint together.

He sank to his knees and started to beg his sister to come back to life but she refused, and he made long moaning noises as his mind was overwhelmed with the shitstorm that was his current situation.

His luck was completely out because he was still on his knees as the police crashed in the door five minutes later, looking for the kilo of heroin Vera had called in. The heroin was the least of his problems though when they found him trying to wrap Donna in the rug from her bedroom. His career and small-time gangsterism was over, but at least he didn't have to worry about a visit from Mikey Duran.

His fifteen minutes of fame would be as the bastard who'd strangled his own sister.

73

Maxine wiped the tears away from her eyes and sobbed like a child. She hadn't stopped crying since Connie had told her what she knew about Jamie Marshall. She couldn't believe it at first, despite what she'd seen and heard from his own lips, and for the first time ever she had become angry at Connie – had accused her of lying and having some other motive for saying what she'd said. What made her even angrier was that it wasn't a surprise; her instincts had been right about the cop. She was angry at Logan for being involved too, and she needed to release it all, though at the end of the day, it was her own fault – and she knew it. Then she accepted it and apologised, knowing Connie would have cut off her own arms for her and didn't deserve what had been said, but to be so wrong again had frightened her, and she wondered if, somehow, she was doomed to always meet the wrong kind of men.

'God, Connie, I think I must have done something in a previous life to get all this punishment in this one.'

She heaved in a deep breath and felt herself calming down. Connie poured them both a drink, sat down beside her and put her arm round her friend.

'Here, drink this. It'll put hairs on your chest, hen.'

Connie slugged half her drink and rubbed Maxine's back as if she was a child. When Maxine had calmed down, Connie stepped outside and called Logan to tell him it was done.

Across the city, Jamie Marshall sat down in his regular boozer near the top of Leith Walk and spread the newspaper out on the table in front of him. He stared at the print for a couple of minutes and shook his head, knowing he was taking nothing in. He had too much on his mind – his world was collapsing around him and he was considering doing a runner. The rubber heels were closing in and he'd been told that two of his ex-partners had been talked into making complaints and statements.

He'd put his ticket in and he was struggling to think exactly where he could run to. He was a graduate, highly trained in the police, yet had no idea how to survive without a uniform. Criminals would know how to do it, and he wished that he was on terms with some of them, but he treated them the way he treated his women. He lifted the beer to his lips just as Logan sat down opposite him. He was startled, couldn't make sense of it and sat back in his seat.

'What's up, Tam?' was all he could manage.

'You know who I am, right?' Logan said it calmly but there was no hiding that this wasn't a friendly visit.

'Of course I know – what kind of question is that? What's the problem?'

Marshall had regained his confidence but even though he was a fit, powerful man himself, Logan seemed to dwarf him.

'You know my reputation then?' Logan had rehearsed his lines before he'd arrived.

'Of course. Back in the day you were the man. Everybody knows. You want a fucking medal or something?'

Marshall knew this was serious but his whole life was serious, so he was fucked if he was taking snash from some ex-minder. It was at that point Logan grabbed both his wrists and started to squeeze. Marshall wheezed with the pain that rushed up his arms – it was as if he'd been plugged into the mains. He was helpless, could do nothing and he realised that all those days of lifting weights in the gym had been a waste of time.

'Now I want you to listen carefully, Jamie. This is what's going to happen, and if you don't do what I tell you, I'm going to hurt you… badly. Hurt you in a way you wouldn't believe possible. Apparently, you're going to prison, an' I'll leave you in a state where you won't be able to stop all those guys you put inside treating you as their new girlfriend.'

'Please.'

Marshall's bottle had gone completely, and he saw clearly that outside the job, he was as defenceless as all the people he'd hurt without reason. Logan saw defeat in his eyes and let go of Marshall's wrists.

'You're not equipped for the real world, pal. Won't survive five minutes with some of the people with scores to settle, an' I'll tell them all where to find you.'

'What do you want?'

Marshall massaged his wrists; they felt like they'd been hit with a mash hammer.

'Compared with all your other problems, not much, Jamie. I want you to stay away from Maxine. I mean completely. If you see her by accident, I want you to run the other way. If you don't, I'll come for you and leave the bits that aren't broken for the cops who want to lock you up. Your choice. Do you understand?'

'Fair enough.'

Marshall's voice was quiet, almost childlike, and he was afraid. He'd always felt powerful, in control and suddenly the world had become a terrifying place.

'By the way, don't phone her either. That would bring the same result.'

Logan stood up and, before he left the bar, turned to Marshall again.

'Have a nice day, Jamie. You don't have many left.'

Marshall headed back to his flat and started to pack a couple of suitcases. He had no idea where to go but staying in Edinburgh wasn't an option. He was frightened, and for the first time he felt exactly what his victims felt.

When he opened the door to leave, two of the rubber-heel team were waiting for him.

'Going somewhere, Jamie?'

When they arrested him, he said please twice as if they'd take pity on him, but no one was listening.

74

Later the same night, Connie had closed up the cafe and joined Maxine in the back office. They were both exhausted and had decided to avoid alcohol, opting for hot chocolate, which lasted about one mouthful when Connie changed both their minds.

'That's enough fuckin' chocolate,' she announced. 'I'll pour us as proper drink.'

Maxine nodded in full agreement – they both needed booze to control their stress levels.

'What if he tries to get in touch, Connie?' Maxine held her nose over the glass and inhaled the sweet notes of the Speyside malt.

'He won't, Maxie – big Tam handed him a red card. He won't cross the Big Man.' Connie stared across the table, wondering how Maxine would take this news.

'Tom… Jesus!'

Maxine was surprised, but when she thought about it, why was she?

'I hope this doesn't cause him a problem,' she said.

She'd given up on doing the right thing and was just glad Logan was there for her – and for all of them. Always there. She knew it was time to stop thinking about his past and start thinking of him as he was and what's he'd been to her. *Maybe even what he could be*, she thought.

Connie had had enough. 'For God's sake, girl. Tam would jump off a cliff for you. You blind or somethin'?'

'I know. God knows I do. I wonder if he can forgive me for being such an arse.'

She was about to speak again when Connie's phone rang. It was Logan.

'Listen, Connie, you in the cafe?'

'Aye, havin' a blether wi' Maxie.'

'Right. I want you and Maxine to leave when you're ready. I want you to walk up to the Lawnmarket, cross over to St Giles' Street and then walk down The News Steps.' Logan said it as if it was an order, and there was enough tension in his voice to tell them he wasn't playing kid's games.

'What's up, Tam?'

Logan didn't fuck around – something serious was happening and there had to be some form of threat out there.

'Just do it, Connie. Trust me and don't look back.'

The phone died in her hand and she stared across at Maxine, trying think how to translate his message.

A few minutes later, Maxine and Connie locked up and headed north along George IV Bridge. It was still busy enough with late drinkers and the ever-present tourists walking back to their hotels or late boozers.

Logan stood in the dark shadows of a doorway and watched Mikey Duran. The Campbells' team had kept eyes on him all day till he'd taken over and told them he'd handle it from there. A couple of them offered to stay somewhere in the area just in case he needed backup.

'I won't need backup,' he'd told them. 'Go an' get a drink on me.'

They knew enough to understand that he meant what he said so they'd nodded and headed off into the night.

Duran was about eighty meters ahead and on the other side of the road. He'd been watching Maxine's place for about twenty minutes and there were no prizes for guessing what he planned to do. There were too many people about for Logan to take him on there. He worried that Duran would just crash in the door and hurt the women before he could get to him, so he worked out the best way to find a place with less people in the heart of the old city. He hoped Maxine and Connie would stick to the script and give him a shot where he'd chosen the ground.

Duran moved after the women – he stayed about twenty meters behind them, waiting for his own chance. They crossed the Royal Mile at the High Court and turned into St Giles' Street. Tam held his breath because this area was always quiet and Duran would either take his chance there or on the long, dark News Steps that dropped down to Market Street.

Connie felt vulnerable when they seemed to be alone in the street. Logan had told her not to look back, but when she got to the top of the steps, it looked as if there was danger in every corner of the old stairway, so she hesitated and looked round. She just couldn't stop herself. Duran was only a few steps behind and when he saw Connie looking at him, he pulled out a long butcher's knife.

Duran grinned. He was a nutjob, this one was sweet and he couldn't wait to do a bit of carving. He was nearly on them and loving what he saw. They were both like frozen statues, unable to move – mouths gaping in fear and not even able to scream. He was about to say something smart-arsed before he got to work when he felt his left knee crack, and he flopped to the deck as if he'd been hit by a bus. But it wasn't a bus – it was Big Tam Logan and the pickaxe handle he'd armed up with earlier in the night and fitted under his coat.

'Get out of here. Go on… run!' He kept his eyes on Duran as he spoke to the women.

Maxine had her hand over her mouth and both women were frozen with terror.

'Go… now!' Logan bawled at them.

They turned and went down the steps as if they were being chased.

'Ya bastard. I'll fuckin' kill ye.' Duran sat holding his shattered knee with one hand as Logan kicked the butcher's knife well away from them. He looked round; they were still alone in the street, but he knew there would only be moments before someone crossing at the junction with the High Street would see them and start nosing or calling the bizzies.

Duran pulled out another smaller knife with his free hand, but Logan had already anticipated the move. Men like Duran just didn't know when they were beat. For such a big man, Logan moved like a lightweight boxer. The pickaxe handle broke Duran's wrist before he could do anything with the knife. He groaned and collapsed back down on the pavement.

'Just so you know, by the time I'm finished with you, your dancing days will be over. Never mind you'll have a long time inside to get used to it.'

Logan walked along the back of the High Court and onto The Mound where he called the police and told them he didn't want to leave his name but there was a man badly hurt in St Giles' Street. When he was halfway down The Mound, a couple of blue lights flew past him.

One of the uniforms recognised Duran and grinned at the mess.

'Came in second wi' this one, Mikey.'

He dug his partner in the ribs.

'I'll fuckin' murder you, ya bastards.' Duran hissed the words through the pain searing through his legs.

'I fuckin' doubt it, Mikey. I really fuckin' doubt it.'

The uniforms lapped it up, their spirits raised after what had been an otherwise dull night in the city.

75

One Week Later

Big Tam Logan cleaned the glasses as usual and nodded to Mick Harkins, who'd just walked in the door. Harkins ordered a pint then put his paper on the bar, studied the piece about Maxine and spoke without looking up.

'Christ, that's amazin', Tam. Jacquie Bell's turned our girl into a celeb! Looks like Joe Public loves the story an' business is boomin'. Seems the girl's a bit of a tourist attraction now. There you go.'

'Life's strange, Mick. Would either of us have imagined back in the day I'd be servin' up pints to you? Christ, you spent enough time tryin' to put me away.'

Logan laughed and felt good; life was back on course for Maxine, although he hadn't seen her since the night he'd shown Mike Duran he was second division. He knew she would be upset and that was natural. Connie had told him she was OK but needed time to settle down again and seemed to be doing a lot of thinking and dealing with her celebrity status. It had almost overwhelmed her, but Bell had been on the money and the public had taken to her redemption story.

'See Mikey Duran's still in the hospital.' Harkins changed the subject but only slightly and there was a reason. 'They're sayin' he apparently met with a bit of an accident – both ankles broken, knee an' a wrist. Must have fell off a building, the state he was in. He'll never play for Scotland now.'

'Sounds like he got what he deserved. Here, this one's on the house.'

He pushed the beer in front of Harkins.

'Well, he'll be banged up in Saughton once he gets out of hospital. Job done.' Harkins changed the subject again and started arguing with another punter about Brexit.

Logan was eating his lunch with Bobo, who was struggling to chase his food round the plate with one arm still in a sling. Maxine walked in the door and sat down beside them. Bobo and Logan looked up without a word and waited. She leaned over and kissed Bobo's cheek; he blushed and knew from her body language that he needed to give them some space.

When they were alone, Logan put his fork down and dabbed his mouth with a napkin.

'I hate violence, Tom. Hate it, and I heard what you did to that bastard. Was that really necessary?'

'Yes, it was. It was really necessary.' He left it at that because he tended not to use a surplus of words.

Maxine sat back and sighed. She'd hardly slept since St Giles' Street, but eventually her mind had cleared. Everything made perfect sense now and she wondered how she could have been so blind.

'Tom.' She paused and gave him full eye contact. 'You fancy going out on a date? You know, a proper date.'

She smiled and reached over to grip his hand. Logan blinked a couple of times and felt his heart race. He stared at her then smiled back.

'You're on, Maxine.'

Printed by Amazon Italia Logistica S.r.l.
Torrazza Piemonte (TO), Italy

11668493R00180